Daimones

First Printing: October 2012

ISBN 978-1-478-3471-0-1

About the Author

Massimo Marino comes from a scientist background: He spent years at CERN, in Switzerland, and at the Lawrence Berkeley Lab, in California, followed by lead positions with Apple, Inc., and the World Economic Forum.

He is also partner in a new startup in Geneva for smartphone applications: TAKEALL SA.
Massimo currently lives in France and crosses the border with Switzerland multiple times daily.

"Daimones" is based on people experience and facts with an added "what if" to provide an explanation to current and past events. It is his first novel. The novel is the winner of the 2012 PRG Reviewer's Choice Award in Science Fiction.

If interested in more details about Massimo Marino, please see his full profile on Linkedin:

http://ch.linkedin.com/in/massimomarino

Connect with Massimo Marino:

Twitter:
https://twitter.com/Massim0Marin0
Facebook:
http://www.facebook.com/massimo.marino.750546
http://www.facebook.com/MassimoMarinoAuthor

ON THE GODS AND THE WORLD

"These things never happened, but they are always."
Sallustius

"Deorum naturae neque factae sunt; quae enim semper sunt, numquam fiunt: semper vero sunt."

Table of Contents

Prologue

Warnings

"Large numbers of animals have mysteriously died recently, from the thousands of birds found dead in two southern U.S. states to 100,000 dead fish in Arkansas. TIME takes a look at other mass animal deaths, many of which are still unsolved." Read more:

'Over the first weekend of the new year 2011, thousands of red-winged blackbirds fell dead from the sky. Two days later, some 500 blackbirds dropped dead in Louisiana.'

'March 2011: Approx. 1,200 penguins were found dead on a remote beach in southern Chile.'

'April 2011: Millions of sardines washed ashore nearby. In addition, thousands of the rare Andean flamingo abandoned their nests in the north of Chile, leaving their 2,000 chicks to die in their shells. Even worse, no one could say concretely why these animals had died.'

'April 2011: According to Francisco Nique, president of the Association of Fishermen of Puerto Eten, in the span of 10 or 12 days, 1,200 dead pelicans along 160 kilometers have been found between Punta Negra, in Piura, and San Jose creek in Lambayeque. Perú 21 press.'

'October 2011: Thousands of dead waterfowl wash ashore at Wasaga Beach, Canada. The Star.'

'January 2012: Dead herring mystery for Norway; locals left scratching their heads after twenty tons of the dead creatures are found on beaches in Nordreisa. The Guardian.'

'May 2012: 60,000—100,000 dead fish found in three creeks in Maryland USA. Baltimore Sun.'

'May 2012: Thousands of Mozambique Tilapia found dead since last week, experts blame pollutants in the river. Ironically, Mozambique Tilapia is considered as one of the most resilient species of fish, known to withstand unfriendly environmental conditions. Pune Mirror.'

'May 2012: At least 2,300 dead birds were found along beaches between Cartagena and Playa de Santo Domingo, Chile. CNN International.'

'May 2012: The Peruvian government reported 5,000 birds, mostly pelicans, and nearly 900 dolphins have died off the country's northern coast, possibly due to rising temperatures in Pacific waters. Scientists scrambled to pin down what caused such a massive toll. AFP.'

— o —

Strange deaths had caused alarm among naturalists and environmentalists in all nations. Birds fell dead from the sky, fish washed up on shores and rivers across the whole planet, but people had other things to care and worry about. Mainstream media focused on economic crises, financial scandals, huge losses from banks, sovereign states at risk of defaulting in the Euro zone, the Arab spring, and the global war on terror.

Why the interest in bird and fish deaths: don't they die every day? Such news was almost whispered as unimportant, or used as filler for a column on some inner page. Local TV channels sometimes reported the facts though as a strange and abrupt twist of the normal course of natural events: interesting—for a second—but nothing to see, move on.

Whoever tried to talk seriously about the animal deaths—trying to discover a pattern—was treated as a weirdo, a delusional simpleton seeing conspiracy around every corner. People reacted to the deaths with raised shoulders, regarding the unexplained quirk about the natural world as worth no more. Some even accused naturalists of trying to profit from the quirkiness to grab more funds for their research and projects.

Regardless, thousands of dead birds and tons of fishes had been found floating ashore, belly up, without any apparent reason. "The sky is not falling," people said. Indeed it was *not* the sky that was falling, only previously live and healthy winged animals. Yet too many fell…well, they were just birds, weren't they?

We had enough reasons to wonder what killed them, clear signs that something was seriously wrong. Initial investigations showed evidence of unnatural events, damage in the breast tissue, blood clots in the body cavity, and much internal bleeding. All major organs though were normal.

In some cases, there was acute physical trauma leading to hemorrhage and death but no sign of any chronic or infectious diseases. Thousands of animals of the same species suffering a traumatic end all together—all of a sudden—around the world with no apparent cause or link. Concerted investigations should have started. But nobody pushed for those. Instead, county veterinarians scrambled to provide plausible explanations. Results from preliminary testing had been released to the news by the Livestock and Poultry Commission's Veterinary Diagnostic Lab. They showed birds, which fell by the thousands, dead from internal collapse—whatever that meant. No explanations were given as to what caused the massive traumas and why.

The Internet covered the deaths with genuine interest to look for causes. Threads and blogs were filled with plots calling for plans between the Zionists, Fascists, Falun Gong supporters, and aliens from planet Zark. Conspiracy theories soon killed all discussions and, in a sense, also prevented genuine forensic work to be conducted: What serious scientist craves association with lunatics wearing tin-foil caps?

Some officials started to release the first explanation at hand. They speculated on causes for the bird deaths ranging from fireworks, the weather, noxious fumes, chemtrails sprayed by airliners, or 'sonic booms.' Anything that could be used to put the stories to rest, and quickly. Some believed the birds might have been frightened to death by the blasts or killed by the scores in traffic accidents.

"We have received information from local residents last night. Our main theory is that birds got scared because of the fireworks. Thus, they landed on the road, but couldn't fly away due to the stress and were hit by a car," one official explained to 'The Local', Sweden's online news in English. The news was also reported by the Sveriges Radio Skaraborg, that stated the birds had been found dead on the streets in Falköping, southeast of Skövde.

He added the animals likely had difficulty orienting themselves in the dark. That in itself would be news. No one talked much about the fishes, like the two million dead in Chesapeake Bay or the dead drums washed ashore along twenty miles of the Arkansas River.

People had more important issues to deal with; the world faced a period of great uncertainty and huge changes affecting everyone at every level. Global terrorism stopped us from seeing what was happening. In those months people were thinking of other things. Everyone wondered whether they'd be next in the vicious round of terrorist bombings and retaliations affecting every country in the world.

Who cared if some wild animals were dying when members of your own family might not come home that night? Humanity had missed its only vital clue. The link was there. We were the sapient species on earth, clever enough to connect the dots, no matter how far apart they were. We should have done our job. Connect them. We were too busy, too preoccupied with other facts to ask ourselves: What the hell is happening?

Nature's red flags went unnoticed and animals—scores of them—kept dying. We kept living our own lives…

Part One

The Purge

No hint suggested the day would be any different from all others. I arrived at work as usual, after leaving my daughter at school. A too bright Monday morning and sunny for early February. The weather had been mild during the weekend, much warmer than it should for the season.

My wife, Mary, complained about the warmth, worried this would be no good for plants and the garden.

"See, everything is waking up. All the buds on my wisteria? The poor thing will become…well, hysterical if the temperature should drop—and it will—below freezing again."

Indeed, those days felt like early spring. I liked that.

The whole winter had been harsh with average temperatures way below freezing. To leave home and take my little princess to school on my way to work was an exercise of will—even more so when activities started at 6:15am and it was still dark outside.

"I go to bed and it's dark. I get up, dark…yet again! You know how it bothers me," I told Mary every time she asked, "What's going on, sweet pea? You're pensive." She still called me that even though it had been years since we were high school sweethearts and I'd played quarterback for our school team.

Thank the Lord, she never said it in public. No one protects a "sweet pea" quarterback or fights to catch his passes! And let's not even think about the harassment from team mates.

Mary had just turned sixteen when we first met.

Something of young lovers remained between us, even after twenty-two years, a twelve-year-old daughter, and life in three countries. We had an easy way to keep count of the time the two of us had spent together: ten years of dating, ten of marriage and then our first and only child. Total number of years? Twenty, plus our daughter's age.

When I got to work, I waited as usual for the gate to open. I kept an eye on incoming traffic and made sure nobody came out at the same time. The gate was a solid slab of metal and it stood next to the guard house, a bulky construction with tinted glasses and dark concrete walls. Sliding slowly on its rails, the mechanism gave a long enough pause to realize you had been accepted to a place not meant for everyone.

I could never tell whether anyone was seated in the guard house or not. The first few times I crossed that gate I wondered if I needed to wave good morning to some invisible man. Now I would simply drive through, conscious of my right to cross the thin threshold separating those inside from the rest of the world.

I drove into the underground garage; my place, Number 98, waited for me the same as every morning. I had to cross another barrier before entering the parking lot. Had to swipe the badge and be greeted by the welcoming green light. A beep confirmed the security system recognized me. I went down the ramp slowly, giving the gate below time to open, enough to let me pass without having to wait. With the years, my timing had become impeccable.

Inside the garage, people had to drive at walking speed to reach their numbered parking slot. Mine was in the last row so I had enough time to realize something obstructed my place. I slammed on the brakes refusing to believe it. I raised my hand ready to smack something and hit the steering wheel in exasperation. For, as I approached my slot, I saw that two wood crates had been left there.

The underground parking also served as a reception area for the Publications Department. Slots in the middle section had been eliminated to give room to the storage areas where all deliveries received by the Pub's colleagues were collected and where confidential publications were packaged for expedition. No one thought that arrangement to be efficient and sustainable. At times, I had to wait for small crate lifters to operate. A short wait but frustrating when colleagues waited for me at a meeting. Complaints to Human Resources and Logistics & Operations had so far produced no results. And now this.

I stepped out of the car to check whether any of the storage workers were around. At 8:10, the place was still rather empty. A few cars were parked in the garage that morning. For sure, they belonged to colleagues on business trips who were accustomed to leaving their vehicles there and taking a taxi to the airport.

The crates were empty. I could move them away or park somewhere else. I chose the first option since no one could see me move them. They weren't particularly heavy. I only had to slide them a short distance, zero risk of injuries or other silly things like tearing my trousers or jacket.

Although I didn't train anymore, my body still enjoyed the results of those past years of football practice—semi-professional level—and the task took only a few seconds: no sweat. I drove into my parking spot. Weird. Things like that were not supposed to happen as workers had a list of unoccupied places which could be temporarily used rather than the ones assigned to personnel.

With my badge in hand, I walked toward the third security point to cross. I swiped it and entered the monthly code on the keyboard. Invisible eyes were witnessing and recording entries for that morning, the same as for every other day. The transparent bullet-proof glass doors opened and let me in to the buffer zone, a concrete walled box with a painted red little square on the floor.

The procedure asked for me to stand still on the red mark without moving while something or someone evaluated my credentials. I hated this last step. After all the security steps I'd gone through so far, I had to be indeed worthy of credit to be allowed into the premises. Maybe guards verified at the same time whether I looked suspicious or dressed nicely? I almost questioned the invisible guard about those crates but I hesitated. This was something to sort out with the Hospitality Team instead. They look after logistics and other annoying stuff.

Besides, if I had moved or wiggled too much while standing on the little red square, the glass door behind would have opened and I'd have to go through the whole procedure again, sometimes suffering the lecturing guard and waste even more time. I am sure they took pleasure in making us wait. I stood as still as I could...and waited. It took a few seconds more than usual and I thought to complain when finally a green dot appeared. I heard the welcoming beep as the opaque entrance glass doors—also bullet proof—slid aside and I was allowed in.

The view had always been spectacular, especially on sunny days. From the parking level entry, one accessed a hallway dotted with settees aligned along its gray walls. In front, a huge glass wall spanned the whole height of the building and showed a magnificent view of Lake Lemano and the mansions of rich Swiss and foreigners wealthy enough to enjoy the scenery from their large estates.

After a last glance at the glorious day unfolding outside the glass wall, I started down the stairs to reach my desk one level below. The entire organization believed in full visibility so, to foster collaboration and communication among personnel, it had no offices...just open spaces and vast halls filled with large desks.

No cubicles, a la North American style, but shared spaces in between with desks arranged in islands of four separated by panels with a transparent top-third. Though you couldn't look at what your colleagues were doing, you had a clear view to establish eye contact; everyone sat in sight of everyone else. Hard to say whether this architect's dream resulted in any real increase of communications between teams. I still have my doubts.

Entering the hall, I peeked to see whether my highest-ranked collaborator and friend, Rose, had gotten in already. We had an established tradition between us: the morning cappuccino.

"Hi, Rose. How's it going?"

"As usual. The guys from Microsoft say they should be able to finish the sprint in time."

"Good, good start for the day. Cappuccino?"

Sprint was the term used to describe the set of tasks to be implemented during a period of three weeks. I led and defined the effort for a major collaboration platform of the highest security. It included all possible technical bells and whistles, video conferencing, and social networking to support all the initiatives running worldwide with our constituents.

Highly confidential matters were discussed on our system, especially on the encrypted video conferences and we enforced an absolute *off the records* policy. Journalists and others, I am sure, would have loved to eavesdrop what we heard those days, particularly Arab League discussions with the Americans.

Everything we did to support and enhance the platform was required *yesterday* and costs or efforts were never a factor. High pressure constantly, criticisms always abundant, congratulations scarce. The kind of demanding task and thankless job anyone sane in his head would avoid. How in the world I ended up in that trap is still an open question. Anyway, as the only director who had been able to *herd the cats,* we had released a working platform in spite of everything and within the agreed timeline.

A few desks away, an American consultant sat, hired and imposed on the team to speed up the project and *automagically* solve all scenarios. He looked at his emails, showing no interest in our conversation or our whereabouts. The guy only knew one thing well and kept selling that as an IT panacea: A framework—and not among the best ones—to create websites. He advocated the solution as the ultimate silver bullet.

It proved no good for us; rather it had been the source of problems and discussions during many of the past months. Much time and money miserably wasted. Yet, somehow, he had secured the ears of influential characters. Despite the lack of promised working prototypes, and even with failing all tests and missing deadlines, he succeeded in imposing his view. A spin doctor, cum laude. Could not happen at a for-profit organization where pennies were counted.

"To a hammer, every problem is a nail," we said on the

team but we called him 'the screwdriver'. We were confronted with stubborn nails and we needed a sledgehammer. Screwdrivers do not understand nails, so he wanted us to cut a slot on the head of every nail. Makes sense? Of course not. He kept neglecting crucial details about the project, things like 'nails have no threads'. We judged his solutions and vision as simplistic. There were other forces at play so our judgment didn't matter at all.

When we came back from our cappuccino, the consultant—even though now formally hired he still acted as such—had left the place for unknown destinations. Surely busy with bending people's opinions and buying support at every occasion. Grinding his way, or 'screwdriving' around, and forcing some head rolling in the process: move away or get crushed.

The cell phone beeped: *Time to start working and accomplish something*, I thought. A message from the HR Chief: "Dear Dan, did you receive our meeting invitation?"

Our invitation? Who was he referring to? From the details, I had to be in the Board Room in five minutes...with him and the 'screwdriver'.

"Rose, I just got summoned to an urgent meeting with Carl and Brad. If I don't come back," I said half-jokingly, "gather my stuff into a box, will ya?"

Rose looked at me with a worried expression. We'd had discussion after discussion covering the unsustainable situation we faced. The entire team, a group of twelve now about to arrive one after the other for their day of work, had envisioned every possible scenario involving changing jobs, projects, duty stations, or even resignation. Everyone expected me to prevent all this from happening.

16

I climbed the stairs to the level of the Board Room, thinking what would be my reaction if I had been shown the door. We'd recently had various meetings with big brass in the organization explaining why we were wasting our time and money, and had detailed the reasons, too. We received orders to halt an evolving project to favor some already failing chimera of an extremely quick solution requiring very little budget and exceeding functionality: the typical silver bullet. So annoying.

To think that not a single person on the upper floors had any idea what silver bullets were. They do not exist in computer science, or elsewhere. I hadn't realized yet what strong external support the new hire had.

I entered the Board Room without knocking at the door. It was a large rectangular space with floor-to-ceiling wood panels; a grandiose oval table throned in the middle, capable of seating thirty people on leather chairs of the highest quality. Screens on the two long walls allowed for video conferencing. The side facing the lake had the usual glass wall overlooking the gorgeous scenery. The institution never saved money and spared no expense. It dealt with big heads used to luxury and, thus, needed to impress as part of doing business with them.

Carl and Brad were already seated and Carl greeted me first. "Thanks for coming, Dan. Please have a seat."

"Hi, Carl...Brad." Now I didn't doubt what the meeting was for that early in the day: I knew the answer but I asked anyway. "Is anyone else going to attend?"

"No, just the three of us," said Carl, "and allow me to go straight to the point..."

I interrupted him. "Brad is here so I think I can guess

why we're meeting. Brad and I have divergent visions on how to proceed and toward which goals." I grinned. "I am surprised this comes right after some recent proofs of the weaknesses of his proposed solution."

I didn't even look at Brad. I cared only for Carl, with whom I had frankly exchanged opinions about the whole thing.

Carl went on describing how everything in the institution should perform as in a Swiss clock. All parts and wheels contributing and turning in unison so that the mechanism could do its job. I had been a great wheel so far but I didn't spin with the others anymore.

An overused analogy and often strident with reality: the clock ticked before hiring *the help* so Carl threw out the baby with the bathwater. He seemed to recite from a lesson of a spin doctor. He kept talking, not sounding convincing at all, or even like he was convinced himself. He came to the conclusion of his speech.

"The Board has decided to terminate your work contract with us. Your last day of employment will be on the 31st of May, in accordance with the legal deadline outline in the staff handbook. So as to provide you with as much time as possible to plan your future steps, we agreed to free you from any obligation to work until your legal deadline as of today. We confirm this does not affect your rights to your salary through 31st of May as well as a prorated 13th salary and holidays not taken during the period. You will find more details in here."

Carl handed me an envelope which I took without looking at it, smiling.

In a way, I felt relief. All these months seemed like

fighting against windmills. The issue had nothing to do with aiming at a better platform. Someone wanted to achieve a firm stance in a power struggle which had begun in the previous months. The COO had been forced to leave only weeks before. I acted as his right arm in many initiatives, besides the one I led. I became an impediment for someone, or considered to be one, refusing to put lipstick on pigs.

Carl raised his eyebrows and caressed his chin. The hint of a smile raised his lips. "You're reacting way better than I guessed. This morning, I tried to imagine how this meeting would unfold and nothing I could think of comes close to this. Are you…happy?"

"Look, Carl…" No one paid attention to Brad, who kept watching Carl and me having this conversation, acting as if he wasn't in the room or had nothing meaningful to say. Probably the latter.

"We both know what is going on in here. We've discussed this endless times."

I clenched my jaw and clutched the sides of the chair fighting the urge to stand up. I sighed. "We, nope, *you* guys will waste even more resources. I can't tell you how painful it is to deal with this nonsense we are forced to pursue. It is not going to be my problem anymore and that is a relief, believe me."

The meeting had undoubtedly come to an end. No further discussions needed, a scenario played already. Brad left the room without saying a word while Carl and I remained seated. When alone, Carl had been more sympathetic.

"What are you going to do now, Dan?"

"I'll go home, relax, cure the acid reflux afflicting me

these past months. Remember my words, Carl. At the next Global Meeting, there will be no system to show. Ours, de facto, is to be wiped out and retired. The new one will be recycled to do something else, much smaller in scope, less ambitious. Unable to work as intended or reproduce what we did so far. It falls short now, it will fall short then. At most, you get a new website." I laughed bitterly. "The most expensive website ever with a newly hired CTO to act as its webmaster. Congratulations."

Carl grinned and did not argue. "I need you to go through some formalities..."

Everything fit now, the parking place occupied with the wood crates; the delays in passing through the gates. Security knew that today I would have only a virtual presence on the premises.

"Your badge is disabled by now."

How predictable. *Poor Rose*, I thought. She had to collect my stuff for me and put everything in a box. The rest of the list was quick: email account, the blackberry, various cards...

"We need those now. I am sure you understand."

Of course I did. Badge, corporate credit card. I also handed him the lunch card. "I have still some 100 Swiss Francs on it. I guess you'll be able to credit the next salary?"

"No problem."

Carl chatted with me all the way to the wardrobe. Then we headed straight to the employee entrance at the garage level, as if to make sure that I would vanish without incident of any sort or wouldn't talk unchecked to anyone. Still early in the morning, the entire meeting lasted no more than ten minutes; employees were arriving and starting their work day. No time for goodbyes. No one noticed.

"Is the Chairman in? I'd like to say goodbye."

"He's traveling. I'll tell him."

"I see. Well, nothing holds me here now. Have a good one, Carl."

The sliding doors opened and I reached my car while texting Rose on my iPhone. "Rose, get that box. I'm fired. Leaving now. Talk to you later."

"WHAT!!!!" I read her laconic answer, immediately received.

I repeated, "Talk to you later."

I had mixed feelings. Had nothing to blame myself for, had done everything right. I refused to oil squeaking wheels or lick boots. If something was wrong in the project, I frankly reported all risks and listed the reasons why, too. I never took offense or anger from constructive criticisms, always considered the facts, trying to never get personal. And it led me to this end result. We were in a world where facts were being ignored and trains were leaving the stations, speeding up toward… Nothing.

The News

I left the site for the first time in years without any of those technology gadgets to make sure 'leaving' became a word devoid of its original meaning. We had to be always in touch with the organization and reachable 24/7. I went through the last moments with an aseptic mental state; the germs of anger, frustration, revenge, and disdain had yet to get hold of my emotions. All considered, was it not for the best? Weren't anger, frustration and disdain exactly the feelings I fought daily for months?

I got used to waking up almost every night—or should I say morning—around 4am. The brain in ebullition with thoughts coming and going without control, one after the other. Revisiting all details, all discussions, all options over and over again. What I endured was far from a sound and sane condition and not sustainable. Worn out and stressed, and the very cause of all that had disappeared from my immediate future.

With these thoughts still lingering, I searched for an area to safely pull over the car and call my wife. She needed to know, no reason to wait to announce that later today. I read news about tragedies related to job losses where the facts had been hidden from family for months, creating a spiral of lies and leading to the worst. Not in this case, I repeated to myself as I had nothing to be blamed for. I had accomplished my tasks and looked after all duties with diligence and professionalism. I didn't need to hide anything.

Unfortunately—in today's business environment—that didn't enhance your job security.

I signaled a left turn and entered the parking lot of the

nearby golf course. One of the most exclusive and expensive clubs in the region, but I never played on its old, majestic course. *'Private. Members Only'* the sign said. I had been for business lunches a few times at their restaurant. Once, I thought I had a chance, however slim, of getting close enough to one of the members to be invited to play a round someday. Now the probability rapidly spiraled down to obliteration.

Stopping the car, I listened to the radio still providing local items of interest soon to be replaced by national news. World News Geneva, the only English-speaking channel in town, broadcast hourly bulletins directly from London. The program listed the crude violence of recent days.

In Libya, word came of an alleged systematic purge of pro-Gaddafi loyalists as entire villages emptied and all inhabitants disappeared. Street fights increasing in Athens between civilians and police and army forces; the government announced tougher measures. Italy, on the brink of economic collapse, became the stage for rough protests with anarchist connotations.

In Syria, the city of Homs was still under bombardment from the loyalist forces committing atrocities against its own people. President Assad denying the allegations; world news and the Arab League supporting them. The Arab Spring seemed on the verge of turning into a rather Hot Summer of violence and death. In the US, the run for the Presidency inflamed hearts and captured all comments and attention. After a moment of hesitation, I pulled out the iPhone from my jacket and dialed home.

"Hello?"

"Mary, it's me…" I hesitated, unsure how to continue.

"Hi, love. I'm about to leave for school. What's going on?"

I decided to be blunt. "I've been fired. They will pay me three months salary and they don't want me in the game anymore."

Silence. I expected a reaction, a gasping sound, a 'gosh', anything. Silence had not been contemplated.

"Are you there?"

"Yes. Catching my breath. Dan, what are you going to do? What are *we* going to do?"

Heard that before, hadn't I? "I'm coming home. Will I find you?"

"No, I'm going to school. My students are waiting for their lesson. I'll come home when I finish."

This time, it was my turn to stay silent. Mary is stoic, always has been. Even in this moment, while other women might go ballistic, she stayed resolute, her mind set on urgent things to do. I loved her so much and her strength was also mine.

"It's going to be all right. In one way or another."

"I know. Need to go now. I love you."

"I love you, too."

The dial tone signaled the end of the conversation.

The radio announcer still reported facts and events of the day. "… all penguins make considerably shorter treks to the sea in December or January and spend the rest of the southern hemisphere summer feeding in warmer waters until March. Chicks begin molting into juvenile plumage from early November, which takes up to two months. Often, the process is not completed yet by the time they leave the colony and the adults cease feeding them.

"It is believed the entire colony perished during what are normally extremely favorable conditions for each individual: warmer temperatures and an abundance of fish. Experts rule out that thousands of Emperor Penguins may have died of natural causes. Captain Ryan from the Queensland Department of Natural Resources and Mines, which also monitors the Australian Antarctic Territory, had this to say: "This is something totally abnormal and we have no records of similar events in the past, even on a smaller scale. If they succumbed due to some sort of epidemic, we fear we could soon discover other decimated colonies. It is too early to come to any conclusion."

Wow, I thought. *This is crazy.*

I turned the engine on, heading home. In my ears, I still heard Carl's voice telling me the Board had decided to get rid of me and yet I couldn't avoid thinking about what I just heard on the radio. What might be the cause of all those deaths? Pollution? Poisoning? Heavy metals in water? There had to be something responsible for thousands of sudden casualties. An entire colony? Adults, females, chicks, no survivors. Pollution and poisoning did not fit.

I made my way into the remaining traffic flow of early morning, past the rush hour of commuters reaching their work place. Something, I realized, I won't do anymore. My mind had started to taxonomize all the implications of what happened.

The radio anchor again grabbed my attention while driving along the winding road down the hills toward Geneva.

"... the eminent gorilla specialist, George Schaller, tells us that the population lived in the area north and northwest of Lake Tanganyika. All three gorilla subspecies are listed as endangered by the U.S. Fish and Wildlife Service and by the Convention on International Trade for Endangered Species and that this is a natural disaster of immense proportions. The gorilla individuals—hundreds of them—have been found dead in various areas by members of the Diane Fossey Gorilla Fund International. Though no signs of gun shots or wounds are reported, all present evidence of physical trauma and distress. The representative of the Fund said it is too early to attempt providing explanations now and that a full investigation will be conducted: "We are deeply sad as of this moment. This is a tragedy..."

The news was interrupted because of a declaration on Syria just released by Secretary-General Ban Ki-moon to the General Assembly of the UN. Syria experienced a condition of civil war: "We continue to receive information about summary executions, arbitrary arrests and torture" adding that, on Thursday, "loyalist forces launched a broad assault against the city" and "civilian casualties were heavy. Homs, Hama and elsewhere have seen brutal fighting with civilians trapped in their homes, without food or electricity, and with no possibility of evacuating the wounded or bury the dead."

I had just been fired but someone in the world definitely lived in a more dire situation. *Is there an end to the worst ever?* I thought. The news went on with other reports of unrest in various parts of Europe. Greece with social upheaval due to the economic crisis and Italy which suffered from an escalation of violence and unrest. Italy faced a huge sovereign debt and unsustainable interests to be paid to the international community and people were getting into open confrontations with the police and the Carabinieri—a military branch of the Italian Army with civil security duties.

I drove through the town in a trance. My mental autopilot would take me home while I was distracted by all sort of thoughts: the loss of job and steady revenue, civil unrests, deaths of both animals and men. Everything is relative, nothing is important. Crucial only if touching you directly. No hard feelings, no strings attached, just life as it is and always has been.

Soon I reached the outskirts of the city. CERN, the European Laboratory for Particle Physics, counted as the last agglomeration before the national border with France. No agent staffed the custom station since Switzerland joined the Schengen Area which comprised the territories of twenty-six European countries.

The Area operated very much like a single state for international travel—border controls for those traveling in and out of it, little to none for all internal trips. Only sporadic patrols were seen at larger crossings.

From there, a short ride led to our house. I got onto the expressway that prevented commute traffic to go through every village in the area with the hope of covering the miles faster than when using the inner roads. The expressway became frustratingly congested at rush hour forcing commuters to waste time in bumper-to-bumper conditions just to cross into Switzerland and reach their work places in town.

Geneva businesses constituted the largest pool of jobs for all people in the nearby French border zone and the town itself was the biggest factor contributing to the high standard of living in the region. This part of France would have been deeply rural and economically deprived if not for the City of Calvin. Every day, tens of thousands of people commuted between France and Geneva. They worked in town, had leisure time, and went back to France to sleep at their homes.

I pulled into the driveway, got out of the car and manually opened the iron gate which was, at first, supposed to be automatic. As time passed by, no one, Mary nor I, ever felt the need for that to change. We bought an old farm for our family, something in between a farm and a village home. We had renovated everything while maintaining the ancient character wherever possible, conferring a peculiar charm to the property. Old and new interlaced harmoniously, marrying different styles and materials with always a subtle contrast that made the house warm and cozy and…homey.

We liked this place, Mary and I. We put in so much of ourselves. The colors, the tiles, the plants in the garden. A nice piece of land of some twelve thousand square feet of grass, bushes, fruit trees, and an olive tree growing in front of the terrace, a tree considered holy in ancient Greece. We planted everything when we bought the property, not knowing whether it would survive the rigid winters common in the area. It did, and majestically so. We took that as a good omen.

Will olive holiness protect us from this, too? The disturbing thought that we could be forced to sell the house struck me with the power of a sledgehammer blow to my chest. The first gut-wrenching reaction to the little speech from Carl, an hour before. I would try to avoid anything but that at all costs.

Costs, right; I had to think clearly about the necessary and unavoidable expenses and what could be cut or reduced from now on.

I headed for the front door, pulled out the keys and fumbled a bit with them. I felt like I needed a coffee, or something stronger. I managed to open the door; the alarm welcomed me with its three-tone beep, the first three notes of the US anthem. I reached the keypad and entered the code. The house was submerged again in silence, Mary already at school. My throat was dry. I went to the kitchen, the room my wife liked the most as she had personally designed the large trapezoidal island for all her culinary adventures.

The kitchen was warm, welcoming and full of utensils. Mary had always been a terrific cook. Keeping in shape was a remarkable achievement and a source of astonishment with a dose of criticism from Mary. To her, I ate too much—"it is not my fault, hon," I often joked. "If you were a worse cook, I would enjoy eating less than I do."

I noticed a small note on the stone counter.

"Don't worry. We will make it through. Together. Love you."

Yes, of course we would, though how and when were still two open questions. I took a mug, put a capsule in the machine and started brewing a coffee. The smell was much better than the noise. At least the coffee was good and a warm mug is always comforting.

I went upstairs. Our house had three levels, the top one being the result of a massive renovation work. We raised the roof enough to get a full additional floor, gaining almost a thousand square feet of living space and it was great. Mary and I enjoyed the entire upper level as our *quarters;* bedroom, dressing room, bathroom, and home office.

On the middle floor, we had our family room with the TV set, a small storage unit, our daughter's bedroom with its own bathroom. At twelve, she had started to ask for us to respect her privacy; she got herself a panel with a *Keep Out* on one side and a *Please, Come in* on the other. When at school, the sign was in her room. She did not use it often, and we took care to always knock if she had the door closed.

I sat on the couch and switched on TV, looking for some news reports. I hopped from one channel to another, the usual cocktail of CNN, BBC News, France 24, Rai International, Al Jazeera. Most were covering the recent election win for Vladimir Putin; with a landslide vote, the old KGB apparatchik had again retained full power and the Kremlin.

Changing the channel once more, France 24 reported the deaths of Mountain gorilla colonies. The causes of death still very much of a mystery, all gorillas presented bruising and blood in their soft tissues. Rangers had started to collect evidence and testimonials. Some reported they saw strange lights, or luminescent shapes, not far from where the gorillas had been found. Other witnesses heard rumbling sounds like thunder, though no meteorological events of any relevance had been reported in the area.

Officials concurred the deaths of the animals were a malicious act and promised a full investigation would be conducted to find and bring to justice the perpetrators. A veterinarian from the Mountain Gorilla Veterinary Project confirmed that, in the past days, locals had whispered among themselves about lights in the shape of a sideways capital "T" up in the flanks of the Virunga Volcanoes. They considered them the cause of the gorilla deaths. The veterinarian also specified that some elders said the *watu wa mwanga*—which could be translated from Swahili as *people of light,* or *from light*—were responsible. This information had not been verified independently.

30

I changed to RAI 24 International: the news focused on another mass bird killing, "… for the last five days, wildlife experts and officers from the forestry commission have picked up more than 1,000 turtle doves as well as other birds, including pigeons. Yesterday alone, 300 corpses were recovered, all of them having a blue tinge to their beaks. Scientists say this could indicate poisoning or hypoxia—a lack of oxygen—which could confuse animals and lead to death.

"The incident in the town of Faenza in northern Italy comes after a series of similar cases and, more recently, in the United States and Sweden. Birds were not the only species to be affected. Millions of fishes also washed up on river banks and coastlines. The turtle dove case is the largest incident to have hit Europe so far. In Sweden, 50 jackdaws were found dead. Italian officials said they expected results from forensic tests on Monday."

"Let's hope it is poisoning or an illness because that would be easier to deal with than it being a sign the world is coming to an end. Tests are being carried out on the bodies by the local forestry commission. Results should be available as of next week, but it is the numbers that make this such a notable event and for the moment it is a mystery."

Although I never had much consideration for these kinds of conjectures, many people were deeply affected by fear. According to many (false) prophets regarding the recent reports, life on Earth would end soon. Something to do with the Mayan calendar. December 21, 2012—the Northern Hemisphere's winter solstice—would be the last day.

The TV screen showing pictures of men carrying billboards urging people to repent because "The End is

Near" had always been common. These animal deaths were adding fuel to general public foolishness. I recognized the streets of Berkeley, California where a group of individuals distributed leaflets to passersby and a large billboard with huge letters filled the scene long enough to read it through:

"The word of the LORD that came to Zephaniah son of Cushi son of Gedaliah son of Amariah son of Hezekiah, in the days of King Josiah son of Amon of Judah. I will utterly sweep away everything from the face of the earth, says the LORD. I will sweep away humans and animals; I will sweep away the birds of the air and the fish of the sea. I will make the wicked stumble. I will cut off humanity from the face of the earth, says the LORD."

The news went on with other facts. Frustratingly, every one of them involved violence, fights, clashes and more deaths. This time, causes were identified without mistake: bullets, bombing, and the general hatred human beings have been so surgically armed with to inflict the greatest pain and suffering upon one another.

I switched off the TV. "Sweep away the birds of the air and the fish of the sea. Sweep away humans and animals." *Now, that is a grandiose plan*, I thought. One that requires quite a sizeable infrastructure to take place and a divine strong will, definitely the case for this last one.

The context did not matter to those people. God had spoken specifically to Judah and the officials of Jerusalem, not to us living in the 21st century. Still, I have to say it was an enthralling conjecture and a very special case of connecting the dots. No doubts, everyone would be interested and concerned about an inordinate amount of dead wildlife though investigations should not bother Bible scholars or any claim of prophecies. Maybe we had better ask ourselves how were we provoking such *natural* disasters?

I decided to Google those animal deaths because I needed to think about something else. Serious enough to justify my turning away from mulling over the morning chat and the ensuing loss of employment. What I found startled me. My little online search revealed, and for 2010 only, reports of not less than eleven strange mass deaths of animals. Thousands and thousands of birds and tons of fishes, mostly in the US.

For 2011, the situation was not better. On the contrary, fifteen unexplained culling of birds and fishes now reaching locations in Europe, too. 2012 seemed to have started in high gear with more evolved animals being victims of something killing them in a quite unpleasant way. Whatever the cause, it had escalated.

With a jolt, I noticed the clock: 4pm. Time to go pick up Annah at school. Annah, our 12-year-old daughter, attended the International School of Geneva. When she was three, we chose a teaching institution for her because, at the time, we were still planning to go back to the US. Our goal was to find a school where Annah would receive an education in English and a good one, too. Our choice turned out to be the perfect one, welcoming children from the youngest ages through diploma years.

Back then, I worked as a scientist with the Lawrence Berkeley National Laboratory amidst a happy staff. As a physicist interested in computer science, I found my turf: fundamental research with lots of computing. I had the feeling I spent my time playing rather than working.

Life in Berkeley Hills and at the lab had been a memorable experience. The weather was pleasant, colleagues and friends were caring, San Francisco a town I fell in love with. We had friends in California. Tony Bennett sung "I Left My Heart in San Francisco"—as I learned—for the first time at San Francisco's Fairmont Hotel in the famous Venetian Room. Mary and I had been there a few times and dined in the hall, with its crystal chandeliers and bronze marble columns. Whenever I traveled back to the City by the Bay, I felt like I was going home...much to Mary's dismay who judged herself as European as anyone could be. Maybe I truly left part of myself there.

Our families were from the old continent, and Europe is far away from California. Even with computers and telephones, the nine-hour time zone difference made you aware of the distance in a profound and acute way. After our daughter's birth, the separation became intolerable. Sending pictures and the frequent phone calls were not able to fill the gap and ease a longing for our families. When the US Lab proposed a rotation of personnel to the CERN labs in Switzerland, I added my name to the list to spend two years in Geneva, allowing for easier contact with our relatives. At least for a while.

Science was devoted to building massive apparatuses with such crushing images like modern cathedrals of molten iron and slabs of lead to demonstrate the world rested on infinitesimal entities and twined dimensions of an ephemeral reality. At CERN, scientists pursued the poetry of the invisible, the poetry of the infinitesimal unexpected possibilities.

The two years became four, then five, and life took precedence with its own plans; other job opportunities came along, then the malicious and evil 9-11 struck. We never went back to live in the US. I always remember John

Lennon's words, so true in cases such as this: "Life is what happens to you while you're busy making other plans." Life indeed had other plans...for everyone.

— o —

I arrived at the school around 4:30pm when students gathered in front of the main entrance. I only had to wait a couple of minutes for Annah to show up. At twelve, she had started to go through a full transformation, the child leaving and making way for the young woman to be. Annah takes a lot after her mother and people say after me as well, though I know better.

She glanced around quickly in search of either my car or myself and a smile rose to her lips when she saw me standing near our Volvo. A mute "hi, Dad" was followed by a hand wave, then she started walking toward me. I decided then to hide from her what had happened that morning. Mary and I needed to discuss it first, figure out clearly all it implied in our life. Annah would be told at the right moment—and this one, with her beautiful smile—was definitely not a good one.

"Hi, Dad. How was your day?"

"Fine, sweetie," I said, giving her a kiss. "And yours?"

The ride back home was uneventful, our usual conversation taking place. I liked to take our daughter to school and pick her up whenever possible. With our schedules, we were all together only during breakfast and at dinner. Those rides with Annah allowed me and her to share some time every day.

Annah was remarkably open with me about all that went

on in her world. Her student life, her friends, the recent discovery of the existence of boys, and the first parties held by the school itself in the large gymnasium. I loved the privilege when Annah asked me how to tell whether a boy was in love with a girl. A hypothetical boy, of course, whose name varied from William, Victor, Robin, Lee… and a hypothetical girl named Annah.

How long would she keep me so much a part of her life? When we reached home, the gate was opened and Mary's car was in the driveway. I parked next to hers. By the time we got out, Mary appeared on the door step with the most incredible smile ever to greet us. "My loves," she said, coming toward us.

She embraced me, then Annah, who drove us back to reality.

"Hi, Mom! I'm hungry. Can I have a snack?"

We walked into our home together.

After a pleasant dinner, given the situation, we kissed Annah good night at the usual time, a bit before nine. The next morning was a regular school day and we didn't need to break any routines now. When alone, inevitably Mary and I turned to my dismissal.

Mary knew the past months at work had been particularly tense. I had trouble masking my anger and frustrations. Moreover, Mary has always been a true life companion; I shared everything with her and she always did her best to help me manage my emotions. She understood the mixed disappointment and relief too. She was scared though and did not hide her feelings.

But it wasn't the end of the world. My career had been irreproachable, with a strong curriculum and diversified expertise. I had developed a solid scientific and IT background, and significant experience in multinational environments. I would find something else in the next few months.

I started to plan my next steps: contact a professional development program agency; head hunters; update my Linkedin account; and use relationships and work-related contacts to create even further connections. More for myself than for Mary. The planning gave me the feeling I had control and was still able to think clearly.

We went to bed early. Mary hugged me for a long time until she fell asleep. I could sense from her body and her breathing she was tense. I rested there, in the dark, cuddling my woman and comforting her, hoping the sky would not fall.

'Life is what happens to you while you are busy making other plans.'

During the night, we woke up to the noise of a strong windstorm. Powerful gusts of wind shook the trees, interrupted by brief moments of calm. Then again, mighty blows blasting against the roof and a roaring with the strength of multiple airplanes landing all together, in one go, on a nearby tarmac. I peeked out the window; the sky was dark, maybe a full hour still to dawn. Mother Nature showed off her might that night, or so I thought.

Mary went downstairs to check on Annah. When she came back, she reassured me that Annah was sound asleep. Her room on the middle floor was protected from the wind blowing strongly outside. No angry boos or whispers.

We had a bit more than an hour before the alarm clock summoned us to our daily activities. Mary curled up close to me and we waited, without a word, listening to the roaring sounds around the house. The wind subsided all of a sudden, as if a gigantic fan had been switched off. Silence, a deep one, replaced the ravaging noises of an angry nature—the calm after the storm—penetrating and intense.

Dawn came with its twilight before sunrise, the brief moments the Roman deity Aurora ruled over and the world awaits the rising sun, holding its breath. The buzz of the alarm broke off the magical silence. Mary stopped the noise with a searching hand, still half-asleep.

"Hummm, we need to get up. Take a shower. I'll go downstairs, prepare breakfast and then wake up Annah. Will you pick up her at school?"

"Sure." For some time, I would be the only master of my schedule. I grinned in the dark and still-sleepy atmosphere of our bedroom. Mary squeezed my hand. She felt for me more than I did myself.

I took a long shower, soothing some lingering internal, invisible bruises. During the day, I needed to get organized and launch the job hunt on many fronts. I had never been laid off before. While common wisdom says in such cases a few days of rest are a must, I wanted to get back into action. Why wait and for what? I needed to revise my resume, visit some head hunters, send emails and, hopefully, arrange for interviews soon.

I dressed casually—unusual for me during weekdays—but I didn't think Annah would notice or raise questions which were as yet too hard to answer. My girls were waiting for me in the kitchen and Annah had just filled up three glasses with juice. Orange for Mary and I, apple for herself.

"Good morning, Dad."

"'Morning, sweetie."

I hugged her and kissed my wife even more tenderly than usual. I set up to prepare coffee for the two of us and got a bottle of milk out of the fridge. Slices of bread were already in the toaster. I loved that smell coupled with the one of freshly-brewed coffee. The dawn sky was beautiful; the morning air, clean and crisp. From the kitchen window, we could catch a glimpse of the Alps and their perfect silhouette.

We were all seated, with jam and marmalade and Nutella ready for the crunchy slices of white bread. Annah started to tell us about the last hilarious video she saw on YouTube and how everyone in her class mentioned it to each other. Ah, and she would love to invite Jessie, her BFF—best friend forever—to stay overnight that weekend.

I shared a confirming glance with Mary. "Sure. You can tell her later today at school."

Mary was not talkative in the mornings so her silence was not a deviation from the norm though she had a hint of a worried frown stamped on her face. I repeated what we had already agreed to before.

"I'll pick up Annah."

"Yes, please. I won't be back home before five today. We have a PTA meeting after school hours."

"All right, it's a deal then. Annah, c'mon, get up and get ready. You know what happens if we're stuck in traffic."

"Yeah, Dad, I know. Besides, don't start reading emails or *I* will be the one waiting."

Annah gave me a gentle push to my shoulder and went to her room.

"We have to tell her one day. She will notice you changed your schedule…and that you're not wearing a costume." Mary looked at me intensely.

If I had believed the sweater would go unnoticed, that proved me wrong. Women, you can never hide anything from them.

"Fine, we'll find the moment. Okay, I'll brush my teeth and we can leave. Will you be still at home when I get back? It shouldn't take me more than forty minutes total."

"I don't know…I need to leave by 8:00. I won't close the gate since you're coming back right away."

Passing by Annah's room she reminded me with her singing voice: "Don't be late, Dad."

"No worries. I'll wait for you downstairs in five."

"Yeah, yeah…No emails, remember?"

I smiled and went upstairs.

In less than five minutes, I was ready to go; Mary was still in her nightgown. Annah rushed so she could be waiting at the door. She had her index finger raised and gestured at me with a mischievous smile.

Mary loved to have our upstairs quarters all to herself in the morning. She said not having a man around while she got ready in the morning meant cutting out at least fifteen minutes in her routine. She was right.

Annah and I both kissed and hugged Mary in turn. I opened the front door to the fresh and invigorating morning air. Outside, the first sun beams traced a placid and serene sky after the night windstorm. The garden was fine though plants showed the stressful moments they suffered. A vase had been knocked down, luckily without breaking into pieces. All was silent and beautiful.

I went to open the gate—"Yeah, one day you *will* be automatic"—while Annah waited for me in the car. When I got in and started the engine, she had already tuned the radio to her favorite station and music filled the air.

We started to drive down toward the plain then turned right onto the straight road through the crop fields to reach the expressway. From that point, it was still a few miles to the Swiss border across which the CERN lab spanned. We encountered no other cars, not uncommon though somewhat rare.

After a rail crossing, the road climbed over a small hill then descended to a roundabout where a countryside Holiday Inn greeted businessmen from everywhere in the world. They claimed *"Outstanding Service at the Doorsteps of*

Geneva" with an expressway directly linked to the airport.

In February, farmers started to fertilize the soil by spreading manure, easy to tell by the acrid smell. On the field to the right, just before the Holiday Inn, a green trailer towed behind a tractor featured a rotating mechanism to distribute the cows byproduct.

Getting closer, I could see the tractor was not moving, its front wheels bogged down into an irrigation ditch, the manure accumulating from being spread over the same place for quite some time as I judged from the height of the dung. I slowed down. The farmer in the cabin was bent on the steering wheel.

My God, I thought.

Annah noticed my alarmed expression and followed my gaze.

"Dad…what happened?"

"I don't know, he must have had a sudden illness. Let me call your mom."

I kept driving, using the hands-free phone kit to dial home. The radio was silenced automatically and, after few rings, Mary answered.

"Hello?"

"Mary, it's me. A man in the tractor near the hotel…you must call an ambulance. There is no one around and I believe I am the first one to…Jeez!"

As I drove into the roundabout and through the underpass toward the expressway, I nearly collided with a car, its lights on, which half-blocked the way. I swerved. The driver had his head thrown back as if he was sleeping.

My heartbeat skyrocketed, both for the scene and the maneuver in the near-miss crash. "Mary! Another accident. I almost slammed into a car on the shoulder."

Annah turned around to look back at the scene.

"Dad, we should stop! He might need help!"

"Hold on a sec, Annah. Mary, are you listening!?"

"What's going on?"

As I got onto the expressway via the ramp, the scene shocked me and I couldn't talk anymore. A couple of cars had crashed into each other, another slammed against the guardrail. Further down, a pickup had overturned and come to rest on the shoulder. Nothing moved. A truck had smashed through the barrier and plowed into the field below, smoke billowing from the wrecked engine.

The sudden silence on the line worried Mary. "Annah, Dan! What happened?"

Annah stared at the scene, her lower lips trembled and tears streamed down her face.

"Mary, we're coming home. Here...it is...it is full of cars...accidents. I'll see whether I can get through to the next exit and be home right away. Call the police now! I'll try, too."

"Oh my god. Are the police there?"

Was she listening to me? I snapped. "*I told you to call them*!"

I took a deep breath. Mary wasn't at fault. Meaningless to pick on her.

"Sorry. No one is here, no one is alive! Stay home, *don't go out!*"

Mary seemed on the verge of panicking, her voice raised to a piercing cry. "*Wait! Don't leave me!*"

"Okay! Okay. Calm down. We're fine."

I turned my attention back to Annah "Look at me Annah. *Look at me!* Okay. Honey, everything is fine, we're going home now. Get down in case I have to drive fast."

No need to speed at all but I did not want her to keep staring at the horrific scene. At one specific moment in the commute morning traffic, everyone at the same time had lost control of their vehicles and crashed…wherever. People were dead or badly hurt in the crashes.

I couldn't think of too many things in parallel at that moment. I shut down my brain and maneuvered in a sort of gymkhana to get through, around, or by wrecked cars. I managed not to indulge in rubbernecking either. In the distance, toward Geneva, a plume of black smoke I hadn't noticed before filled the sky. I reached the exit. Shortly after, I stopped the car on the overpass and got out.

"*Dad, don't go! I'm scared!*"

I jolted, bumped my knee against the car door, looked angrily at Annah and shouted "Calm down, Annah!"

I managed to regain composure after a few seconds. Annah trembled like a puppy on a cold night.

"I am here. Not going anywhere."

"Dan! Annah!" Mary shouted on the phone.

Raising my voice had the opposite effect, of course. Suddenly a small and scared child took over the happy young woman she was moments before. She kept sobbing and shaking.

From the bridge, a frightful and grisly scene; cars and trucks crushed with everyone trapped inside. No one alive around. I counted not less than fifteen vehicles, maybe more. And the silence…the humming of the car engine sounded blasphemous while I grasped the full magnitude of what I was witnessing.

I got back in the car and reached to hug Annah, covering her with my body to comfort and protect her. "Let's go home. And stay down, honey." She felt so small and vulnerable in my arms. "Mary, I'm bringing Annah home. Don't worry, try to reach someone now, please! I love you. Be there in a few."

I interrupted the call and music filled the air again. No commentaries, no live anchor voice. We listened to the recorded program that usually goes on at night. I switched it off. Music sounded awfully out of place now. I forgot to call the police myself.

Driving back home, what started as a peaceful morning turned into a nightmare of unknown proportions. We passed other car accidents and the corpses of a couple pedestrians, too, lying on the pavement at the bus stop. Some early commuters waiting for a bus that did not come and would not be coming either.

Annah moaned softly and I kept talking to her until we got back to the straight road through the crop fields.

"It's fine now, we're almost there."

Annah did not reply. She looked at me intensely as if trying to absorb strength and composure from me. We met no one on the last miles before reaching our place. Mary rushed out of the front door crying.

"Where is Annah? *Where is Annah*!?"

"*In the car!* She's in the car!"

Mary almost threw herself inside the vehicle. She grabbed and encircled Annah with her arms. They both burst out crying.

Getting to the passenger side, I opened the door and put my arms around both my women.

"Let's go inside now, don't stay here. Let's go."

The black smoke in the distance was now visible from the garden and was expanding slowly. While taking them indoors, I became aware of the absence of any planes coming into the Geneva airport...maybe all air traffic had been diverted? Surrounding houses showed no sign of activity either. For the time being, I did not mention any of that to Mary.

Once inside, I locked the door. Mary went to the kitchen with Annah and gave her a glass of water. Why do we all drink after some shock? I could not swallow anything after what I had seen and heard. Everything was so silent.

"Mary, did you call the police?"

"Yes, and I tried them all...15, 17, 18, and 112." She peered out the window.

She had done well as those were the numbers for the ambulance, police, fire department and the European-wide emergency operator.

"What did they say?"

Mary hesitated. "Dan...no one is answering." Then she looked out the window "What is with that smoke?"

Unreal. This was not possible. Made no sense.

"I don't know about the smoke. Are you sure the line is

working properly? Those services are on 24/7. An operator must be answering calls."

Mary stared at me and did not reply; she was pale. I picked up the phone and the familiar tone greeted me. I dialed 112. "Pick it up...pick it up." The phone kept ringing on the other side. Mary watched the whole scene, visibly scared. She had to sit. Annah was recovering slowly. An impossible scenario unfolded before us.

I tried another emergency number even though by then I did not expect a different result: no answer. In France, call centers are interconnected. Switchboard operators assess the situation then decide upon which resources to send out. In all cases where victims are present, the ambulance service is dispatched, too. There was no operator to answer our calls.

"Stay here. I'll try the computer."

Mary and Annah didn't react. I rushed upstairs, climbing the stairs two at a time and almost falling at the last one. "*Shit!*" We had a reliable and fast Internet connection and I would have had all answers in a matter of seconds. I sat in front of the iMac and launched the browser on the BBC News website.

Thank God, the Internet worked. The familiar page fired up almost immediately. "Greece unrest continues unabated", "Pakistan charges Bin Laden widows", "Strong solar storm hitting Earth", "'Fresh massacre' in Syria's Homs", "Powers urge serious Iran talks", and other news. Nothing strikingly unusual, no mention of any massive incidents anywhere. All seemed normal; the usual killing, fighting, massacres, riots. The solar storm? Not possible. At most, it would cause more Northern Lights and disturbances in telecommunications.

Then I noticed the date...it was yesterday's. Since last

night at 2:32, taking into account the time zone, nothing—or rather, no one—had updated the page. Now it was past 8:30 in the morning and journalists are early birds. It wasn't plausible that no reporter at the BBC had cared to add anything to the pages yet.

I tried other sites. Italian, French, Swiss news, and various newspapers online. The time seemed to have stopped sometime in the early hours of the day. Not one mentioned major catastrophic events, or any new recent event!

Email! I checked my account. Some automatic delivery, the usual commercial crap, the latest ones. Twitter! I logged on. It worked! Last tweets, worldwide trends, not a tweet from the people I followed nor the organizations. Even news channels were silent. Nothing recent. I tweeted, "PLEASE SOMEONE REPLY TO THIS IMMEDIATELY. THERE ARE CORPSES ON THE STREETS. I AM IN GENEVA AREA. PLEASE ANSWER BACK." I had fourteen more characters to use, but I hit send anyway.

My heart dropped a beat as I stared at the message on the screen: "Sorry! We did something wrong. Try sending your Tweet again in a minute."

I tried again, and again.

"Daaann!"

"*Yes!* Mary! What?"

In my chest, heart was pounding; my ears buzzing. I went quickly downstairs expecting the worst. Mary and Annah were standing in front of the kitchen door leading to the yard, staring out the glass panes.

"What?"

Mary pointed at something in the garden.

"The cat. That is our neighbor's cat."

The neighbors! Right! The neighbors.

"Have you seen them? What's their number?"

"It's stored on the phone."

Mary played with the commands for a few seconds. "Found it!"

She dialed. We waited. Mary's expression grew more tense with time. Her lips twisted tightly, then she started to bite them in anguish. I didn't like that so I took the phone from her and put it down.

"Mary! Look at me!"

I turned her toward me, my hands on her shoulders.

"We are all together. Only this counts. We are safe."

I pressed her body against me and gently pushed her head on my shoulder, caressing her hair, and held her tight. She began to cry.

Annah awoke from her stunned lethargy and reached to hug us both. I opened one arm to embrace her, too. The enormity of what we were going to face started to emerge in our minds.

"Stay here, you two, and try to calm down. I don't see any immediate danger. We need to know what happened to the neighbors."

Mary straightened up, her eyes imploring, "No! Please don't go."

"Dad! Stay!"

They complained but I needed to search for one thing which had just popped into my mind. And I did not want to tell them anything about it right then.

"I'll be back soon, don't panic."

I pointed at the beautiful morning out there. The sun was warm and everything calm outside, though eerily so. I managed to have them agree that it made sense to cover the short distance to our closest neighbor's house and…check on them? I gave no other details. I kissed them.

"Don't stay here. Go upstairs so you can watch me going, make sure everything is okay."

I led them toward the stairs. They were frightened and I could not blame them.

"Be careful and come back right away!"

"Don't worry."

Without Mary and Annah knowing, I wanted to grab the sturdy butcher knife we had in the kitchen as a precaution. Maybe paranoid, but was I really? *Yet only the paranoid survive*, I thought.

Checking on the neighbors was not the plan. Joe had been in the army in the sixties, and he once showed me his gun and bullets with pride. He kept everything in pristine condition. His pistol would be better off in my hands now.

He was proud of that pistol. "Dan, let me show you something," Joe once said. We shared a beer on his patio one warm weekend the year before while the wives were away. He went inside and came back with a bulky object wrapped in a cloth. He unfolded the tissue and put a wooden box on the table. He held his hand on the cover for a moment, then opened the lock with a small key.

"This is my MAC-50. Did I tell you I served as petty officer?" Yeah, he'd told me few times. He took out a black pistol—automatic, I thought—and turned the gun into his hands as you would do with a piece of art. His eyes widened with some untold memories.

"The Manufacture d'Armes de Châtellerault originally made this baby. Then they changed the name to MAS when the operations moved to St. Etienne. This gun works perfectly, you know?"

He paused.

"9-rounds detachable bullet magazine with 19mm Parabellum. Look here, I still have plenty." He showed me several boxes. "I probably did wrong but, when I left the army, I managed to keep everything. The box is safe and locked in the cabinet with all my documents. But be careful, Dan. Beth doesn't know about me shooting with it so don't tell Mary."

I did not tell Mary.

I was sure Joe and his wife were dead so why weren't we? That question did not need any immediate answer, of course. The answer would come to us, whether we wanted it or not, and it might not be one we would like either. I took the knife in the kitchen, hid it under my sweater, and left home.

I walked out onto the front terrace, took a few steps, then turned around. Mary and Annah were at the first floor window, in our family room, anxiously watching. I waved and Mary threw me a silent kiss; I nodded and resumed walking. I wanted to reach our neighbors by crossing properties, climbing over the low garden wall, and get to their house from the backyard unseen by anyone in the neighborhood. Not that I expected to have any witnesses.

Their property showed signs of the previous night's

strong winds, too. A couple lawn chairs were overturned as well as some of the vases Beth cared so much about. Plants had broken twigs and the enriched soil she prepared meticulously for all her flowers was now spread on the patio floor in a kind of sad, dark bleeding.

The back door showed no signs of break-in. Apart from the shattered vases, everything seemed normal. Without much hope, I called out. "Joe! Beth?!"

I waited a few seconds before knocking hard on the door and called out to Joe again. No replies, nor any sound, came from inside the house. A friendly meow and a rustling startled me. Cats! Could they ever provide some warnings about their presence? What's her name again? *Peluche*, I recalled. Our neighbors' cat welcomed me in her fiefdom, graciously reassuring me I had been accepted.

I tried the door handle, locked from the inside. We lived in a safe neighborhood so no houses had reinforced doors or anything more than a standard lock. I was sure my body type was too much for the kind of obstacle blocking the way. As a precaution, I gave a solid kick to the door first before going with my shoulder. The wood around the lock cracked and Peluche ran away hissing. I guessed I would be a less-welcomed guest next time.

Encouraged by the first one, I kicked a second time and, with a loud crack, the door slammed open. No one heard anything. No alarmed voices, no hurried steps or the familiar voice from Joe yelling, "What the *fuck*!" I walked inside and took out my knife. Dan the Butcher! I had the feeling I'd stepped into some horror movie and I played the bad guy.

"Joe!?"

Nothing.

Proceeding cautiously, I reached the dining room then peeked into the kitchen and noticed the breakfast set on the table, ready and unused. Beth must have prepared everything the night before as we were used to doing ourselves. But no one had any breakfast that morning. Without further hesitation, I went upstairs toward Joe and Beth's bedroom.

Daylight flooded the room as Joe and Beth slept without pulling the window shades or using any blinds. The scene was explicit; no doubts on what happened. They lay in bed, no visible commotion, as if death had occurred within a few seconds. Not much to do. Although I expected that, my hands started to shake and I had to lean against the door frame, covered in a sudden sweat. My hand rose to wipe tears of anger and sorrow. I took a deep breath and put the knife away. These were not anonymous corpses; there was Beth, and Joe, and I could hear their voices in my mind.

They both had bloodshot eyes and some blood seeping from the ears. Joe's mouth was open and he looked as if he had been gasping before dying. Beth was more self-composed than Joe as she had been in life. She seemed to have passed away quietly even though she too showed sign of a rather stressful death. I guessed she'd died faster than Joe.

Joe had been a character. Always ready to share a beer and always busy with gardening chores. He loved gardening but he never missed the chance to tell me how it was Beth who made him dig that area, plant a new young tree, killing weeds, or doing laps with his small lawn mower. No task was so urgent not to stop for a beer each time he saw me in our garden. "Dan, time for a beer? You see, I'm not allowed to stop, I have Beth breathing down my neck but she can't stop me from sharing a beer with friends."

Of course, Beth never pushed him to do anything; she simply pointed at stuff and Joe would jump at the chance to get himself occupied. And Beth never failed to make a remark on our Italian origins when she served coffee on their patio "It has nothing to do with your strong Italian coffee but, oh my, I couldn't drink that. My heart would jump out of my chest."

They were always smiling and sometimes it was really funny to eavesdrop on their joyful quarrel about where to plant this or that flower in their garden. Joe, especially, mastered the art of bringing to the table the most absurd reasons to support his views. I sighed, fighting and chasing away the horde of memories that assailed me.

I closed their eyes, covering them with their own bed sheets. What else could I do? My mind went back to the main reason for this visit: the pistol. Joe said he safely tucked away his gun together with his documents. So it had to be in his home office. The cabinet, he'd said. In the office, there were a couple wooden cabinets, all locked, and a desk.

The desk drawers were open. Inside the right drawer, I found a few pens, some new envelopes and stamps, stationery, scissors, a stapler, a block of post-it notes, and unpaid bills. In the left one, more documents and papers, a bible, other office stuff, and keys! Could they be…I tried all of them on both cabinets. None worked, some did not even fit.

Well, the door hadn't provided much resistance so neither would a couple cabinets. Moreover, they were not intended to sustain burglary and I was sure I wouldn't have a police officer in front of my door the next morning. In any case, I had a pretty good story. I used the knife as a lever to force the middle doors open. I did not go for the additional drawers of the cabinets as I remembered the size of the box where Joe kept the gun. The pistol case wouldn't have fit in those.

The doors opened with a cracking sound, though much quieter than the patio door before. Inside, some folders labeled "Tax 2010-11", "Utility bills 2011", "Utility bills 2012", other loose documents and there! What I was looking for! Poor Joe, he had no reason to hide his gun any better, especially as he liked to clean and regularly use his 'baby', as he used to say. It only needed to be stored in a safe location and easily reachable at the same time. Moreover, both being retired, their kids had their own lives and no youngsters lived with them anymore. A nice old couple, good people they were.

I took the case and examined the small lock. The keys...

As a first guess, I tried the smallest one which fit and worked. Inside, wrapped with an immaculate white cloth, I found the MAC-50—or MAS-50, whatever the brand now—two full magazines and plenty of additional 19mm bullets boxes...parabellum. I put everything back in place and closed the cabinet. I had no reason to do that, except maybe out of respect for Joe. I headed toward the patio.

With the door cracked open, soon the house would become shelter to all sort of pests. Seeing Peluche alive and well made me think that other animals must be okay, too. However, Peluche was nowhere to be seen. Yet I believed she would survive. I closed the entry door as best I could and went home.

Mary and Annah were still looking through the window, waiting for my return. I guess too frightened and worried to do anything else. They got excited as they saw me climbing over the garden wall. They frantically waved at me but Mary frowned when she noticed I carried the wooden box. I raised my free hand to signal everything was alright. With Joe and Beth lying dead in bed, I still actually signaled all was fine.

As I approached the house, Mary and Annah came down the stairs and opened the door. "*Dad!*" said Annah as she ran toward me. She was getting stronger, her hug squeezed me. Mary waited at the doorway.

Back in the kitchen, Mary and Annah wanted to know about Joe and Beth. I did not go into the gruesome details about how I found the neighbors, dead in their bed. Especially not now, not in front of Annah. Maybe later, when I was alone with Mary if we had a brief moment of privacy during the day. I told them they passed away in their sleep and I covered them as best I could. I didn't think they suffered or realized anything. Nothing more to do for our neighbors for the moment but bury them. Mary couldn't hold her tears. Then Annah asked the question dangling from the tip of Mary's tongue.

"And the box, Dad? Is it Joe's?"

"Yes. Joe once showed it to me. I'm glad he did."

From Mary's expression, I believed she had guessed the content. She wiped her tears, sounding tense and nervous when she asked, "What's in there, Dan?"

"A gun," I replied bluntly. No reason to lie.

The answer immediately raised voices of concern from both: "I don't want a gun in the house!" and other remarks. With a calm voice, I managed to explain why I took Joe's pistol. Although we probably did not have any reason to use firearms right now, or in the future, I could not exclude the possibility. In case—just in case, I repeated—the need should arise, better to have a serious means of protection and dissuasion rather than confiding in human reasoning and intellectual power alone.

I had visions of a catastrophic and inexplicable event that had caused the scenes on the streets and throughout the village. I didn't have to invent any hypothetical danger from other people.

"Think of estranged dogs," I added after a moment. "It will not take long before they turn wild and dangerous if they start to fend for themselves. And wild dogs do hunt in packs."

Mary didn't seem convinced so I rapidly changed the subject.

"Anyway, we should try to get in contact with someone, anyone. Did you call the emergency numbers again?"

"I did. How is it possible no one is picking up, Dan?"

"I don't know. I can't be sure but what happened to Joe and Beth might be the same with the commuters on the expressway. Besides, I haven't seen anyone around, not a single person. I mean, alive. I can't… "

They seemed confused. I was confused, too.

"Mary, give me the phone, please." I thought about my parents who lived in Italy. "And try calling people on your cell. You, too, Annah. Call your friends."

I wanted them busy with something to do. I hoped all those deaths were somehow local, confined to a relatively small area even if wide by several miles. I still hadn't noticed or heard any incoming planes and, by then, quite a few should have reached the airport for landing in the morning. That, and the black smoke rising to the sky from that direction, played against my hope.

I dialed my parents' number. After what seemed to be the longest moment ever, I got a connection. The phone rang but no one answered. I glanced at Annah and Mary and I saw they too were not having any success with their own calls.

We tried all numbers we had stored on our phones, both the fixed-lines and mobiles. I even called professional relationships, anywhere, with no consideration of time zones. I would have loved if I woke up someone and verified that, somewhere, the world was running as usual.

Nothing.

"How can it be, Dan?" Mary was pale.

Annah didn't say a word but her lower lip trembled as it had earlier in the morning. I was not prepared to provide any explanation. *We* were not prepared for this. How is anyone supposed to face the possibility of being…left alone? Could that be? The eventuality defied all beliefs.

Armageddon and conspiracy theories combined pictured less extreme scenarios. This was the real world though, not a theory. Our reality, not some science fiction horror movie. How could people die en masse everywhere at the same time?

Granted, not getting any answer on the phones did not mean we were truly alone. The number of people we contacted had to be infinitesimal considering the billions of inhabitants on the planet. Rational thoughts clashed with everything we were experiencing.

"Dad…why don't we try the TV?"

Damn, what an idiot. Another obvious thing to do which I did not think of, yet my 12-year-old daughter came up with it.

"Of course! Come here." I hugged her. I needed that contact more than anything else in the world.

The TV set was on the first floor, in the family room. We all went. Finally we would have known, we would have been reassured, received explanations, and discovered people busy taking actions and things would turn to normal soon. We had TV via ADSL connection; I hoped everything worked there, too.

I switched on both the TV and converter box and started to jump from one channel to the other. We received blank screens, black screens, a couple non-stop infomercials, and one or two music only programs. In most cases, the screen showed a message stating *Technical Fault*, *No signal* and the like. A few times, some logos, numbers and codes, or an emphatic *End of Broadcasts*.

The channels were essentially dead in all the countries we had access to. The impact on us had been huge. We were speechless, muted, and I saw despair in both Mary's and Annah's eyes. Had the planet reset on us? Had something or someone called off human beings and their civilization?

"Dad...my friends. Are they dead? Even those on Facebook?" Annah cried softly.

Facebook! The largest social network on Earth. Annah and Mary had accounts on Facebook to stay in touch with co-workers, school mates and close friends. Others used the site for everything, even as a dating service! How many hundreds of millions were on Facebook and how many connected with each other daily? Those numbers are not matched by anything else online, I reasoned.

If someone was still alive and had—as we did—Internet access and a Facebook account, chances are he could be using it right now. Searching for others.

"Honey, I love you," I told Annah and I rushed upstairs to the computer.

Facebook, Facebook, Facebook...there was something I

had read about it recently.

"Mary! Your password, quick!" I shouted.

Mary and Annah joined me and, excited, I described the theory I came up with, surely we would find someone alive on Facebook.

"Dan, I am not friends with the entire Facebook community. How can you reach…?"

I stopped Mary short and started to explain what I read the week before and just remembered: The ads!

"You see, if you have an account and you pay online with a credit card, PayPal, whatever, you can run your own ad campaign and Facebook does the rest! In principle, we can reach everyone on Facebook."

The idea turned Facebook into the digital version of a message in a bottle. From our virtual island—Mary's account—we would send thousands, millions of messages to any Facebook page in the world…that is, if the servers were still working.

In the worst-case scenario, at least for as long as they worked until the next malfunction when nobody would be around to fix it. Then even Facebook would go silent and dead. Time was of the essence now. The plan might work for few days, hopefully weeks before the digital entropy stopped everything everywhere.

I got to the Facebook ads management page and clicked *Create an Ad*. Oh God, it worked, and the process was rather simple:

1. Design your ad with info like title, message, destination URL, etc.

2. Define the target. This was a godsend, choosing the

country where to send the ad just created.

I started with the US, Canada, and the EU countries. A panel on the right gave me the estimated reach...306 million people and counting. I eliminated all restrictions to select focused groups. My interest group was the entire planet!

I proceeded alphabetically and eliminated countries contributing less than a couple millions accounts. Next ads will cover those. I was going to send my "Calling for Survivors" message in the *Facebook bottle* to a comforting reach of four hundred sixty-two million and change!

I put a picture of us taken live with the built-in camera on the Mac and this message in all capitals. "WE ARE ALIVE. PLEASE CALL OR GET IN TOUCH WITH US AT..." then the date and time. I added our phone numbers and the email addresses we had access to. I hit the *Review Ad* button. A popup message stopped me short. Because I targeted users without any age restriction, minors were reached, too. My ad had to go through an approval process before going live.

I could not rely on Facebook employees still working to approve ads. Frighteningly enough, that seemed no longer to be wild hypothesis and conjecture. CNN was dead and it meant only one thing.

I adjusted the target age and placed the order. After a few seconds, the greatest thing on Earth happened: the Mac *Glass* alert sound, signaling incoming messages, cheered us as the most beautiful sound ever. We received an automatic message from the Facebook Ads Team! I wondered if anyone from that team had survived, God bless them.

The email said:

"Thanks for creating a Facebook Ad or Sponsored Story!

Your confirmation is below. Please note that you will only be charged for the impressions or clicks your ad receives. The total charge will not exceed the daily campaign budget you have set.

Remember to create multiple versions of your Facebook Ads. Successful advertisers recommend starting off with 5 to 10 versions of your ads to test which combinations of images and text are most effective.

If you have any questions about your Facebook Ads or Sponsored Stories, please visit our Help Center.

You will be sent an email receipt for any charges from Facebook, and the information about the charge is also available in the billing tab of your Ads Manager.

Sincerely,

The Facebook Ads Team"

A copy of my beautiful help message followed, exactly as people would see our message on their pages. I created a few more ads to reach more countries and managed to target an additional hundred million Facebook users. Soon, depending on how the system actually worked, those ads would be seen by someone sometime. God, please!

The email from Facebook also provided an embedded button: *Manage Ads*. Clicking on it, I was sent to a dashboard. There I could see my intended audience, my personal interest group of hundreds of millions of people, the reach and the number of impressions, single Facebook pages where my ad was going to be shown, number of clicks and cost, plus additional information pertaining to the management of multiple ads.

I did not care about the payment or the number of clicks

my previous employer's web page would have received. I cared about someone picking up a working phone and calling us or sending us an email message, a signal of hope, a signal of life. I guess we had nothing more to do now than wait for the miracle to happen. For the time being, the dashboard showed a frustrating *Pending* status for my planetwide distress call.

Annah brought us back to reality with practical things and stopped our minds from wandering away from other important needs.

"Mom, I'm hungry."

It was beyond lunch time, sometime around one o'clock. Annah used to be at the school cafeteria with hundreds of students from all over the world at the International School. It was also a quite welcome interruption from the spiral of scary end-of-the-world doomsday scenarios we had been abruptly plunged into that day.

"I can make some toasted panini for everyone," Mary said while giving me an intense look as she nodded Annah out of the room. I understood. Mary's main preoccupation now was to save Annah from all I had exposed her to.

I assessed our situation. We had electricity and Internet. Phones worked too, though of no use if no one answered our calls. I nodded back at Mary, meaning I understood what she meant. I wanted to check another thing first, worried in case our Internet access would die for good sooner or later. I was glad they'd be occupied for a while with normal life things, for however long it lasted.

Think about some practical issues, divert the mind from focusing on what we faced at the moment. That was crucial. We had enough to drive anyone crazy, or worse, suicidal and

I had to be glad my family seemed to be holding out amazingly great under the circumstances.

Before she left, I told Mary we needed to know how much food and provisions we had and the kind of autonomy we hoped for. Annah would help her mom to take note of everything and evaluate our situation and what to do later to improve it. I would do some more research online and join them soon after downstairs.

While working on the Facebook ads, some internal thoughts brought to mind that I actually had eyes out there in the world: Webcams! I googled "live webcams". It appeared to me as a desperate, hopeless task. I got pages with static webcams with 12-hour picture intervals, with non-working links, and question marks where images were supposed to be. Frustration mounted rapidly.

Then I found "LIVE Webcam Network" in all its HD glory. The main page showed live pictures from Times Square, New York! My heart jumped.

It was sunny in New York. The scene showed a crossing I did not at first recognize; seemed familiar though. The site did not specify the exact address. Next to the curb, a USA Today vending box, two phone booths, one having on the side an ad for "AWAKE, The Movie".

No live traffic. Quite a few cars at a stop, either in the center of the road, or against the curb and on sidewalks, where they had bumped buildings and other obstacles. I expected to see more and scores of corpses on the streets. A car in the distance seemed to have hit a streetlight pole of some sort. "*Wait!*" I figured out where the webcam pointed. In the top corner, I recognized a statue I knew—George M. Cohan.

He was a famous figure in the New York City theater scene just after the turn of the century. The memorial had been erected in recognition of his contributions to the American musical theatre. I had to be at Broadway and 46th Street in Manhattan.

Something lay on the floor partially behind the pedestal. I could not tell the nature and there was no option to zoom the picture either. Legs? Wooden planks? Impossible to say. One single dead body?

A yellow cab was stopped on the sidewalk at the far right of 46th Street as if the driver had awkwardly parked the car. I couldn't see anything inside any vehicles. Some smoke or vapor came out from something, maybe a light pole. White condensation flew outward, not at street level, a bit higher up, and I didn't figure out the cause.

On Broadway, there was a construction area with large scaffolding going from the top of the building down to the ground. No movement or people walking around; the area was deserted. Further down on 46th Street, other stuff obstructed the visible part of the sidewalk. No way to distinguish what it was. People? I felt a cold sensation in the lower parts of my spine and shivered.

I tried with another link. This one labeled "LIVE from SXSW in Austin, Texas." I had never been in Austin so had no idea what the webcam showed. The live picture covered a downtown block with old two-floor buildings flanking the street. One had a red vertical sign "RITZ" on the corner. Traffic lights worked. Cars, parked on the right side. A static picture, if not for the flashing red, yellow, and green lights.

While I watched, the site switched by itself to a different webcam. This time, "WRIGLEY FIELD. Home of the Chicago Cubs" main entry came to view. No one around. I waited a bit more and the next scene jumped to downtown New Orleans, a little street crossing with its characteristic French district flavor. This too looked deserted.

The next one pointed at the bronze bull on Wall Street. The statue almost filled the screen. Back to New York. My heart sunk. A police car with lights still on and flashing red and blue had crashed against it. This last was surrounded by metal barriers, all contorted now because of the crash. There as well, not one person visible in the scene. No activity, just an empty eerie view.

I tried with Moscow. I could not get much information from there either. The scene was beautiful, a panoramic of the Novodevichy Convent and Cemetery, as reported by the site. It came from a webcam installed too high above and offered little to no street view. Some white smoke slowly rose up from in between distant buildings, no visible movements, even around the few stopped cars. Too far away to tell if they had crashed or if they were simply parked.

The connection from the site was slow and, at times, I got a spinning wheel or no reply from webcam links. The Amsterdam cam presented only a white empty page. No scene at all. Other linked webcams reported a nasty error: "Run script "void(0)" on the browser status bar and no response of any kind. I didn't think anyone ever would fix those scripts now.

I wanted to get some certain and definite answers from those views. I got only hints, nothing conclusive. I expected a mass of corpses on the streets. More catastrophic scenes. Those hints were bad nonetheless, even more troublesome, probably. I saw nothing like busy and active street views anyway. Where were all the people? If deaths had been so sudden, shouldn't the streets be full of dead bodies? I would try later on other sites and webcams. In the meantime, Mary called from the kitchen downstairs.

Annah had almost finished eating her sandwich and had a glass of milk in front of her, too. Mary waited for me. We had enough food to be fine for a week, she said. Water? Yes, for as long as it was running from the tap. We could not count on municipal utilities to run indefinitely. We should get provisions of non-perishable food, rations, water, medicines.

I had already started to think in survival mode. In spite of Mary's abhorrence for everything resembling a gun or any other form of offensive weapon, I thought I would soon become an armory shopper, too.

I told Mary all that but the idea was to find a gun shop in town and turn into an apocalyptic version of Rambo. I had no idea whether we would be facing real danger from then on. I did not want to find myself in any dire situation and having to think, *If only I had that.* Whatever *that* was going to be. If around us the world had stopped being served by humans, I would serve myself instead. Everything waited to be taken. The world did not suffer from a global nuclear blast. No "Day After" scenario, thank God. We ate in silence.

"I'm going to the mall," I said abruptly.

"No, you're not!" Mary then continued with a more conciliatory tone. "Dan, please don't. We don't need anything right now." I stared at her and raised my eyebrows. My head bent to the right as I did unconsciously whenever I believed someone had no idea what I was talking about and why.

Mary looked at me and lowered her gaze for a brief

moment. She sighed "Okay then. We'll come with you."

"No, that is out of question. You will be safer here at home with Annah. I won't be long."

I pulled out my iPhone and dialed her number.

"What are you doing?"

"Just seeing if it works."

Mary's phone rang.

"Don't answer it now. I'll call you again from the mall. If it's safe, I'll wait for you and Annah at the entrance. We will need both cars."

"Why the urge? What do you want to do?"

"Because we need stuff and because it is much safer today. Trust me."

I took the pistol with me. Mary noticed but said nothing. Annah did not react at all and that worried me. She had been apathetic the last few hours. She was lost in some inner world of her own. She stared blankly at us. I signaled Mary to follow and, outside, I told her to keep an eye on Annah; not to leave her alone while I was away. I muted her words with a kiss and left. I closed the gate behind me and hit the road again.

— o —

The mall was only a ten-minute drive from our house. The road took me through the closest village, then traversed more crop fields before reaching the large shopping center, the hardware store and a gas station, all on one site. "The Valley Shopping Center: Over 80 businesses at your service!" the billboards told customers in both English and

French.

If computers still worked and managed general operations, I wouldn't have the need to break in as the automatic doors would work and lights would still be on. Everything ready and waiting for customers that would never come.

I drove slowly, the gun tucked between my legs. I felt safe in the car but I did not want to take any risk. Houses along the road looked empty. Joe and Beth were not the only ones who had found death in bed during a February windstorm. A number of cars were still parked in driveways. Others must have been among the early commuters on the expressway. People lost to an impossible fate.

I slowly traversed the village eager to catch any possible sign of life, smoke from chimneys, a boy on a bike crossing the road, the parking lots where the local grocery market greeted its customers, the elders and the ones who preferred and supported the small shops against the giant mall. My eyes searched for scenes common for the time and place, people, shoppers, moms pushing baby strollers. Nothing of the sort. As if everyone had vanished.

It probably would have been good if those believing in "The Rapture" were right: "We who are alive and remain" will be caught up in heaven to meet "the Lord." After all, a good vision, to be chosen to meet our Lord. Hopefully alive in the physical sense of the term. Instead, every house, every apartment was now a tomb. I wasn't driving through a village, I was driving through a cemetery.

I got to the mall without crossing anyone apart from cars off the road with their drivers dead inside. One in the middle of the field had left behind grooves like scars from his unwelcome passage. Another one overturned after having smashed the bus stop. At the mall, the parking was occupied by very few vehicles. Maybe those of cleaning personnel, security guards, and other employees. I drove through and stopped the car right in front of the entrance and stepped out.

Crows, calling each other! I didn't expect to see any birds still alive! Up in the sky, a couple flew in circles and a few more in the distance. Indeed, I didn't see *any* dead animals. Peluche had been fine, and birds must have flown away the night before and might now be slowly returning. I looked around. No one. I reached to switch off the engine and stood there in silence for a little while. No noises, no sounds but the crows. No voices. Nothing. I closed the door, got the gun in my hand, and headed toward the automatic doors. They opened.

Inside...music from the loudspeakers. Music had always been part of mall operations and, with the shopping crowd, it had become an almost unnoticed presence. Now music struck me with violence: loud, arrogant, profane. I moved forward a few steps. The shops' rolling shutters were all down for as far as I could see. No employees had opened them that day.

The mall gave the impression to be huge and able to satisfy any customer needs. Especially now when no one crowded the place. I walked cautiously along the hallway. My steps resonated and were the only noise I could hear apart from the musical entertainment. I stopped, checked the bars on the phone and called Mary.

"Dan! Are you okay?" Mary's voice was anxious.

"I'm fine. I'm fine. Everything is fine. Don't worry. I'll check around here a bit more and I will call you again."

"Dan, please… Oh Lord, be careful. I love you."

"I love you, too. I'll call you in few minutes."

Amazing how a gun can give you a sense of security and control. Weird to handle one there. I reached the central plaza where the coffee bar was ready for customers with its many little tables, Parisian brasserie style. Next to those, across a barrier, "Paul's" vending point resembled an old, last-century truck. The pastry and French bakery had the exclusivity. The windows of its main shop was full of fine food, croissants, beignets, tarts, their signature double-sized *macarons*. Annah loved those. *They'd be good for few more days*, I thought.

From there, taking the hallway to the left, the Migros supermarket welcomed its patrons with its tons of fresh produce and exotic foods. I was interested more in canned and packaged goods and household merchandise. An advertisement showed me how to profit from this week's sales; products marked with a red dot enjoyed a fabulous 50% discount on the original price at the cashier. How convenient. The place was flooded with light and painfully deserted.

A vision of the multitude of shoppers, overloaded carts, children running, the always smiling cashiers came to my mind. All gone now, vanished. Raptured. I grinned at myself. I walked back to the central plaza. On the far left, stairs led to the office levels, maintenance and services. I headed that way first.

I climbed with caution, still expecting…what? After all I had experienced that day, I would never consider anything impossible anymore. From the top, I looked down for a broader view of the mall and its hallways. How could this be possible? I did not know the location of the security guard's quarters but I soon found them at the end of a corridor. I put my back against the wall, pistol ready, and knocked hard on the door.

We could not truly be the only ones alive, could we? Maybe a panicked guard trembled inside, with a loaded gun in his hand, about to shoot. My heart was beating fast and I learned then what cold sweat truly meant. Nothing, no reaction. "*I am opening the door!*" I called out. Extending my arm, I turned the knob. The door opened, squeaking on its hinges.

I peeked through and didn't notice anything abnormal at first, no signs of commotion and no one inside. I went in. Then I saw him, or at least his foot. A guard was on the floor, must have been about to start his shift. He was lying in a fetal position, behind a desk. Young, in his mid-twenties. His back curved, the head bowed, his legs bent and drawn up to the torso. The face, as Joe's, with the same gasping expression and blood from his nose. Eyes wide open, blood seeping from them, too. Same kind of violent death.

At the back of the room, a door was ajar. I advanced slowly, glanced briefly at the dead guard, then tried to peek through into a sort of office or changing area. I had glimpses of lockers along the wall. I moved to the other side and pushed the door open with my foot. Another guard, his legs over a bench in the middle of the floor. He must have fallen backward when he died. Another desk and a chair were the only other pieces of furniture in the room.

I had seen enough. I checked briefly around for the presence of more guns, but there were none. These guards were only armed with bludgeons. I didn't care to take them from their bodies. Not what I needed. I left and went to the central plaza on the ground level. Still looking around me, I called Mary.

"Mary. There is no one here." I didn't mention the dead guards. Yet, suddenly, I was uncomfortable with the idea of having Mary and Annah driving alone to join me at the mall, even if only ten minutes away. A pinch of paranoia could do no harm at the moment.

"Stay home, no need to come over here now. I'll load the car and I'll be back soon."

"Okay." She sounded relieved. "Dan, be careful."

"I will."

I headed for the supermarket area and took a cart. I knew more or less where to go as sometimes I helped Mary with our grocery shopping. I walked each aisle and collected canned food, anything with a long shelf-life...fruits and vegetables, pre-cooked food. I left the cart at the exit and went back.

I loaded one with gallon water containers, then another. After water, I went for flashlights and batteries, dozens of matchboxes, candles, and canned heat by the carton. Handfuls of gauze and bandages of assorted shapes and sizes as well as scissors, safety pins and tweezers. Anything that seemed prudent to have at hand.

Over the counter, I found antibiotic ointments for treating scrapes, scratches and cuts; bottles of vitamins; acetaminophen, ibuprofen and aspirin for pain relief. Leaving the area, I noticed hand sanitizers and disinfectant wipes; added those to my cart. In the aisle with detergents, I collected soap bars, sanitizer bleach and was able to find nose and mouth protection masks.

I judged I had done a good job on that ride. One day, I would also need to visit the outdoor store for travel and first-aid kits. I knew they had water filtration and portable purification systems among other things. Had to sit with Mary and compile a comprehensive list for the next visits. The car was loaded to the roof and I flattened down the back seats.

I was happy to be able to leave the mall without incident. Now was the time to test my theory on automatic services. I drove to the gas station and pulled in to the pump right next to the credit card payment column. The system was up and running; its computer voice welcomed me and asked me to select the grade, put in the payment card and enter the code. I was quite euphoric to be able to fill up the tank. For my next visit, I had to come with some jerrycans.

As I got behind the wheel, I heard a dog barking, not so distant and getting closer. Not welcoming either. Closing the door, I saw a rather large animal running to the car. The beast threw its paws against the window and barked loudly at me with fury. I started the engine and slammed the pedal. The Volvo jumped forward with the dog running behind, roaring with rage.

I left it behind in the distance. What the hell?! The event shocked me as some dogs can become dangerous in a relatively short time. Nothing could be considered safe anymore. Glancing around, I shivered as I seemed to be surrounded by hostility. While driving, I could not fail to notice the empty blue sky. Condensations jet trails—better known as contrails—developed during the day and spread in the morning hours with the start of jet traffic. The resulting ice-crystal plume lasted for several hours as testimony of the passage of an airliner across the sky. That morning, nothing!

At times, contrails criss-crossed the sky as air traffic peaked but there were only a few clouds, no jet trails. There had been no air traffic at all, and the Geneva airport received traffic from all over the world. This, plus our failed attempts to get in touch with someone, the dead TV channels, frozen Internet news. It all meant but one thing: What had happened here must have happened everywhere on the planet.

The enormity of the tragedy overwhelmed me. The world population was estimated to be about seven billion people. I had no idea how many survivors were alive today, thanks to whatever glitch had saved us. For what I knew, there could be only a few million left. Possible? I doubted we would have any chance to meet survivors, ever. I caught my breath at the thought. Better not to share these considerations with Mary and Annah. After all, I could be dead wrong. Note to self: Bad choice of words. Don't use with the girls.

The dog was nowhere to be seen now; I slowed down and scanned around for more dogs or any other animals. I did not risk crashing into incoming vehicles even when driving with my attention equally split between the road and the surroundings. Everywhere in sight was deserted. I drove through the village again. Nothing had changed since my passage shortly before. The same desolation, the same sensation of an immense void and no one alive.

When I got to the front of our gate, I sounded the horn to warn of my arrival and immediately regretted it. In spite of all evidence, I still expected to see people show up, maybe wounded, sick, or worse. I guess my imagination had started to recollect past images from horror and catastrophic genre movies, massive contagions, and zombies alike. With those in mind, I made sure all around the car was clear before getting out, the gun still tucked in my waistband. I heard Mary and Annah running on our graveled driveway and calling for me.

"Dan! Dad!"

What kind of world had we inherited and what kind of life could I promise them now? What kind of dangers lurked? I was in a negative mood, to say the least. I couldn't show my distress in front of wife and daughter though—especially Annah. She always looked up to me. I put on my best smile and concentrated on the good things. Provisions? Not a problem! Food and any medicine or anything else? Not a problem either, provided we were not against breaking the windows of the various shops at the mall in the future. Our situation? We were safe and sound.

"No worries, I am back. All went fine and I have access to plenty of stuff at the mall." I forced myself to smile.

I hoped to have the internal resources to keep going for them. The gate opened enough for Mary to rush out and hug me while Annah fully opened the panels to let the Volvo in.

"I was so worried. Why didn't you call again? You promised! I was afraid to call myself...I imagined things. What happened?"

"It's all fine, check the trunk. But let's get in now, let's not stay right here."

I used a little lie to give reasons to my request and urgency. "There was an unfriendly dog not far from here, and I think I spotted a few others. Mary, drive the car all the way to the house to unload. I'll close the gate."

Did not want to have Mary and Annah out any longer and confronting—possibly—a wild dog. I guess I was under the influence of too many Hollywood doomsday renderings. I told Annah to go to her mother while I closed and locked the gate. In the meanwhile, Mary had parked the car and opened the trunk.

"Oh my!"

"Dad! How much did you pay for all that?"

I smiled at Annah. "I guess for a while we are going to be entitled to borrow things rather than buying them."

She looked at me, astonished. "Really? You mean you just grabbed stuff and left?"

"Yeah, more or less."

Annah suddenly changed expression and frowned. "Because nobody was there…"

Hers was an observation, not a question. I believe she had reached her watershed moment where everything changes, events collating in her mind. Interesting that—with Annah—the trigger for all the pieces to fall into place had been shopping without paying. Nothing will be the same as before. *My kid is gone*, I thought.

"I need you to be brave, Annah. We all need each other more than ever now."

Annah nodded. Mary examined the load and what I had collected. With certain items, she agreed; for others, she wondered why we needed them at all. I admitted that some might be an excessive precaution but knowing we had that stuff readily available at home made me feel safer. Besides, the basement still had plenty of space. Actually, I wanted help from both of them to make a list of what could be useful or needed for the next weeks.

While we got the provisions inside the house and down to the basement, I told them—adding more details—about the encounter with the dog at the gas station and again touched the subject of firearms. It was crucial for them not to leave home without some means of self defense, and never wander alone. I believed it best to carry guns, even on our own property until I made sure the fence could not be easily trespassed by wild animals.

"Dan, are you going mad? Annah is only twelve! You are not giving a gun to our daughter!"

"Yes, but not long ago in the States, boys and girls knew well how to use rifles and pistols, ride horses, and tend to cattle on ranches. They kept mountain lions, wild dogs, and coyotes at bay. Mary, I might be wrong and probably even going mad as you say. I am not so sure though. I don't know what is out there."

Mary paused, not ready for my reaction. She turned away from me, glanced at Annah and stepped into the garden. Mary looked at her plants, her arms crossed tightly at her chest. She approached our old stone wall and caressed the sturdy leaves of the olive tree, then turned around to gaze at our house, Annah, and me. Her eyes were red. She walked over and got right in front of me. Raised one hand and traced my profile with her fingertips, looking straight into my eyes.

"I don't know, Dan. What is happening to us?" She walked back to the car trunk.

Mary did not vehemently reject the idea as I expected. She proved to be more adaptable and flexible than I hoped for. I didn't know how much it had cost her. Mary had changed, as Annah had. But we needed to be able to change and adapt to any possible situation.

We finished bringing everything inside and arranged what I brought from the mall; some in the kitchen, the majority in the basement. While we unloaded, Annah wrote down all we had gathered and completed the list she and Mary had already started. We would last over a month, rather easily now. Probably even more.

Mary told me she and Annah kept trying to call people while I was away and sent other emails around. Still no answers. Annah cried a lot because of all her friends who must have died and she asked why we hadn't died, too. Mary managed to calm her but she worried for Annah...as I did. This had been hard for us so I could not imagine what went on in Annah's mind and how tough it must be.

Annah's only island of normality, where she could rest and feel safe, would be Mary and me. For as long as we acted normally, stayed calm and resolute, not showing weaknesses and fear, I was sure Annah would handle difficult situations well. We only needed to take care that we, the adults, did not fall apart. For the day, we'd had our share already.

What Mary had told me about emails and phone calls reminded me of the Facebook ads, our virtual message in the bottle. She hadn't checked them. I went upstairs, anxious to see whether they had been activated. The status of our ads campaign was still pending. Man, I hoped Facebook would work. Certainly our greatest opportunity to get in touch with anyone alive out there. Wherever *there* was.

Mary joined me "Annah is in her room. She is tired, I'd say exhausted even. And, mentally, this is too much for her."

"I guess so. It's tough on us, imagine how it is for Annah. How are you feeling?"

Mary looked through the window and said, "So calm out there, and peaceful...and the black smoke from this morning? There isn't as much as before."

"I will need to check on that too one of these days. And go back to town as well."

She turned with darting eyes, her head swiveled. "Why? What for? People will come, relief will come. We only have to stay here and wait. Right?" Her voice had veered to a high pitch, almost begging me to reply 'Yes, of course', but I couldn't.

"Mary, I don't know. I don't want to give you false hopes. I don't think any relief will reach us any time soon...if ever. We need to be prepared for that eventuality."

She looked at me, visibly scared, her arms folded tightly around her. Her body language was of complete denial and refusal. She didn't say anything, and stepped back away from me, staring at the floor.

"Mary, listen to me. I will never give up. Remind yourself of this, we can survive and we will survive. I will do all I can to ensure that, no matter how frightening the situation or how certain the outcome might appear. Should death ever stare us in the face, I will look back resolutely and without blinking."

She burst into tears. I stood up and held her tight in my arms. She trembled and sobbed, unable to stop.

"Dan, what are we going to do? What are we going to do?"

I sighed. *"God,"* I thought, *"if You are there...what's happening, and how did You ever plan for this?"*

I took Mary to our bedroom and cuddled her. I kissed her and dried her tears with my lips. And kissed her more. Even in the most dire situations, people cling to life with all their strength and resolve. Our kisses became passionate. I started to unbutton her shirt. Mary responded gently to my touch and helped me undress her. We made love fiercely and passionately, impatiently, as it happened with our very first time.

Dusk came upon us and we left our bubble. We had shut out the world, briefly but intensely. Mary caressed me. "I love you, Mister."

I pressed her against me "We have each other, Mary. It is all I need. I need you, and Annah. Then I can face anything."

We kissed again.

In the evening, Mary and Annah prepared a light dinner. I recovered an almost forgotten set of binoculars that were lost in the glove compartment of the car. Only slightly better than a toy, but fine for now. I would have to get more serious gear in the next few days. Better stuff could turn out to be most useful. The scenes I got from the 10x magnification I enjoyed with those lenses confirmed what the silence kept telling us all along...*there is no one alive, you are alone.* Households were plunged in darkness, garden lights were off, window shades closed or open into dark interiors. The neighborhood, apart from the few street lights, was somber. The silence was unbelievable.

For the first time ever, I started to close the shutters on windows at the ground and first floors, and secured them closed. I did not know what to expect and I did not want to have only a thin layer of glass between us and whatever could come to us. Mary watched me without saying a word. Annah gestured to Mary, then pointed at me; out of the corner of my eye, I noticed Mary signaling her not to pay attention.

Dinner had been brief and, for how crazy it sounds, I decided—more for Annah than for us—to spend an evening no different from others before. So I announced I felt like watching a movie, that I had too much on my mind and needed to stop thinking about our next steps. Mary and Annah did not have their heart into the plan, but I insisted, and we selected a James Bond movie with Pierce Brosnan.

I activated the burglar alarm of the house. We could not rely on a non-existing police force. For as long as we had electricity, the siren would warn us of any intrusion. We sat close to each other on the sofa, without saying a word. I kept the volume of the TV too loud and the movie was full of gun fights and blasts with improbable action scenes. In the end, we managed to relax. At least I did. Bond prevented me from thinking too much about our own incredible scenario. I tried to keep an ear to any sound coming from outside, but after a while I let go. I enjoyed those moments of normality.

The movie ended and, when the credits started, we heard a fearful howling. Some neighbors had dogs; we had seen them walking with their animals sometimes during the weekends. We had exchanged brief conversations in the past, and the dogs had been friendly to us. Well, at least with their masters by their side.

We liked pets and had cats before. But dogs, we felt, were a lot of work. I never pictured myself in the dog-walking routine every day, no matter the weather or how tired I happened to be. Dogs would never understand and say, "No worries, master, tonight we can do without."

"Poor dog," Annah said.

Mary nodded. "He must have started while we were watching the movie." With a glance, she reproached me for keeping the volume too high.

"It would be good if we had a dog now…" I thought aloud.

Annah got excited immediately. "Really!? Dad! Are we

going to have one? Please!"

Indeed, having one or two dogs, our dogs, on the property would not be bad at all. I had a problem though. Getting puppies made little sense and grown up animals…how to trust they would become 'part of the family' and consider us their masters? Dogs thrive on routines. Routine was missing now. Maybe, if we created a new one…that was something to seriously think about.

We got ready to spend our first night in the new world order. Annah did not want be alone in her room, especially because hers was not on the same floor as ours. She begged to sleep with us, in our bed. She was five or six years old the last time, and never with the two of us together. And always in exceptional cases, if one of us were absent.

The floor landing separated our room from the home office and we kept a sofa bed there. Annah could start using that from now on. Better than sleeping alone in her bedroom one floor below. Neither Mary nor I had the courage to resist and say no to Annah's plea. At least for the first few nights. I had one more reason I didn't share with Mary. In my heart, I hoped we weren't going to experience another windstorm and we actually would awake the next morning. I hoped nothing or no one would 'discover' they had 'forgotten' us alive. I preferred to be all together that night.

If it had to happen, so be it. Life must be lived at the right time. Death is not scary when one dies after having lived fully. One must choose to live though and face all adversities. With a sunken heart, I kissed Mary and Annah good night. They were both soon asleep, while I couldn't find rest. The dog still howled and his was a gloomy sound. My brain couldn't stop sending and processing images of dead people, deaths, the animals, something killing penguins, and birds, and gorillas. And now us. Why was I still alive? And Mary, and Annah? What if something worse was going to happen? How would I have been able to protect them? We were resting on a thin crust, below us the unknown. And I was scared.

I soon found myself fighting to stay awake. It was peaceful outside, and after what seemed to be a very long time, I collapsed and fell asleep.

Part Two

Routines

I jumped at every noise—even the ones we were accustomed to—like the cracking of wood-frames on the roof, or a gentle breeze rustling tree branches. Almost each time, a dog howled. The dog. Was there more than one? In the complete eerie silence, I believed I detected two different barks. Yes, two at least. Lamenting their desperation to the night, sometimes they overlapped. I would look for those dogs in the morning.

At times, Mary and I whispered a few words to each other. She'd had an agitated night herself, and we both checked on Annah often. She whined at times or had some jerky leg movements which kept us awake. Apart from that, Annah had a full night of sleep, thank God. The resilience of children. We all needed to become resilient now. Dawn came; I heard birds sing as they used to do every morning since the temperature had risen again. I was tired, and happy we were still alive.

Life! The world was not dead. Nature assimilated the apparent extermination of the human race with a shrug of her shoulders. In a few decades, if humans disappeared as the dominant species on Earth, many of our artifacts would be absorbed by the advance of Mother Nature, no longer pushed back by countless human opponents. Vegetation would take its place and plant new roots. It would be weird to watch this transformation happen.

I got up slowly, trying not to wake Annah...or, especially Mary, who appeared to have at last found some peace in her sleep. I went to our home office and, with trepidation, opened the Facebook ads management page. *"Yes!"* I clenched my fists. The ad campaign status had finally turned to active! Our message in a bottle had already reached some fourteen thousand home pages. Fourteen thousand…didn't seem such a good start to reach hundred of millions. This would take years!

Maybe ads began slowly; maybe their rate would pick up soon. I missed the moment when the campaign had started to appear on Facebook. If the message reached hundreds of thousands of pages a day with a target of some four-hundred million it would take…four thousand days! Dear God! The Internet will not last that long. Best scenario, ten years.

If we were lucky, this campaign would survive only a few months before digital entropy struck and services started to degrade or stop altogether. Didn't matter. I didn't have better options at the moment to reach other people. We prayed for those across the world who were in our same situation; those whose lives had turned into the equivalent of a tiny island of pseudo-normality in an infinite ocean of human vacuum and deaths. Still, we prayed they had access to their Facebook pages too.

I took the binoculars and scanned outside through the two windows. One faced southwest, the other northwest. From the one facing south, I covered a large part of the valley. Empty roads in the distance and, further away, a couple of villages perched on low hilltops. Nothing, no movement, and the same truck on a field. Like yesterday. Too distant to distinguish any details but I was sure a body rested in the cabin, collapsed.

I could see nearby houses toward the north side. No vital signs from roofs, no white smoke from chimneys, no one preparing breakfast. Only the sounds of nature. It must have been that way thousands of years ago, when human colonization of the planet was still confined to small groups of huts together. A bunch of frail humans helping each other, fencing daily dangers and threats, and surviving. Year after year.

I sighed; we had no human companions. Maybe we were more isolated than anyone had ever been in history. Maybe. I was not an expert in the matter but I doubted this kind of solitude was experienced by the first humans. My mind faltered and my heart sunk. Alone! I would not allow such thoughts to weaken my resolve and determination. Resilience! I had to do it...for Mary, for Annah.

I wondered what I would have done if they were dead too. Probably would've committed suicide. Resilience! Stop thinking about this stuff! Mary suddenly appeared in the office.

"What are you doing?"

I jumped. "Oh, you're awake…"

"Well, I guess since here I am. Sorry if I frightened you."

I didn't reply. I put the binoculars down and turned to hug my wife.

"Good morning, love. I was afraid I wasn't going to be able to say that today."

She nodded and looked gravely at me. "We cannot leave Joe and Beth like that," Mary told me suddenly, raising her chin to look into my eyes. She put a hand to my chest, where my heart would be. "We just can't, Dan."

She was right. I could not bury the entire village or those other friends who lived in town. But I *would* take care of Joe and Beth.

"Okay, first thing this morning. But I'm hungry now, aren't you?"

Resilience. Act normally, don't divert too much from normal routines, and normality will help us survive and find new paths we would walk and live without going insane. I deactivated the alarm to reach the ground floor. Annah was still sleeping. We left a note on the pillow saying we were in the kitchen, then went downstairs to fix breakfast.

I opened the shutters, one by one, and the morning light flooded all the rooms. Another morning, sunny and fresh air. Spring peeking early at the door and winning over the last weak remnants of winter. The smell of freshly-brewed coffee invited me to start the day.

Breakfast with my wife. Such a normal thing, just like any other day, and yet it felt so weird. Apparently, skin deep, the world had not changed. The billowing black smoke, toward the airport, had disappeared during the night. No visible signs of disruption around. At least from our place, everything was peaceful and quiet. Birds sung in the warming sun of that early spring weather. No ominous signs, apart from the blank TV screens and the white noise from most radio channels; nothing screaming everything had gone terribly wrong. And the silence, of course. Yet from our kitchen, the world was beautiful, and yesterday only a very bad dream.

I had a Mephistophelian experience. The demon of the Faust legend, Mephistopheles, the name derived from the Hebrew mephitz, meaning *destroyer*, and tophel, meaning *liar*. Indeed, I had witnessed destruction, and from what we had seen on the Internet, it was happening all over the world. Still, looking through the windows, the scene screamed at me 'it is a lie; everything is as it has always been'. I shivered.

Mephistopheles did not search for Faust, did not search for men to corrupt. His ultimate task was to collect the souls of those who were already damned. Who condemned us humans, and who collected all those souls?

"I'm going back to the mall, Mary. There are lots of things we still need."

"Why? What!? You said we were fine for a month."

"Yes, if everything stays as it is now. But I can't guarantee things will keep working. Electricity, for example. What if a branch fell and cut a power cable? We would be in the dark and I can't repair that."

"We'll come with you."

"Then…you need to learn how to use a gun. And Annah, too."

Mary backed off, physically stepping away from me. "No, no."

So I told her the full details of the dog attack that I averted only by luck. Soon there would be more than one; other animals might become aggressive too. We lived in a rural area and woods extended not far from our place where wild beasts had been spotted a few times before.

Foxes, badgers, and wolves were known to thrive. Not in large numbers, but they would soon realize the major contender of their habitat was no more and nothing would block their path. They would start to venture further down to the plain and extend their range of action. I would not last with a woman and a girl fully and totally depending on me for their own security.

If she wanted to come with me and bring Annah, too, they both had to become self-sufficient. Even to the point of one day being able to help me, save me from danger, if need be. Besides, we might not be alone after all. Whoever could be out there, near or far, could we be sure they are jolly good fellows coming to help?

I had been able to instill doubts in her mind and I hated myself for doing that. I didn't want to scare her too much or frighten her to the point of ceding to panic. But we needed to start shedding a bit of our own civilized crust. Find some primeval instincts and skills for survival, and better to happen sooner than later.

"Think about it," I said as I left to get ready for Joe and Beth's burial.

Joe had a small vegetable garden, so I went straight to his tool shed. I found his shovel and started digging the grave, and then another. With Mary, we chose an area of the garden under a cherry tree and decided to place Beth next to one of her flower beds. The ground became harder to excavate as I dug about a foot deep and the task took me all morning to finish.

Annah had made two crosses and used small wood planks to inscribe their names. We weren't sure of birth dates so she put the current day along with their approximate ages. Before going into our neighbor's house, Mary and I wore the protection masks I had found at the mall the previous day. I had no experience with dead people and didn't know when a decaying body would start to smell heavily. It was already emotionally difficult without the need to factor in physical repulsion.

Annah waited downstairs while Mary and I went to Joe and Beth's bedroom. Mary began to cry softly when we got into the room and she saw them lying on the bed.

"Oh Beth, Beth…"

But she did not stop helping me even though our friends showed signs of rigor mortis. Dealing with them had been a hard test on our fragile emotions when we had to force their limbs into a better position. Although I should have composed the bodies the day before, the rigor mortis made it easier for us to transport their bodies, one by one, wrapped in their sheets. A relaxed body would have been more difficult to carry.

Beth, a petite woman, wasn't heavy at all and we carried her out first, into the trench near the flower bed, as Mary suggested. Annah followed us to the garden without saying a word. Joe was heavier, of course. Mary had some difficulty dealing with his weight. We had to stop three times for her to rest. Finally, we completed the gruesome task and laid our friends to eternal rest beside each other. I did not feel religious, but Mary insisted we needed to say something. *Didn't Beth go to church every Sunday?* So I spoke.

"Beth, Joe. I do not know what fate has snatched you so brutally from life. I hope you can rest in peace. The Lord, if you meet Him, will explain to you what part of His plan foresaw all this to happen. Please, pray for us. Amen."

"Amen," repeated Annah and Mary. I started to fill the graves. Shovel after shovel. When I finished, Annah helped me put the crosses in place and she arranged some flowers she had picked. We stood in silence for a moment…it felt so absurd and so monstrously abnormal. Yet abnormality was the new 2012 normality and we had to get used to that.

After a shower and a light lunch, I checked the Facebook campaign again. Thirty-two thousand impressions. No clicks. No wonder…Dan, what did you expect? The dogs howled again. I planned to find them that afternoon. Of course, Annah wanted to come along but Mary helped me convince her that really wasn't advisable.

"We'll stay in touch with the cell phones," I said, as the connections still worked fine.

Although the dogs could not be too far away, I took the car along with Joe's pistol. The dogs, if the howling ones were those I knew, should recognize me. Still, I didn't count on much of a welcoming party. I brought some food with me and made a mental note to get dog treats at the mall in case all went well and looked promising. If not…

I wanted to win their trust with the food and then visit them every day. They only had one chance and I hoped they took it. If I decided it was worth the effort, fine; otherwise, I was resolved to kill them both. First, to keep them from suffering or starving to death; second, for our own protection in case they turned out to be unconditionally aggressive. In that case, it would have been out of the question to let them remain free in the wild.

Shortly after, following the barking, I found the house. There were indeed two dogs, and the ones I remembered. They looked like German Shepherds but they both had a curly white coat. I knew I had once asked their owner about their breed, but I couldn't remember what he said. I stopped the car on the left side of the road, in front of their house.

This neighborhood, too, was desolate with no signs of people or their presence. No corpses either; indeed, as if everyone had been caught in their sleep. In a sense, that was sheer luck. If what struck us had happened hours later, bodies would be everywhere, many more than the few early commuters dead on the streets and in their cars. Thinking of this last point, why hadn't I seen any corpses from the webcams? Another question with no answer.

I stepped out of the car, the gun in my hand. Both dogs barked at me from the other side of the fence. They sensed death. I know little about animal behavior and psychology but I understood they were not raging dogs. They were simply nervous and scared.

I tucked Joe's pistol into my back waistband and got the food. I showed my hands, slowly opening the wrapping. They still barked. I started to talk, almost whispering, in what I hoped was a reassuring manner for dogs. I stepped forward a bit more. They got excited, jumping, running toward the house and back. I reached the fence and put down two large handfuls of food on the low supporting brick wall.

Mary had prepared a delicacy of minced meat and rice. I thought she was wasting good food but she said the first impression had to be stellar..."Works with humans and will work with dogs, too." I didn't complain much; with an entire mall at our service, I had no reason to worry yet about food supplies.

They smelled the meat, and hesitated. I knew they must have been hungry in addition to being scared. I kept talking and chanced getting close enough to allow them to sniff at me; they showed no aggressive behavior.

Then they started eating. *Weird,* I thought, as if they decided it was okay to take food from me only after they had sniffed and assessed me. *These are not stupid dogs.* Good. They took their chance and scored a point. I gave them the rest of the meat and rice and stepped away.

"Okay, guys. I'll be back tomorrow. Stay dry."

— o —

By the end of the week, Mary and Annah had started practicing shooting with the pistol at plastic bottles filled with dirt. I put them on the stone wall we shared with the local cemetery so, if they missed, no one would have complained. The wall was high enough to hide tombs and crosses from our sight, and the little church with the tall cypress tree had become a familiar presence. The church received a visit from the priest once a month, on the first Sunday, and the streets filled with vehicles. We liked the sound of the bells calling for mass. Bells, I missed them.

Every Halloween, Annah liked us to organize a sleepover with her friends and the wall was an integral part of the celebration. The kids would sit on it, their backs to the tombs, and squirm at every little sound. I loved to read scary stories to those little girls, excited almost to paroxysm at the idea of having tombs only few yards away from them. Even better if it was a bit windy; waving and swaying trees at night were quite frightful, especially with me making gruff voices when reading the most scary passages of the story.

All those moments rushed to my eyes like a sudden strong gust of wind, startling, and making you wonder where it came from. They exploded like mortar shells in my mind when the first bullet hit the stone wall and chipped a sharp edge away. The first straight hit came days after and Annah had scored it, bursting into cheers. She pounded fists with me in laughter. It had taken only few hundred bullets.

The dogs now waited for my visits, cheerful when I showed up. I started to do regular trips to the mall, and got replenishments of dog food and treats. I also visited the hardware shop a few times, and the Earth Adventures store.

95

In a week's time, I collected jerrycans of gasoline and filled Joe's tool shed with them—I did not want the equivalent of a bomb at home. Each jerrycan contained twenty liters of fuel and I collected forty of those. I equipped two portable electric generators with standard gasoline engine. They both rated for five thousand watts and gave me the peace of mind I wanted in case our power went out. The nicest part was that I did not need to put a price tag on them.

At the Earth Adventures, I had to break in and silence the screaming alarm bell. I found hunter knives, two wind-up radios and flashlights, portable water purifiers and solar cell chargers. All of this could be a help, too. The best find had been the wind-up walkie-talkies with a nominal range of two miles. Better not to be relying on mobile phones to work indefinitely. Also, our property fence was now secured with barbed wire to keep animals away, just one more precaution. And I got real binoculars too. Paranoids survive.

We listened to the radio daily, scanning channels, and we kept sending emails and browsing the Internet. Time seemed to have stopped digitally as no site received any updates. I even tried to join online forums to post messages but most of them required an authorization to do that. I received plenty of automatic emails and, within hours, I would receive the approval, or not, by the moderator. Of course, no moderator ever sent me anything. The Facebook campaign had reached almost a million people. Great results but no clicks.

I guessed it was time for me to head to Geneva and have a look around town. I knew of an armory...and having only one pistol in the family was not enough.

From the border with Switzerland, the road turned into a long straight line until almost reaching the Cornavin rail station in downtown Geneva. The new tramway lines had been inaugurated only the previous summer. Streetcars now connected passengers from the CERN laboratory to the city and traffic had improved considerably. The Swiss road authority had also built a tunnel going under the satellite city of Meyrin. This alone cut the trip time to the center by not less than fifteen minutes and everything had been delivered respecting time and budget. Didn't matter now. I did not want to risk going through the tunnel which might have been blocked by car wreckage. Instead, I chose to drive in the middle section devoted to streetcars in order to rapidly cross Meyrin.

To reach the border, I avoided the expressway and opted to drive through the village. It had been two weeks since that gruesome February morning and degradation started to be visible. Nothing spectacular, just weeds surfacing wherever they could. Quickly, efficiently, and spreading undisturbed.

Vegetation was not trimmed, of course, and leaves and debris accumulated in various spots as well as loose pieces of paper and garbage. I suspected animals were responsible for that, most probably domestic ones which had searched through trash bins contributing to the general feeling of a place that had been forsaken.

I kept radio contact with Mary but I almost lost the signal when I approached the border. A car had smashed right against the custom booth. The impact almost brought it down and part of the large canopy had collapsed, but it left a narrow passage free. I slowed down and went through. After having done that, I realized I could have simply crossed the border in the other lane, unobstructed. *What was I afraid of, a fine?*

"Mary, I can't hear you anymore. I'll call you in a sec."

I stopped the car in the middle of the road, almost in front of the main entrance to the CERN laboratory. I felt a sense of utter desolation. Sickening but I was getting used to it. Over the phone, I told Mary I would stay in touch about every twenty minutes or so and tell her of any findings. In any case, she should not be worried as I didn't expect to find company in Geneva and I would have been on my toes regardless.

A streetcar was at rest at the CERN stop, the first one of the line, or the last if you were coming from the city center. It was quite a busy line which served the lab personnel and one also used by border-zone French citizens. Nearby was the bus stop of the 'Y line' which reached into France and normally used by commuters. I drove by slowly. No corpses there. I accelerated and proceeded toward downtown and my ultimate destination.

I wanted to go to the armory first thing. Joe's pistol would have been enough for self protection in normal situations but we were not living in normal situations. Both Mary and Annah needed to have their own gun. Everything was still confused in my mind. I admit I was being guided by catastrophic movies and the survivors' behavior from Hollywood blockbusters. Yet I was now the one living in my own blockbuster and a very real one, too.

I reached Meyrin without seeing any bodies on the streets apart from those in the few cars crashed against a wall or on the curb, and one rotten fellow at the tram stop. People used to drive slowly on those inner roads so there were no spectacular accidents. Cars had simply ended up gently bumping against the first obstacle they met when the driver died. Whatever happened to us in this part of the world had happened early, in the wee hours of the morning. I couldn't imagine how it would be in other cities if everyone had been caught on a busy weekday.

After Meyrin, the road overpassed the highway to Lausanne. I stopped on impulse and got out. I never heard birds or crows before during the day in town because the everlasting humming of traffic covered their calls. Now there was none at all; no artificial noises, no human buzz. That day was different also for other reasons. I reached the railing and a disturbing scene greeted me. It was similar to what I had seen on the expressway but this time crows and other scavengers were feasting.

Some of the crashed cars had broken windows, opened and contorted doors, the bodies within exposed to the elements. And nature is very efficient at breaking down human remains. Luckily, I was not close enough to see the maggots, beetles, ants and wasps that were surely participating in the feeding frenzy, in and out of every orifice. Still, I shouldn't get too upset as it was a natural process bound to happen in a similar way everywhere, at that very moment. Soon there would be nothing left for animals to feast on.

I went back to the car and kept driving until I reached downtown. Geneva was a city of ghosts, an even larger cemetery than the village near home. Hard to believe that almost two hundred thousand people were dead there.

At the first large intersection in town, I stopped the car. Lowering the window, I blew the horn loud and often. The screaming sound bounced off the buildings. I stepped out but kept blowing the car's horn...hoping for someone to show up, to see a face at a window, some sign of life.

Nothing. No one. I was alone, and I screamed.

"Is anyone there? Where is everyone?"

Geneva did not answer me. Slowly I got into the driver's seat again and resumed my journey. I continued down the street and turned left at the Notre Dame church onto rue de Lausanne, driving slowly. Traffic lights were working normally though I didn't bother to stop and the cameras flashed each time I ran a red light. After the first one, which triggered my reflexes to brake, I thought that actually it could have been a way to leave a signature. From then on, I did it on purpose. Who knows, if anyone was alive and still checked those cameras, I was leaving the proof that not everyone in Geneva was dead.

I looked for signs of recent human presence, anything suggesting someone was still alive in town. I didn't know really what to look for. In any case, whatever those signs could be, I had seen none. For the most part, the streets were empty though crows and other birds were now more present. Encouraged by the lack of humans in the surroundings, they were slowly taking possession of the place. I saw a few dogs, alone or in a pack, but they kept away and never tried to approach the car. I did not try to get closer to them either.

The gun shop was not far now and I called Mary to reassure her everything was fine. Right after that, I arrived at "Armurerie du Lac".

The windows were intact and displayed a multitude of blades, a ninja costume, knives of various kinds, a range of Japanese samurai swords, curved katanas, and a nice group of Glock pistols. I was not a gun expert but I had found the right place.

I parked the car on the sidewalk in front of the shop, took the pistol and got out. I glanced around and listened for any possible noise. Nothing, all quiet. An empty town can be quite oppressive, I discovered. Geneva weighed heavily on my senses and seemed almost quizzical. Buildings' windows looked straight at me, as if they were hundreds of accusing eyes asking "Who are you, why are you here? Why are you alive?!"

I tried to push open the glass doors to no avail. What would happen if I were to break in? The alarm would protest and scream against the intrusion and I would have been uneasy to *shop* with a siren piercing my ears. I have never done anything like that but I didn't have many options.

At first, I thought about shooting at the doors but then decided it was better to ram them. I backed the car up to the entrance. I did not want to make a mess or risk ruining the vehicle, or worse, the radiator. If I damaged anything I would have to call Mary to rescue me and leave the car there. Not good. So I slowly backed up to the doors, then pushed the pedal down and rammed them. The entrance shattered and the doors went off their hinges with a slam. I ended up half inside the shop. The alarm went off. Loudly.

My heart was pumping heavily. Definitely, I was not a burglar and had to breathe deeply for a while before I was able to get out of the car. My boots crackled on the broken glass and the alarm scream pierced my ears. I could not act properly with the alarm shrieking in my ears so I located the siren. They had mounted it close to the ceiling, on the right corner. I took the pistol, aimed carefully and fired a couple of shots.

The siren almost exploded. It was all silent now, even

though my ears were still buzzing. Maybe an alarm now blinked furiously in some police stations where no agents would answer the call. Having never been there before, I examined the place. The shop seemed to have everything I needed, at least at a first look. Hunting rifles were aligned vertically behind the counter but were of no use to me. Various locked glass cabinets contained handguns of various types, including pistols and revolvers. This is what I was looking for.

On a pedestal, the famous .44 Magnum and, behind it, a few pictures of Inspector Callahan from the "Dirty Harry" movie. An inscription stated it was "The Most Powerful Handgun in the World" and a paraphrased Harry quote ("Go ahead. Make YOUR day.") was followed by the inflated price...a moot point now.

I was tempted by that Magnum, like having a cannon in your hand. *But first things first,* I thought as I needed pistols light enough for Mary and Annah yet with considerable impact power nonetheless. Unfortunately, there was no clerk to ask for help or to guide me in my gun shopping spree. I had to read all those terse descriptions if I wanted any information about the various models. My eyes fell on a "Glock 36 Cal. 45 AUTO. Compact and powerful." Two terms that fit perfectly.

Reading further, the description said: "Slim and powerluf". Yes, the note wrongly spelled it..."powerluf!" How many typos were left trailing behind? How many wrongs will not have a chance anymore to be made right? How many "I am sorry" burned how many lips in the last moments, forever untold, forever burning...I kept reading. "Fits to the hand of any user. The new GLOCK SLIMLINE presents grip ergonomics of the next dimension. The Glock

36 measures only 28.5 mm/1.13 in. in width. Together with the secure grip design this makes handling the pistol very easy." I got four of those and, with excitement, I collected thousands of rounds. Boxes after boxes.

I also found two Berettas. They were smaller than the Glocks and I was not on a budget, so why not? Might they be better for Annah? Had no idea. We would have to try which one she handled best. She had done well with Joe's pistol, and seemed to learn fast. She could decide for herself.

Next I found two Skorpion VZ61s. I had seen those in movies. I guessed they would be a nice addition to the family arsenal. The sign said it could use either a short 10-round magazine or a 20-round capacity magazine. I grabbed a large number of the latter.

After storing all those boxes in the car, I took the time to inspect the Skorpions. They felt so light, like lethal feathers. Why were we so skillful in creating perfection for killing other human beings? I found the fire mode selector, a lever installed on the left side above the pistol grip. It had three settings: "0", "1" and "20". Obviously standing for weapon safe, semi-automatic and full automatic mode. I set them both on "0". I would prove my assumption later at home.

Home. It was close to an hour since the last time I had spoken to Mary. I took the phone and dialed her number. Mary answered immediately.

"Dan! Where are you? Oh my God, I was worried. Are you okay? Why didn't you call before? You said twenty minutes!"

I acted as a shopper under the influence of a Harrods's sale virus. Guilt rose like a tidal wave engulfing my thoughts like debris tossed around by conflicting flows. Finally, I uttered an apology. "I'm sorry. It will never happen again."

I told her where I was and how I had found the town completely deserted. There was no evidence that others were alive but that couldn't be conclusive. Others...I had only driven on the main roads, then straight to the armory. Surely there had to be folks like us, somewhere. Why not? But I didn't sound convincing even to myself and Mary did not comment.

"Anyway, I think I've found what I was looking for. But, how are you both doing?"

"We're fine, Dan. Just come home."

"I won't be long."

I sat on the bumper of the car and memory brought Mary's voice asking, "What's going on, sweet pea?" Sweet indeed, like the fragrance of jasmine in our garden, carried by the evening breeze. Days had passed by uneventfully and new routines had set themselves in place. Mary and Annah checked the Internet, and browsed the countryside with the binoculars while I had been busy with the visits to the mall and bringing food to the dogs trying to win their trust. They also took notes on what they saw in various places so to easily distinguish if anything had changed in the scenery from one day to the other. Accountants for signs of life. Their checkbook remained miserably empty. Nothing was ever different. Ever.

The world was changing of course; spring was all over and nature gave the impression of not caring a bit about the fate of humans. To tell the truth, it was gorgeous, better than any previous seasons we remembered. Visibility was amazing. Even taking into account that Geneva was not famous for being a city invaded by smog, two weeks of no human presence had had a significant effect. The air was perfumed with the first blossoming flowers. It was painful to notice how nature was so better off without us, and cheerful she had got rid of a major nuisance.

I crushed those thoughts as if they were ants attempting to cover the last piece of cake at a picnic, ruining the day, and resumed searching at the shop for what could be of help to us. I got some vests with multiple pockets, about the right sizes for the three of us, and some kind of military boots and rucksacks. I handled some machetes and decided to get them too, just because. I also found proper ear protection for shooting practice. They would replace the ear plugs we had been using so far in our gun exercises. Especially now, practice was bound to increase in frequency and number.

In a second adjacent room, I found a real arsenal, a large choice of military stuff and I couldn't decide at first. Honestly I had very little clue what to go for. I went for what I knew from blockbusters memories, so first a couple of Kalashnikov AK-103 with 30-round magazines. I loaded the trunk with enough to supply an army.

I thought about Mary's reaction; she would think I went crazy. Maybe I was, maybe we all were, each of us mad in our own distinct way. Unable to see it ourselves nor did we have anyone to tell us.

Just before leaving the room, I saw out of the corner of my eye a name I knew from my infancy: Benelli.

It was a brand for motorcycles and hunting rifles, too. My uncle was a hunter and he had a couple Benelli's. He loved them. Beautiful guns but I knew they could be deadly. On a hunting trip, he killed my mom's Golden Retriever with one single shot, point blank. He got furious the dog did not obey him on the spot, at least this is what he explained when he got back home with game but no dog.

He destroyed the poor animal with one shot, and my mom's heart too. She remembered vividly how pain crippled her when she was told her friend got killed, and how she felt the pain physically, squirming like earthworms on the ground after a heavy rain. I think this is why I never went hunting with my uncle when I reached the 'right age', as he used to say. When is the right age to start killing?

The Benelli in front of me, though, was not a hunting rifle; I had never seen this model before. Not surprising, it being a military rifle. The card was labeled "Benelli M4 Super 90—CHF 2419" and continued: "Benelli SpA of Urbino, Italy, designed and built the M4 Super 90 Combat shotgun for the US Armed Service." The shotgun had beaten all competitors and the US Army, the label noted, had awarded the contract to Heckler & Koch, USA, subsidiary for importation of the Benelli M4 to the US. The first batch of 20,000 units had been delivered to the United States Marine Corps in 1999 and the shotgun was labeled in the US as an M1014.

1999 was the year Annah was born in Berkeley, during our life in California, and my mother was from Urbino. An avalanche of memories flooded my brain and my heart. It was overwhelming and my eyes filled with tears. I'll probably never see those places again. They are now secluded in a dreamland of memories, sheltered and private. Never to be seen again. As if someone had erected a tall barrier around me and I had no chance to break free. I could go everywhere and had no constraints of any sort, yet I felt trapped and chained to a boulder.

I needed to control my thoughts so I focused again on that Benelli. If it was good for a Marine, I reasoned, it was good for us. Well, for me at least. I thought I would never leave home without that shotgun ever. It looked light, like a piece of art, a nice killing machine, if one can use nice with 'killing' and 'machine' in the same sentence. For good measure, I got two of them and plenty of rounds. I had to admit it was a lovely piece of work, too. Italian taste showing off, all matte black, and looking extremely powerful. I also found the round magazine extension so the rifle had nine rounds available.

I do not know whether I could have made a better choice at the armory. It seemed perfect to me and I was sure no target, dead or alive, would ever complain with me that I could have hit them with other kinds of bullets and guns. I felt our chances of survival were much higher now. I looked at my wristwatch. I had been away from my women long enough. Next time, heading to other destinations, we would ride together. After they were prepared, that is.

I replaced Joe's pistol with the Glock 36; I had one loaded and ready to fire. In the street, I aimed at a stop sign. The recoil was lighter than Joe's MAS-50. At thirty yards, the impact was right where the aim was. Very accurate. It had six rounds and I made six holes on the target. The sound too was more contained. Joe's pistol had been mentally relegated into a lesser category, to scare dogs and other animals.

I had fired it with two hands and the Glock behaved perfectly. I was amazed I was shooting a .45 with such a gentle recoil. Or maybe it was normal; I didn't have much experience with guns. Sure, some shooting during military service, but that was years and years ago. The Glock was so thin and compact in comparison to the MAS-50 that I could hide or carry it without any difficulty. I loaded another full magazine, got back to the car and hit the road, leaving a shattered shop. I went back home through the international organizations district.

— o —

In front of the United Nation's Plaza, s 40-foot tall memorial made of wood stood defiantly; a monumental sculpture, a chair with a broken leg, in commemoration of all land mine victims. The broken leg represented the wounds and lost limbs of the victims. The plaza was empty. I didn't stop and moved forward on the Route de Ferney, toward the airport. It was a lonely drive, and I smelled the new guns with a pinch of satisfaction for a job well done.

At one point, the road crossed the A1 motorway to Lausanne on an overpass and, from there, the single landing strip of the airport was fully visible. I wanted to discover what caused the black smoke we saw the first day, smoke that had lasted almost 48 hours. Something big must have been burning. The only wreckage along the road so far had been a trash truck which almost knocked down an old stone wall. As I slowed down, I noticed the driver was still in the cabin. I could not see where the other members of its crew were.

I stopped at the overpass. The Geneva International Airport's only strip was visible and there it was, a partially burned plane. One of those private corporate jets among the first to reach Geneva early in the morning for some top executive's business trip.

It must have landed by itself on the ILS to end its run onto the fields beyond the strip, smashing through the airport perimeter. Its nose had dived into the ground and the strip was scorched where the landing gears had collapsed. The fuselage had broken in half roughly where the engines were attached to that section, toward the rear. I assumed it had caught fire on impact, and burned after getting separated from the plane. That separation had saved—in a manner of speaking—the rest of the plane from complete destruction.

I couldn't read any aircraft registration or the nationality. Must have been located in the rear, darkened by the fire. There were no other planes but those parked in front of the air terminal. Apparently no flight had reached Geneva that fatal morning.

The timing matched that of the windstorm, I reasoned, and I started to believe the wind was unnatural. It had probably hit us between 5-6am. Commercial flights never arrived in Geneva before 6:30am. I knew that because I was usually awake every morning at 6:20, and used to hear and see the first arrivals some fifteen, twenty minutes after I woke up. That meant airplanes had not made it on time into the airport. *Where did they crash?*

What on Earth could be so pervasive and powerful to not only kill people in their beds within a few seconds—and across vast areas—but pilots and passengers on airborne planes, too, roughly all at the same time? That was huge, incredible. If my conjectures were right, the implications were…what were the implications? I had nowhere to turn for help. What sort of power could erase or suck out human lives like that? This was the stuff of science fiction and my mind refused to believe it.

It also meant that airplanes must have continued their flights under the control of onboard computers, going through all waypoints till reaching the last one. At that point, the plane would fly on the same course and at the same altitude until it burned out all its fuel. Then the crash would occur when the engines did shut down.

I knew that because I played X-Plane on my computer for a couple of years. I had some knowledge of airliner characteristics and their FMS, the flight management system. X-Plane is highly sophisticated and it is used for real training of actual pilots. An FMS is a specialized computer system that automates a wide variety of in-flight tasks. One primary function is the management of the flight plan.

The FMS can guide the aircraft along its flight plan, waypoint after waypoint, until reaching descent and even following the STAR, the standard terminal arrival procedure. In short, pilots enter all flight details into the computer and a later-generation FMS can fly an airliner until landing when full ILS is available, a system of category III to be precise. One day, when everything is standardized, it will be possible to touch the landing strip at all airports.

I corrected myself. That was in another world. It was not going to be possible anymore, at least in my lifetime and the lifetime of who knows how many generations after mine. The world had changed. There were no pilots left. In that moment, I realized the planet had to be covered with airplane crashes. Some around major airports if caught while already on the descending slope, especially for the 24-hour facilities...burned-out wreckage wherever the last waypoint had sent them to a doomed destination.

It was mind boggling. These were pieces of a gigantic cosmic puzzle and I had no idea how to connect them. In anguish, I had visions of 9/11 on a planetary scale. The culling of animals...weird. Escalation in number of deaths and locations. Weird again. Escalation in more evolved life forms such as Emperor Penguins and Mountain Gorillas, and those were the ones we had the time to discover. Who knows what else and where? Then us. Humans, the dominant species. This time, precisely and massively culled. What on Earth? This led to an external force, a deliberate plan put into action.

I got back in the car, dizzy by the enormity of the catastrophe. Were we supposed to survive at all? I gasped for air. The mind is really a funny thing and, as I started the engine, my memory pulled out from nowhere a passage from "The Hitchhiker's Guide to the Galaxy" by Douglas Adams:

"The Hitchhiker's Guide to the Galaxy says that if you hold a lungful of air you can survive in the total vacuum of space for about thirty seconds. However, it does go on to say that with space being the mind-boggling size it is the chances of getting picked up by another ship within those thirty seconds are two to the power of two hundred and seventy-six thousand, seven hundred and nine to one against."

Why had I thought of "The Guide"? Anyway, that was not correct either, I told myself. A sudden exposure to a very low pressure, or to the vacuum, such as during a rapid decompression, could cause a rupture of the lungs due to the large pressure differential between inside and outside of the chest. A rapid decompression can rupture eardrums and sinuses, bruising and blood seeping.

I don't think we could hold our breath for thirty seconds in those conditions. At home, relaxed and prepared maybe, if one is fit. Following a rapid decompression? Unprepared and caught by surprise? Not a chance! We would lose all air in our lungs in a blink, we would lose consciousness after a few seconds and die of hypoxia within minutes. I remembered the old flight lessons I once took. I continued following them up to the point of having a solo airport circuit flight, then stopped when an acquaintance died the day of his final flight exam. Burned alive. That, added to the high costs of getting flight lessons in Geneva, made up my mind about getting a pilot's license.

Stewart Payne! The name popped out of nowhere. My subconscious was trying to tell me something. Payne died in his plane together with the pilots and other passengers, apparently from a sudden loss of air pressure in the cabin. Hypoxia. The crash and deaths had been an unsolved mystery, impossible to determine the cause of the cabin decompression. Did someone test something there? That was hyperbolic and the conjecture didn't last as everything returned to the part of the mind we do not have access to when fully awake.

I called Mary to tell her I was coming home and all was fine. The smoke? A private jet had an uncontrolled landing, ended its run on the fields and partially burned. I would say there were no survivors either. In any case, no emergency vehicles or crew had intervened. Everyone must have been dead already before it happened, both in the airplane and at the air terminal.

"I'll be home in twenty minutes. I love you."

"I love you too. Be careful," said Mary.

— o —

When I got home, I showed Mary and Annah the arsenal I brought back. Annah was excited and wanted to try the pistols right away. Mary was not excited at all. She looked at me, really worried, with her exploring gaze trying to read my mind. I pretended not to notice and addressed Annah.

"Slow down, little girl. One thing at a time."

I wanted to unload everything and do that properly and methodically. "Guns call for respect and need to be treated seriously, Annah."

Before starting to shoot, I had to familiarize myself with the new gear. Then I would be able to help Annah and Mary learn. But first, I wanted to go visit my dogs. Hadn't had the chance yet that day. I called them *my dogs* then, even though I never entered the yard where they were confined nor tried to get them out either. Sometimes Mary and Annah had come with me so the dogs were getting to know them, too. This was the big day for all of us.

For some time, I had been bringing two leashes with me and showing them to the dogs. I let them sniff the leashes, bite them, get used to them. I had rubbed the leashes against my body so that my odor would stick and be identified by the dogs. I usually put the leashes down together with the food so that their presence had become, or at least I hoped so, natural and non-threatening.

At the hardware store, I had retrieved two large kennels. I also stayed there for half an hour, every day, reading a book aloud. Annah made fun of me as I had her stay in the kennels too. It was good to laugh pretending we were kennel neighbors. I loved to see Annah smile again. Mary kept looking at me, clearly worried about my mental sanity.

After finding a safe place to store the guns and bullets, and enjoying a light lunch, it was time to go full monty with the dog affair. "Today is the day," I told Mary and Annah. "I am bringing the dogs home." I was happy to see Annah was more excited with the idea of having the dogs home with us than with the gun business, which was good. She had already chosen the names for both: Taxi and Tarantula. The dogs seemed to love those names and had started to respond to them.

Annah's choice made me smile when she first told me about the names. Taxi and Tarantula, T and T. TNT, the world express delivery corporation. Their motto "Sure We Can" was a brilliant motto for our family too now. I told Annah and we adopted it at every occasion. She often repeated it to me: "Because sure we can, Dad."

I had placed one of my used tee-shirts in each kennel so the dogs would recognize my scent, hoping it would be a comforting message for them. I had put myself out for those dogs and I wanted them to become part of the family, plus add to our protection and chances of survival. They would be an important factor in the whole equation. For all of us.

I gave Joe's pistol to Mary and put the Glock I used that morning in my waistband. This time I walked to meet the dogs.

"I believe I won't be long," I said. Mary smiled at me and nodded without replying.

I put their food, the leashes and a large pair of pruning shears in a backpack and left home for the fifteen minute walk.

The property was surrounded by a metallic grid fence, very common with some in the village. For some reason, their owners thought it was a much cleaner or *lighter* solution than stone walls and old looking wood fences. Quite the opposite of the approach Mary and I had taken for our house. *What did the Romans say?* "De gustibus non disputandum est": It is worthless to discuss personal taste. It is called 'personal' for a reason.

The plan that morning was to cut the fence while the

dogs where busy eating and then call them to the opening and decide what to do based on their reaction. Perfectly detailed plan, right? If all went well, Taxi and Tarantula would sleep that night on our property. Everybody happy. If not…honestly, I hadn't contemplated that possibility. I didn't want to repeat my uncle's exploit.

The dogs were waiting for me as I had successfully created a routine. Taxi and Tarantula, soon to be our two white German shepherds, barked joyfully when they saw me and wagged their tails as I approached. I had searched for their type on the web and found all sorts of information about that breed. Google still worked as were most of the various websites, and worked well.

"Hi, Taxi. Hi, Tarantula…Good boy, good girl…Yeah, yeah, I'm here, c'mon, c'mon."

I definitely had hit it off with both and that made me very confident. They were medium-sized dogs, well-balanced and muscular, their fur dense and straight. Tarantula, the female, had a light-cream tan to her coat; Taxi was a pure white male. They greeted me standing tall on their feet, paws on the fence.

I put down the backpack and caressed and held their big heads with both hands. Standing on the perimeter brick wall of the fence, which was roughly like a large single staircase step marking the property limits, it was a threshold that had never been crossed. I hoped everything would be fine as they happily licked my fingers. Time to have them eat now and then proceed with the plan.

"Here, here, look at what Mary prepared for you," I said, unwrapping the two large balls of rice and meat and cereals.

I had taught them to wait for me to signal when they

could start eating. They were both clever and easily trainable. They watched me attentively without looking at the food. Well, they did but discreetly. I did not make them wait too long; I signaled them and they plunged into the food. I stepped back and walked further down the property limit and took out my shears from the backpack. Slowly and without making too many movements, I started to cut the fence's metal grid. Both Taxi and Tarantula, paused for a second to watch me at first, then they decided whatever I was doing was okay and kept eating.

After a few cuts, I was able to open the fence enough for the dogs to come out or for me to get in. In that moment, I took an unknown risk and changed plan on the spot. Taxi and Tarantula were just too happy to see me...would they change attitude if I had stepped in their yard? Would I be treated as an intruder even after all we had gone through in the past weeks? Slowly I sneaked through the opening and got in. Now, in principle, I was indeed an intruder.

They saw me come in...hesitated, then ran toward me panting and breathing heavily. My hand went to the Glock on my back waistline. I didn't show fear, just determination in case they turned against me. They encircled me, barking, and pushing, and touching, and jumping like puppies. It was amazing. I was so elated, they were greeting their master! I let go the grip on the Glock.

I hugged them, pushing back and wrestling with both. I was so happy, I laughed and it was marvelous! "Yes! Yes! Here Taxi, here Tarantula." It was overwhelming, it was so natural and rewarding, as if nothing horrible had ever happened to us, Taxi and Tarantula included. I was like a child.

I took them back and let them finish their food then went

for the leashes. I had the dogs sit down, side by side and in front of me. It was a serious moment. I kept talking to both in reassuring terms and explained all that was going to happen as if they could understand me. They sure gave me the impression they did. In their eyes I could see only trust. I secured the leashes one by one...then I said, "Go."

At first they started to move ahead of me and pull on the leashes. I stopped and pulled back. "Stop!" I cried. They startled a bit but complied. I moved a step in front and again said, "Go!" They did as before, running ahead and pulling. "*Stop!*" I pulled harder. Now they were both staring at me and I had the impression they were trying to formulate what to do with me, and process the signals I was giving them.

I stepped forward and repeated "Go" with a low voice, and walked with a slow pace. This time I only had to pull a little and keep the leash tight. They started to march at heel, at my same speed. I stopped, they stopped. They surely must have been trained a bit before as these were evidently acquired behaviors. I simply had to make them recollect those and apply them with me.

This was great, majestically great! We strolled in the garden for a little while, starting and stopping. Then we went for the opening in the fence. I stopped. "Sit!" and gestured with lowering my hand down. They obeyed. Definitely trained dogs. I mentally thanked their previous owner for having made things easier for me. "Wherever you are, buddy, you did a good job."

I opened the grid fully so we could go through easily. Me first, then both dogs followed. I had them sit again, this time on the other side of the fence. Also to make them realize where they were and what had just happened. We were on the street, no fence...they could have run away at that moment. They didn't. I called Mary at home.

"So?" she immediately asked without giving me time to say a word.

"Mary? We did it. I am coming home with Taxi and Tarantula."

I heard Annah screaming excitedly. Mary held the phone so she could hear my words. They had been anxious too.

"Come home quickly, you three. Don't waste time on the way."

Mary's voice, if possible, was smiling and happy. The dogs and I walked home.

With the addition of the two dogs, our survival unit grew to five elements. The two German shepherds amazed us. I read they had a distinct personality, marked by self-confidence. Taxi and Tarantula were poised and, when the situation demanded it, they were eager, alert and ready to serve in any capacity. They proved to be exceptionally loyal and tended to be especially protective toward Annah. I believe they also understood she was the youngster of our pack and paid extra attention to her.

Days passed by and I started to venture around with Taxi and Tarantula. If anything, it increased our mutual understanding and trust. Annah came on patrol with us a few times, even more so whenever the intended route hit the countryside to visit farms. Sometimes we found the farmer had died while attending the cattle. I was careful not to overexpose Annah to scenes of death, though it was inevitable.

We freed farm animals whenever we saw them confined. Carefully, as the animals were frightened and they literally jumped out onto the pasture grounds. What else could have been done? I fantasized about having a horse for when cars disappeared forever and horses once more became the principal means of transportation. I dreamed about getting milk from cows and producing our own cheese. The reality was we had little knowledge about those things.

We checked from time to time that everything was fine at the farms we visited. Animals had grass to eat at their leisure all year long in our regions and, with help from both Mary and Annah, we opened barns and gave them access to the hay supplies. They would have to fend for themselves as they, too, had to learn new habits and new routines if they wanted to survive. One thing was certain, we could not visit every farm in the surrounding area. But even that limited activity gave us things to do and reasons to plan for the days ahead. It made our presence in the world meaningful; we still served a purpose. Those trips also increased our bonding with the dogs.

I really didn't believe I would have to resort to riding horses in my life time. I thought if my car broke I only had to find another one. What the heck, even a brand new one. Gasoline was not a problem. With my portable generators, I could operate the pumps at gas stations even if the electricity went out. In the worst of cases, I could use the manual pumps I found at the hardware store and access the station reservoirs directly.

With the company of our dogs, I grew more confident scouting the area with Mary and Annah. I relied on the dogs to increase our overall awareness. At times, I had the impression they were scouting on their own, then coming back to reassure everyone all was fine. Sometimes Mary stayed home, waiting for us, especially when the surveillance raids we planned weren't going to last too long.

My wife and daughter became really proficient with the guns, though Annah was more natural and achieved higher accuracy than Mary. In the end, after trying both the Glock and the Beretta for hundreds of rounds, Annah preferred to use the Italian pistol. Moreover, she started to try shooting with both hands using the Berettas, and with decent success.

With all the free time, I had arranged our own shooting range in a nearby field. We used old frying pans of different sizes for targets, hanging them from poles and supports obtained with materials from the hardware store. We placed them at various distances with the intention of providing increased difficulty.

For myself, I loved the Glock pistols. Once, I fired 200 rounds in succession without the gun ever getting jammed. To me, that was incredible as the barrel was hot, but not unbearably so. They were reliable guns and I don't think it was due to my skills in keeping them clean.

The other star of our arsenal was the Benelli shotgun, the M4. Jeez, those beauties had real firepower. I destroyed a few pans with them. Taxi and Tarantula got quite nervous the first times and barked a lot, but I needed them to get used to the shots, the noises, and the smell. Once they showed they trusted us and stayed calm in all situations, I would know then we had become a tough bite for anything or anyone who might one day cross our path with less than honorable intentions.

The Skorpions had little recoil. Mary and Annah could use them easily in both single-shot mode and rapid fire. A bit different for them, and more difficult to handle, was the full auto-mode. They sprayed bullets all around. Not efficient against an isolated target but they would improve with practice. They fared much better with the stock extended than without. They gained in accuracy that way. Mary accepted, willingly or unwillingly, the presence of guns in our life. There were reasons to have them and she stopped arguing about it.

Although I didn't make a point to visit and verify every house, those nearby and the village were deserted, the property owners obviously dead. After a while, we took those deaths for granted. A few times we had to scare away estranged dogs. In the meantime, they had started to hunt in packs and I suspected some must have fed on human corpses. Usually, they were not trying to approach us and only as a matter of precaution did we fire a few shots in their direction without attempting a kill. We had seen no wolves so far, just some foxes, and deer were now frequently spotted crossing the fields or wandering around, suffering no more disturbance from human presence.

We ventured back to the gun shop to replenish our ammunition supplies; practice makes perfect but requires lots of rounds. I thought we were doing pretty good. March got well under way with a warm spring that made everyone happy but Mary, who always suffered from allergies this time of year. The pharmacy at the mall proved to be useful. Medicines and drops and pills aplenty, much more than actually needed.

— o —

We started to lose interest in the Internet and emails. Without any updates, it had become a frustrating and disappointing task. Also, in a sense, we took for granted that our chances to establish contact with anyone had to be as calculated in The Hitchhiker's Guide to the Galaxy: "... Two to the power of two hundred and seventy-six thousand, seven hundred and nine to one against." Getting in touch with someone would have felt like winning the lottery.

Mary and I reinstated formal education for Annah. Well, mostly Mary, because she was a real teacher. She was the Head of School, the Dean, and the Minister of Education. I helped with math, physics, science and technology subjects; Mary covered all the rest. Our first goal was to finish the current year's program at the International School which had stopped abruptly that past February. We had all the textbooks available at home so we were not starting from scratch, nor did we need to reinvent procedures or teaching methods.

Exerting ourselves to provide Annah with a proper education had other side effects. For example, it helped in giving us reasons to watch the calendar. We kept count of the days of the week and respected weekend rests from lessons and teaching. I believe we would have soon lost track of time if not for the school schedules. It also provided Annah with continuity, a structure where she could recognize her place in it. Of course, we had to fight resistance.

"What's the use, Dad? Why learn things I'll never use..."

That kind of remark from kids had always been heard by parents and was easier to counter in the old world. I could not talk Annah into future perspectives, better jobs and opportunities, to stand out in the crowd, and all those things. So I gave Annah a sad and honest answer that cut short all further discussion.

"Because there is no one else to remember all that. Because we can share what we know with you, and you will remember us better when we will not be here anymore. Annah, we've lost everything...I do not want to give up on you. When I think about the future, all I see is you. The best love I can give you is the one which will awaken your soul. That will make you want to reach for more, plant a fire in your heart, and make you stronger. That's what I hope to give you forever."

Annah rushed into my opened arms. We both cried. Every day was an inner fight to find the strength to carry on, to not give up. Every day, the world simply moved on, ignoring us. Yet everything was just perfect around us, though humanity was no longer a factor into the grand equation of the planet. If I didn't know quite how to face that, how could a twelve-year-old girl? Still, I had hope. I refused to passively accept the facts, to believe we were the end of everything. I refused it, I refused to give in to desperation.

— o —

With Taxi and Tarantula, Annah and I went to the local golf course on occasion. Grinning with sadness, I thought I must have been among the best players in the world with my 16 index. And Annah was a close second, even if she did not have an official index yet. Yet... She will never get an official index, but I will give her one when she's able to score less than 18 shots over par on the 9-holes near the CERN lab. Starting from the high-handicap ladies' tee-off, of course. Some things never change and I clung to them to avoid sliding down a mental ravine, tearing me apart...at which time I would have found only madness.

Those rounds, with Taxi and Tarantula watching and on alert for us, were moments of true serenity. It almost felt as if nothing had happened. Those were the moments to cherish, sharing a passion with Annah. Seeing her trying so hard just to learn how to play golf. I knew she did that mainly to spend time with me, time together. Probably because she was also rewarded by my smiles and laughter and cheers for every good shot from her.

Time was the one thing we now had more than ever. And maybe we were all a bit crazy, playing golf when the rest of the world as we knew it had died. But what were we supposed to do? I guess that craziness is also what kept us going.

— o —

By the end of March, we had not yet ventured to downtown Geneva. Neither did we ever go to the shopping district. I had only explored part of Meyrin, a nearby satellite town. Mostly to identify shops and businesses which could become an additional source of provisions for us. There was a large multi-store center in Meyrin and we didn't really need anything from Geneva as food, medicine, clothes and general supplies were available at both malls, the one in France and the one in Meyrin. Thus, it was only out of curiosity that we decided to plan a day in Geneva.

The last weekend of March, Saturday the 31st, we loaded the car with food, water and ammunitions to spend a full day scouting the town. How different from visits only a few weeks before. Some shopping, a restaurant, just some good times together. Now it was like preparing for an expedition to enemy territory, planning for danger and the unexpected.

With our two canine petty officers, my lieutenant daughter and second-in-command wife, the patrol squad got ready with supplies and armaments in our Volvo XC 90. We locked and secured the house, closed the gate. As a last measure, I parked a brown UPS truck in front of the driveway gate; one I'd recovered a week before from its dead driver. The truck completely obstructed and protected our entrance. Now, nothing could ram into our gate.

Call me crazy but UPS had contributed to good nights of sleeping for yours truly. I borrowed the idea from memories of the Mel Gibson "Mad Max" movies I had seen. Never would I have imagined one day Hollywood would have provided me with instructional tips on how to survive. Ours was a much safer world than the one Max experienced in those plots. His scenario had been quite different from mine. He had lost his family and avenged their deaths in a killing rampage of all villains, thus the title...I do not think he was mad at all.

He lived in a world where an unknown conflict had destroyed the entire civilization. I believed I wasn't going to share his fate in our new world. There were no villains around, so far, and our civilization infrastructures were still standing. It was not just villains to have perished in my world, it was everyone. It seemed plausible to me to believe that we had better prospects of a more peaceful life than the one depicted in those movies.

We started our short journey to town. The last time we'd all went together, we planned for some shopping and a dinner at our favorite restaurant for family outings: The "Relais de l'Entrecote". We were armed with our credit cards, not guns, quite confident about the future and the stability of our lives. I had a job and a very good salary. Honestly, at that time, I had already started to dislike my job and even thought about quitting, but I was in no hurry. It was an entirely different life, the life of a different me in a different world.

We crossed the border, passed in front of the CERN lab main entry and went straight to downtown, the same way I drove through for my first visit to the gun shop. I'd had more time to grow accustomed to scenes of death, car accidents and overturned vehicles than Mary and Annah. My wife held my hand and she squeezed it hard at times. Annah was in the middle of Taxi and Tarantula and I could see in the rearview mirror that she hid her face in their mantle so as not to see too much of anything. Was it too early for her?

We arrived in town in silence; there were no appropriate words to comment on anything. This time, I kept going forward after the Notre Dame church and didn't notice any change from my first and last ride through town. Human changes, at least...yet how fast would nature be in reclaiming all its spaces? The impression I received was of an untidy and sloppy town.

The streets were deserted, and plants had started to grow wild. Weeds made their appearances in pavement cracks, finding the smallest possible fertile spots where to grip the earth with their roots. Like cat claws on a doomed prey, indifferent to their pain and destiny. The previously neat and trimmed green areas, flowerbeds, and urban decorations had grown naturally but in a chaotic way, at least to our civilized eyes. Dead leaves bunched together where wind had collected them along with papers, plastic bags and everything else not securely fixed in place.

We caught glimpses of cats and small dogs which must have escaped from their masters' apartments—now tombs— and we resisted Annah's pleas of starting an animal shelter business. Besides, we had two dogs already. A few cars were around, those of early commuters culled that watershed day when human civilization had been cut short. I don't know who the ghosts were now, us or those unlucky drivers locked in their vehicles, their path interrupted by a fatal destiny in the shape of a wall, a curb or a street light post. Some seemed to have parked in impossible locations, left there to rot by an uncaring fate disposing of garbage. Pigeons and seagulls, from the Lemano lake, had left their mark and there was no one around to clean up after them.

We arrived at the Pont du Mont Blanc, a bridge crossing the point where the Rhone River leaves Lake Lemano again to continue a few miles further into France. It was free of cars but intact except for a broken and twisted balustrade on the right side. Something had smashed into it, like slashing open a wound into its metallic flesh, no signs of it left on the pavement. Whatever vehicle, it had plunged into the lake without any attempt to stop as if the driver had been eager to reach his liquid tomb. Probably a delivery truck.

We crossed the bridge slowly, going in the direction of the shopping district. Geneva rivaled London and Paris as a prime shopping destination in Europe. You'd find the finest things in life and, though they are not cheap, the selection was staggering and made for world class retail stores. No shopaholics around that day.

The windows were magnificent as ever, but there was no one to attract anymore. Business shut down for lack of customers. I had the impression of walking onto a movie set, all perfectly staged down to the smallest details, yet deserted as the actors and crew had not arrived. The parallel streets of Rue du Rhone and Rue du Marché, becoming Rue du Rive further east and Rue de la Confédération to the west, made up Geneva's most famous shopping area.

Designer retail stores and world famous watchmakers lined the streets usually packed with window shoppers. The entire district almost resembled a fashion runway, perfect and beautiful. The resemblance though was loathsome, as if fashionable jewels and clothing brands had finally admitted they did not care whether customers liked them or not. They reclaimed a reason to exist for themselves, becoming altars and shrines to vanity and vacuity.

My goal, our goal, was not a shopping frenzy. Our goal

was to see whether anyone could still be alive in town or finding evidence of their presence: any broken shop windows, any sign of the passage of people looking to sustain themselves. Who knows, maybe even looting. That would have been a clear sign of people alive. I did not want to get out of the car before a good sweep of the area so we kept driving, Mary and Annah ready to intervene at any moment, my paranoid side alerted. Taxi and Tarantula sensed we were tense and they were uneasy.

I drove all the way to the end of Rue du Rhone, than back onto Rue de la Confédération and Rue du Marché. That was the first time ever for me, as that last part of our driving loop had always been closed to traffic and only streetcars went up and down. Once. In another world.

"We're not getting any clues this way," Mary said.

I agreed. "I don't like it very much either but we need to get out of the car. We should first go to the main grocery stores."

We decided to stop in front of the Confederation Center. Itself a shopping mall and near two other big ones, Globus and Coop. People, if there were any alive, would have looted in those to feed themselves at least. We headed to the Center first as time no longer had any meaning. Everything was of the highest priority or of no priority at all. It did not matter, we did not matter. We had become inconsequential matters to the rest of the world.

We got out cautiously. Taxi and Tarantula sniffed the air, waiting for us to move. I looked at them; they did not seem to have sensed the presence of anyone and the dogs would have provided us with an early warning. I had one of the Benelli shotguns with me, and my Glocks. Mary and Annah each held one of the Skorpion pistols. We were no longer the ordinary family of two months before. We investigated, seeking clues—and, hopefully, people—and acting as if we had ventured into a war zone. We were ready to face danger if danger dared to face us.

The day was gloomy. Clouds had started to gather earlier in the morning and now they completely covered the sky forming a dense and thick layer. Spring had arrived too early in the region and that brought weather instability. It was much colder than during the previous weeks, and dismally and depressingly dark as if the world itself wanted to remind us we were in a cemetery. We would have better weather in the days to come. Not that it would change much.

We didn't reach the Center right away as I wanted to get in from the top floor, not from the lower level. The Center was at the footsteps of the old town, perched higher than where we had arrived, accessible from there via a set of old stone stairs winding up and leading from one little old road to the other, intricately arranged. From above, we would've accessed the Center and made our way inside from the top, its 2nd level.

We were used to the silence by now, hearing just the noises coming from nature: birds, breeze, rustling leaves. It felt less macabre than before. Slowly we climbed the winding stairway to the upper level. The old buildings overlooked our advance and were deaf and mute, as if we were an oddity not worthy of commentary.

The old town had turned into a huge bird's nest; pigeons and doves cooed, heedless of our presence among those old walls. I wondered whether they marveled at us, walking below them, a remnant of a past they surely had already forgotten. High up, the cry of a hawk pierced the air. A new equilibrium had established itself between prey and predators in town.

And what were we now, predators or preys? I chased the thought away; I needed no distractions at the moment. Taxi and Tarantula climbed together at our heels, not leaving the pack. They would have preceded us and scouted by themselves only if I had ordered them to with a "Check!", then to rush back when I whistled.

Finally, we reached the higher levels. It took a long time with the slow, careful pace we had adopted. At the top, a little pedestrian paved square was located where the Brasserie Lipp and the Capocaccia restaurant faced each other, separated only by a short distance. The Capocaccia terrace was ready to welcome the epicureans from the old town businesses; it was depressingly empty now.

We stopped and stood with our backs to the low wall of the Capocaccia terrace. Everything was silent and calm. The upper level of the Confederation Center opened to the paved square we had just reached. From our position, we could barely distinguish the interior even though the lights were all on.

"Check!" I called Taxi and Tarantula into action. They jumped ahead and entered the Confederation Center's top level, ears pricked up. I signaled Annah and Mary to stay back, glued to the terrace wall, and I slowly moved forward to the entrance of the shopping center. I knelt down and got a glance of both Taxi and Tarantula searching inside. Nothing abnormal, apparently. I let my eyes adjust to the interior lights before taking a step inside. It did not take long as the day was not a bright one that Saturday. I advanced a couple yards ahead to have a clearer view of the top level.

I glanced back toward Mary and Annah, waiting for me. The Lipp entrance stood next to the elevator on the right.

The escalator to the mid-level went down on the opposite side of the hallway, to the left. The internal main entry to the Capocaccia restaurant, a remake of Italian stone steps with its forged iron balustrade, was as inviting as ever. I whistled to the dogs and signaled both Annah and Mary to rejoin me. Taxi and Tarantula dashed toward me, happy. I gave them a treat.

"Good boy, Taxi. Good girl, Tarantula. Nothing to see here, huh?"

Mary knelt next to my side, Annah right behind her.

"All seems clear at this level. As if no one has been here since…" Since that early day in February, when our world had been replaced by this new weird one. Mary nodded.

"Let's stay together now."

Neither Capocaccia nor Lipp showed any sign of a break-in. The Center had two levels above the ground; the interior space of the building was empty so that each level consisted of shops along the outer perimeter and a large hallway-balcony circling around, like a gigantic rectangular donut with rounded edges, allowing for a continuous flow of shoppers without intersections. On one end, there was an open-view elevator with a glass cage, connecting all levels for patrons to see through the transparent cabin, maybe catching a glimpse of their next shopping destination.

The ceiling lights and the marble columns gave the whole place a sort of an Art-Deco taste. There weren't many places where anyone could hide from us with that open architecture, but we proceeded cautiously anyway. At the first level, Taxi and Tarantula searched the area before us and we kept advancing along the hallway. We constantly kept eye contact with the dogs who sniffed all over and glanced at us regularly while they were scouting the place.

"La Maison du Gateau", a well-known pastry shop, looked as if it was about to open. When we reached its windows, at a closer look, the cakes seemed stale and no longer safe to eat. There was no other visible sign the shop had been abandoned. On the other side of the balcony I saw a small and local Havana Cigars business. I mentally took note of it. Another stop for my own gratification.

Apart from being dirtier and now the home of a few birds, the Center hadn't received any visitors since February. No looting or other degradation from possible human intervention. There was nothing more to see.

We exited at the street level and returned to the car. A light rain was falling but the clouds were even darker than before. Maybe we would have a wet weekend. Probably. No shooting training that coming Sunday, no reason to practice in the rain and get wet for nothing. Instead, I would light the fireplace at home, Mary would bake a cake, and we would watch a rental movie on Apple TV. It seemed crazy it was still working along with the Internet and electricity. Almost as if the world and its infrastructures were telling us, "We do not need you. Good riddance."

Though initial engineer degradation had begun on the Internet, it only affected specific sites and probably some servers, not its accessibility as a whole. When the entire service went dead, I planned to add regular visits to CERN as a new routine. The lab enjoyed higher uptime services and dedicated lines. It even had its own power grid.

At that point, our next stop was the Coop City Fusterie shopping mall. It was a short distance from where we were. We walked down Rue du Commerce, which started off Rue de la Confédération, almost in front of the Center. We arrived at the mall entrance at the corner, at the end of the block. The automatic doors opened with a squeaking and scratching noise. *These will stop working soon*, I thought.

Suddenly, Taxi and Tarantula started to growl. We turned slowly and there they were, a group of four dogs staring at us, showing their teeth. Annah and Mary froze.

"Stay calm," I said in a very low voice. "Be ready to shoot but stay calm. Do not stare at them!" I knew a direct stare was considered by dogs to be an act of aggression or perceived as threatening.

"Dad, what do we do?" Annah asked in a whisper.

Mary kept silent, her eyes fixed on the group of unwelcoming animals.

"Annah, if they attack, you aim and shoot. Don't rush and don't panic."

"Now, Mary, very slowly, get inside with Annah. Slowly."

"Dad, no!" Annah started to protest but Mary put one hand on her shoulder and pushed her gently toward the mall.

A dog bite can have serious consequences, potentially fatal in our situation. I did not want to risk any of that. Four dogs faced us from the other side of the street. T&T would have confronted the group if I had ordered it, or if any of those four had attacked, but our shooting might have put both Taxi and Tarantula in danger.

Our two dogs split in front of us, almost at the same time as Annah and Mary reached the mall. I got the Benelli at waist high, ready to shoot. Only one dog of the four was the size of Tarantula, herself slightly smaller than Taxi; the other three were of smaller breeds.

Taxi and Tarantula growled even louder and made little steps forward. I followed, maintaining a distance of two or three steps behind them. The Coop automatic doors closed behind me as we moved away, as if the curtains fell on our stage, preventing Mary and Annah from getting involved. I aimed the shotgun. If I needed to shoot, I wanted to be able and ready to do it without having my dogs in the line of fire.

On the other side of the road, the four dogs must have considered the area as theirs and took us for intruders to be challenged. The biggest of the pack advanced, antagonizing Taxi and Tarantula: in reaction, they side-stepped increasing the distance between themselves. Now the large dog could not stare and face both Taxi and Tarantula at the same time, and the new situation must had created an additional problem in its brain.

I took a stance in the middle, the shotgun pointing right at the dog's head. I had a clear and free line of fire. My hands started to ache as I realized I was squeezing the Benelli's grip with too much strength. Drops of perspiration erupted on my forehead and my eyes started to itch as the sweat made its way down my face. I was about to resolve the stalemate, my index contracting on the trigger to eliminate a potential danger before it could mushroom.

I could not say exactly what changed, but the pack leader suddenly took a less aggressive posture and barked a couple times at a high pitch. The other three were no longer menacing at all and started to show signs of submission. They made themselves smaller by crouching low to the ground, and tucked their tails between their legs while my two dogs seemed like wolves getting ready to pounce on prey.

They were all looking away now, everywhere but

directly at my shepherds, avoiding their sight as if it hurt them. T&T kept showing their teeth and snarling. They were actively displaying dominance. I watched the whole scene in amazement. Certainly, Annah and Mary were watching too from inside the mall, but I didn't dare to turn and check.

The pack leader moved slowly toward both Taxi and Tarantula keeping his head low and ears turned backward, the tail waggling in what seemed a stressed pattern, held at mid-height. Taxi and Tarantula seemed more relaxed now and stared at the approaching dog. When it arrived close to Taxi, Tarantula put her opened mouth on the now submissive dog, her teeth around its neck and head. She physically pushed it with a paw to the ground while Taxi stood tall next to it. I had never seen anything like that.

Fascinating. The entire scene was simply fascinating. Tarantula moved then toward the other three dogs to complete the show. They exposed their belly to her and let Tarantula sniff their genitalia.

I turned toward Mary and Annah inside the mall and gestured, "Did you see that?" Mary shook her head while Annah smiled, visibly relieved and proud of her dogs. I backed toward the sliding doors till they opened again. Standing at the entrance, I whistled. Taxi and Tarantula startled, undecided for a split second then rushed toward me, faithfully. The other dogs stayed still and did not move.

I entered the mall, followed by our white guardians and protectors, and reached my wife and daughter. The automatic doors closed behind us, panting as if exhaling their last breath. Mary providentially had a cloth in her hand and began to wipe my face.

"I'd say we know now who keeps their cool better in this family," she said, and glanced at our furry companions. I was glad she could joke; I gave a second pass to my face with the cloth and kissed her.

"Eww. Gross, Daddy." We turned and smiled at our frowning daughter.

The entry level of the shopping center hosted the women's department store and we started walking down the aisles. In spite of our specific goal that morning, both Annah and Mary were distracted by the display of clothes, dresses, jackets, sweaters, shirts and skirts and were touching them while passing through.

Annah turned around and smiled shyly. It was at moments such as this when the reality of what our lives had become hit us. The world was practically intact and it made things smoother for us, easier to cover our basic needs. Yet at the same time, it was a painful reminder of everything and everyone we had lost and that we would never have with us again.

The store, at least that department, seemed untouched.

"Do you need anything?" I suddenly asked.

Mary and Annah stopped and looked at me with a question in their eyes. I pointed at the rows and rows of fine garments and fashion brands on display.

"I think it's okay if we split up. Look around here, stay for a moment and see whether anything is out of place. Keep Tarantula with you while I get down to the grocery level below with Taxi."

Annah eyes widened in excitement, and a brief look at my wife confirmed she understood what I had in mind. I smiled.

"C'mon, Taxi. We'll let the ladies do some shopping." I

moved toward the staircase with Taxi by my side.

We reached the lower level. I saw Taxi was relaxed, leisurely glancing around and at me, breathing calmly. I guessed he did not sense any presence of animals or humans.

"Heel!" I commanded and walked toward the produce and food area. Taxi got closer, glued to me.

The automatic barrier opened gently and everything was flooded with light as if nothing had ever happened. At first sight, all goods and shelves were intact. I entered through the aisle where sweets and candies were on display. Taxi walked by my side, keeping my pace. Alert but calm. Further down the aisle, to the right, my eyes fell on rows and rows of chocolate bars.

I stopped. I could not resist, never been able to: I got a few dark bitter ones and put them in a pocket of my vest. I never much liked the taste of milk chocolate and, as I child, I felt desperate each time someone brought milk chocolate thinking they made me happy. I never understood why my parents never told anyone I didn't even bother trying the taste of those gifts. With that in mind, I took and unwrapped a Cailler Crémant plain bittersweet chocolate bar.

I closed my eyes, smelled the fragrance and bit to enjoy the rich dark chocolate flavor. I supposed Mary and Annah must have been having a similar tension relief moment with some fine clothing up there. Taxi touched my leg with his nose looking up to me, imploring. He pulled me abruptly from my dreaming. Like Sid in "Ice Age" did with Scrat, the saber-toothed squirrel, saving his life right when he was about to eat a giant acorn in heaven. Scrat lost the paradise and the giant acorn and got mad with Sid when he returned to his senses. I couldn't get mad with Taxi.

"Not for you buddy, I am afraid. This delicacy would kill you." Instead, I gave him a dog treat which I always carried with me.

"Let's see what Lady Luck is treating you with…ah, lamb. Your favorite!"

Taxi took the Meaty Bone with obvious pleasure. He licked my hand, too, something I never particularly liked and had yet to get used to. I glanced at my wet and sticky hand and sighed.

"Let's move now," I said, attempting to dry Taxi's drool on my butt.

The pause had been short, and I wanted to examine the place quickly and thoroughly. Although there was no reason to worry about Mary and Annah upstairs, I did not want to stay away for too long. The produce area smelled foul; everything was rotten and moldy. Pineapples, peaches, grapes, tomatoes, and cucumbers, all ready for the bin. Potatoes had germinated but they would still be edible, I guessed. Carrots, on the contrary, were mushy and covered with mold spots.

That area seemed untouched and unvisited, no signs of looting. I proceeded to examine other parts of the store and, with a bit of disappointment, I had to conclude the place had not received any visits. Got a bottle of mineral water from a shelf and drank a sip. Then I poured some water in my hand and let Taxi have a drink, too; it didn't bother me this time.

There was nothing left for us to do. We did not need to get anything either: our mall near home was a more convenient location, and we still had plenty of supplies. I returned to my girls.

"Mary?" I called out.

"Here, Dan. We're here." I followed her voice.

Taxi and Tarantula greeted each other, and Tarantula licked Taxi's mouth. Before handing the bottle of water to Mary, I had Tarantula drink off my hand too. Annah was radiant, and so was Mary. Both had spent time trying on jackets and trousers, some shirts and accessories as well. It looked like they truly had a good time up there, but I believe Mary was just happy to see our daughter smiling and carefree, as any twelve-year-old should be. She was showing her things to try on, and how to wear them, combine colors, and styles. Together. Laughing and joking. As before.

"Dad! Look what I found." She showed me a beautiful leather jacket, a three-quarter sleeve suede jacket, and a luxury cashmere coat. Plus other things, of course. Many others.

"May I keep them? They are so gorgeous." I looked at Mary and pretended to think a moment to decide.

"I guess so, but it means we need to go back to the car first. We can't carry all that around!"

"Please, please Daddy."

Why say no? Annah was handling difficult situations extremely well, especially since the arrival of Taxi and Tarantula. I went to the cash register to get a couple large plastic bags and handed them to Mary.

Annah's fist pumped. "Yes!"

"Did you find anything down there?" Mary asked. I answered "No" with a head shake. I believe she expected that. She did not comment further.

"What now?"

"Well, I guess we put everything into the car and try

with the Globus mall. Then we go to the Eaux Vives district and head for the shopping center."

Mary nodded in agreement and brought Annah the bags. "Annah, sweetie, help me fill these. We have a few more stops to go."

When we stepped out onto the street, the stray dogs had gone and the rain had subsided. Just a spring shower. The cloud layer appeared to be getting thinner and the day was a bit brighter than before. We started to walk toward the car with Annah still chatting with Mary about her new clothing. Suddenly she stopped short and changed moods abruptly. Mary tried to ask her what was wrong but Annah kept replying, "Nothing." Then she turned around and burst out, "Mom! I don't want to talk about it now, okay?"

Mary frowned and caressed her hair but Annah tilted her head away. Mary glanced at me, worried and puzzled. I raised my shoulders but didn't want to say anything with Annah listening. We resumed walking, reached the car, and put the bags in the back. We got in and drove further up on Rue du Marché toward Place du Molard.

The Globus mall occupied almost an entire block. We parked in front of the square, near the "Bon Genie" entrance, another department store. Just to give it a try, I went for the main entrance.

This time, the doors did not open. I examined a secondary entrance, the one opening straight into the cosmetics department. Locked as well. Obviously, no one had visited in the last two months. On the other side of the road, Globus. We went straight for the entry on the Place du Molard which opened directly into the restaurants' area. That entrance was locked, too, and the tinted windows did not allow a clear view inside. We tried with the main entry back on Rue du Marché: No luck there either. No Globus for us that day unless we smashed through, but it was not in the plans.

In the shopping district, Place du Molard was a favorite stop as it had a couple of restaurants and a pub that occupied the middle area with their tables and chairs when the weather encouraged eating outside. We were facing the "Café du Centre", then the "Pizzeria Molino", and the "Lord Nelson Pub" where I had shared quite a few tasty beers with friends in the past. They were all closed, business shut for good. For a while, we were each lost in our own memories about the places.

"Ok, why don't we take a break and eat something now."

We sat at the fountain near the florist and ate in silence. Taxi and Tarantula did, too. I hadn't forgotten Annah was troubled. Later, Mary and I would have to address that. Bad thoughts can be dangerous if left to simmer and weaken the heart slowly and invisibly from the outside. Like termites that destroy the beams of a house, secretly, in the dark until it's too late and everything collapses. We would do that at home, though. Now was not the right moment. We needed a place where we could pretend everything was alright and normal around us. A place where we could be us.

"The Eaux Vives 2000 doors will open," I thought aloud.

The Eaux Vives 2000 was a shopping center with multiple stores and a number of little shops inside. A completely different style than Globus and Bon Genie. Less upscale, and addressing more to customers with lower budgets. It had bank ATMs, a pharmacy, a florist, laundries and a grocery store, and little artisan shops.

"Can we go now?" Annah asked. She was definitely in a

bad mood. I exchanged a glance with Mary and signaled her not to press the subject.

"Let's go." I simply replied.

From there, and driving in the streetcar lanes, it was only a couple minutes by car. On our way, I glanced at the Davidoff store, with its luxury tobacco goods. Cigars. I wondered whether the room where they stored them was still working and keeping the tobacco just perfect. I indulged in memories while passing by and told Mary I would have stopped there someday. I always wanted a humidor, a large one, holding around 150 cigars. And full as an egg of course.

My smoking habits never fully justified the budget it would require although a humidor would look fantastic in the living room, full of Corona Esplendidos. Who knows, maybe I would start savoring them more often. Further up, the Apple Store; no long lines now. I wondered what happened to people like Tim Cook, Phil Schiller, Jonathan Ive, and others I had seen on stage quite a few times in previous years. I guessed they'd all joined Steve now. *Apple family reunited*, I thought sadly.

Driving or walking in downtown Geneva, in the shopping district always packed with people, was usually mission impossible. Especially on Saturdays. Now it was deserted; no voices, no need to make your way amid a dense pedestrian flow of wealthy people. By this time of day, Latino music bands would have entertained bystanders, and on the corner, maybe a Conservatoire student playing the cello. But no one played music for us. Not there. Not then. Not even a living new Mozart would be able to gather onlookers that day. Or the day after. Or ever. Music was dead.

Again looming thoughts, ready to bring me down. I

didn't know why they kept coming, unannounced. Like cold, bony fingers trying to pull me toward the abyss of madness.

— o —

My Annah was the most precious girl ever, sunny and happy, always fantasizing about a bright future, first loves, boys who had recently got her young blossoming-woman attention. "Hot boys," she had said, ready to add immediately, "but nice boys, Dad. They are very gentle." I looked in the rear mirror and saw a veil of sadness in her eyes. I smiled, she noticed and tried unsuccessfully to smile back, under attack by her own demons.

My God. What kind of future was she going to have? We—Mary and I—had our own memories. We had a happy life; we traveled, tried things, enjoyed what life had to offer. We did not really miss anything in the previous years, especially when Annah wasn't yet with us. We were not rich, far from it, but we could afford things without worrying much about month's end. But Annah? She was just starting her life; in a few months she would be thirteen. Once she had asked me, "Dad, do you think I will have a boyfriend when I am thirteen?" I felt a lump in my throat. "When I will be thirteen..." Mary pressed her hand on my thigh. She knew.

We were about to arrive at our destination and that broke the circling of my thoughts, like vultures hovering over a dying prey below. I slowed down even further and parked at the corner of the building, opposite the mall. We looked around. All quiet and all abandoned. I stepped out and opened the trunk to let Taxi and Tarantula step down. Mary and Annah got out too. We closed the doors and the noise echoed back, briefly tumbling from building to building.

At our backs, the street climbed toward the Natural History Museum; in front of us, it went down for the entire block length, to end at the old City Hall. The entrance we faced led to the middle level of the mall, the one where the produce and grocery store was, our main target. On the next block, to the left, there was a little Migros. A similar supermarket chain like the Coop. We'd search that grocery store later.

We crossed the street and approached the sliding glass doors. They opened and, when inside, the florist shop offered a depressing view. Everything was rotten, dead and dry. Petals on the floor, the plants all dead for lack of watering. Taxi and Tarantula were busy sniffing everything, sneezing occasionally. We turned to our right and advanced toward the small bakery and pastry. Once more, the spectral silence was astonishing. On the displays, green mold covered the once good pastries that filled large platters and beetles rushed to hide as we approached.

The town must have turned into a giant beetle shelter and incubator. These scavengers, together with flies and maggots, arrived within the first day, looking for orifices to deposit eggs, and soon larvae started the feasting. In twenty-four hours, the eggs would hatch into slithering flesh-eating insects and the cleaning process would start.

Luckily, we did not have to witness any human decomposition details live. No corpses were in sight. After two months, with the warm weather we'd had, the majority of them would be almost skeletonized or mummified by now.

I had no urge to go around houses or break into apartments to look for confirmation of this theory. By now, even the remaining skin on cadavers had to be converted into a leathery or parchment-like sheet which clung desperately to an otherwise clean bone. Anyway, that was the case with the dead commuters I had seen the last few days. I suppose in warmer apartments, the process must have been even speedier. I was unaware of the reasons why I was alive and was extremely happy that Mary and Annah were, too. Sure, we were in a crappy world, but we were together and to me that was all that counted.

We kept moving forward toward the produce market area. Taxi and Tarantula sniffed around as we went. We reached the cashier counters at the entrance and, together, walked slowly looking for telltale signs.

"Shall we split?" I said.

"No, let's stay together this time," replied Mary.

So we did, Taxi and Tarantula at our sides, protecting their human pack. The fresh produce area presented the same scene that had unfolded before me in the other shopping centers including a display of decaying fruits and vegetables. Yet the refrigeration system, still running, had prevented the place from becoming infested with flies and other insects. That is, more than it was. Mold was unavoidable.

Unfrozen packed meat in the closed and cooled displays wasn't fresh of course but it was without maggot infestation. But, as in the mall near home, frozen meat in the big fridges behind the counter was perfect and I had safely "shopped" for meat from time to time. We proceeded toward the beverages and drinks section. Did not need to get any bottles then; we had stored in our basement more than we have ever had in our previous life. I did notice though a couple shelves dedicated to the higher priced French Bordeaux wines. They were almost empty. I pointed them out to Mary. She had noticed, too. A connoisseur?

Past the wines and liquors, the shelves were full of juices, sodas, and water. Something felt odd though. Nothing certain of course, or evident, but it looked as if someone had been browsing the items on display. There was a sense of lack of order. We just looked and pointed to each other the areas where mineral water packaging had been removed. The odd feeling also came from one brand being in unusually low supply compared with the others, and the remaining packages were not perfectly aligned as were the other brands. Unless on *that* particular day *that* spring water had already been in shortage, there was no reason why supplies of all others brands should have been in larger quantities. They should all be, on average, at similar levels and all neatly arranged.

"Daaad!" Annah called out from the aisle next to ours. Taxi and Tarantula sat at her side. She was standing and staring at something out of reach from our location. We rushed over to her. The sign above listed: "Cereals, biscuits, jams, instant coffee, cookies, oatmeal, dietary soluble fibers." In the middle of the aisle, the vision of a partially crushed Kellogg's cornflakes box struck us as a miracle. Someone had been there! It was unmistakable! Cereal boxes had been taken from the shelves and what was left was not arranged in neat orderly rows. As for the water packages, they had definitely been messed with. One or two cases can be coincidental, more than that was proof.

"Someone has been here, Mary."

She looked at me and nodded. Then she pointed to another shelf:

Biscuit boxes were in the same untidy state. Excited, we

realized we had even more evidence. It could only mean we were not the only ones alive anymore. We were not the only ones who got spared that night in early February.

"Dan, who...?" Mary was about to start asking the crucial question.

"No idea, but there is no doubt now. Someone's been here."

How many? Just one person or a large group? Maybe an entire family as in our case. It was impossible to tell but we could be sure of one thing: we were not alone. Other areas on the canned food shelves also showed signs that someone had taken items in a fair quantity. All at one time? In multiple visits? We had no way of knowing.

Who knew? If this were a regular spot for other survivors, then we would have been able to get in touch with them easily. It was... phenomenal. I could tell from Mary's and Annah's eyes they were both excited at the prospect. What they had in mind became clear, at least for Annah:

"Oh my God, Dad. Maybe these are kids, I like those cereals too...Dad, we need to look for them, maybe they are still here, and...Dad, you need to do something!"

"Calm down, Annah. Everything is possible, and no, they are not here now or the dogs would have found them. Wait, please, let me think."

"Dan, Annah is right though. We need to look for these people."

"Okay, okay, wait a second..."

I knelt and took the crushed cereal box and presented it to both Taxi and Tarantula. They smelled it at length. I could see from their reaction that they had actually discovered an intriguing scent. "Search!" I urged them in a rush. The drills we did repeatedly together with Annah at the shooting range camp were not for nothing and paid off entirely now. The dogs started to sniff on the floor, scratching as if they were trying to un-dig the odors. When they did that, I noticed some faint thin traces on the floor that had been invisible to us before. How could I have not seen them before? They seemed to be older scuff marks left by shopping carts and the dogs were very interested in them for whatever reason.

They sniffed everything intensely, over and over, then went back to the cereal box I'd put on the floor for them. Suddenly they rushed back toward the produce section. Annah startled, and we all ran after them. The dogs kept sniffing in mounting excitement trying to capture remnant molecules of a scent we would never be able to perceive with our incapable noses as canines can identify smells 10,000 times better than nasally challenged humans.

The place was full of past human odors but our shepherds must have detected a recent scent and something that had stuck on the crushed box, too. At least, that is what I hoped for. Presenting them with the cereal box triggered in their brain the notion that what they had detected was unique and important as they were now selectively separating it from all other smells. I wondered how their instincts guided them. Why were they picking up some spots and not others? To me, they looked all the same and I was blind to the clues Taxi and Tarantula were collecting. We were still watching around the vegetable area to check whether we had missed some hints before when the dogs moved again.

They must have recovered the trace because they were now leading us decidedly toward a sort of conveyor belt, a moving sidewalk to take customers to the levels above. On the floor, I distinguished again faint traces of...what, cart wheels? Were they the same ones or different? Maybe I just imagined things. I pointed those out to Mary who looked back at me with a silent question. I had no idea, so I raised my shoulders. The dogs rushed to the conveyor belt, and we rushed after them.

Taxi and Tarantula hesitated for a second on the landing of the upper level, as if undecided about which direction to take. We stopped, then they accelerated toward the women's clothing section, panting heavily in excitement. It was rather difficult to keep their pace but I did not want to interfere at all with their search.

When we reached them, our dogs were busy sniffing various stuff on the floor, which at first I could not identify: Someone had indulged there, as Annah and Mary had in the previous department store. A woman? Different clothing—vests and sweaters, coats, tops, jumpers—had clearly been tried on and flung over the rails or the store counters and on the floor. Some hangers were empty. I was a hundred percent sure we were not alone anymore. The world's known population could soon increase roughly by at least an estimated 33%, maybe even more!

Taxi focused on a piece of garment left on the floor, and he was soon joined by Tarantula. It was a gray fleece hoodie. Not a brand new one but not worn out either.

"Look, Mary!" I rushed toward our dogs and there was no need to urge her to follow. Both Mary and Annah had reacted the same way.

The previous owner must have found something better to replace the hoodie with and dropped it there. I had never been so careless in my raids to the mall, nor so sloppy when out for food provisioning. I did not want to leave traces of my passages at the mall near home. In a sense, those considerations reassured me. From the size of the hoodie, I guessed the other survivor had to be a young woman judging from the kind of clothes that had been tried on. Not particularly organized either, again a bit sloppy? Maybe just neglectful and arrogant? Alone? I tried to imagine the kind of person we were going to face.

I found a shopping bag and put away the hoodie for later. It would be an identifiable object for Taxi and Tarantula if I needed to go chasing down anyone.

"What do you think we should do, Dan?" Mary suddenly asked.

"Well, we will try to make contact with her or them. But not right now and not here." I nodded toward Annah.

"We do not know who, how many, or what their intentions are. It will probably be all right, but I do not feel like taking the risk and jumping into the dark either." Especially with Annah there, but I explicitly didn't say that. Actually, at that moment, I wanted to take them both home.

"Dad, do you think there could be more than one?"—she hesitated—"Do you think there will be others…of my age?"

I think Annah was trying to let me understand what had troubled her all day. We were not alone, Mary and I; we had each other. But Annah must have felt isolated. She had us, of course, but from her perspective she was alone all the same.

"Maybe. I don't know, sweetie. That would be great, but I just don't know." I didn't want to give her too much hope only to be disappointed later.

Mary touched my arm. "Dan, let's go home." She cut the conversation short and put us back on track, or maybe she felt the discussion was taking a dangerous turn for Annah. I was grateful to her.

Yeah, that was the best thing to do now and think calmly about our next steps without rushing things. Potentially, our world was going to change again, and abruptly even. But in what way?

Later that evening, all discussions revolved around what we had discovered that afternoon. We weren't alone anymore! Other people had survived! And if someone was in Geneva, maybe more were alive in other locations, too. Maybe not so far either, just not so close as to make interactions and encounters easy and probable.

In the next days, we scanned the horizon more intensely and frequently compared the notes Mary and Annah had previously written down. Had anything changed? Were there more visible lights at night? Were there any houses with lit windows? Nothing. For what we could see from our home, everything was as dead as ever. I was tempted to put something visible from afar on the roof. Anything that would grab the attention, like a flag or a banner. At the same time, I was scared. Yes, in a deserted world where everyone around us had been killed, I was afraid to face other people and of what they were capable of. Paranoids do survive.

I was not going to the mall daily and we had to presume it was probably the same with "the survivor" in town, as we now referred to the person who'd looted the drugstore and the Coop department store in Eaux Vives. And were we ready to meet other people now, whoever they turned out to be? Those doubts came from me almost unconsciously. I was as surprised as Mary and Annah when I mentioned it aloud.

"You don't want to?" asked Mary.

"It's not that I don't want to…" I suppose I was afraid of the change.

We had just started to regain some normalcy in our lives.

Things to do, things to focus on and hope for. Hope is a good feeling in itself. What if our hopes, about not being the only ones left on the planet, turned out to be ill-fated? Humans proved to be the most dangerous species of all in every century, most efficiently toward each other. The various "what if" implications worried me a lot.

The Facebook ads campaign was now a multi-million page affair and still we had no results. Maybe survivors were not that common. Maybe at the mall it was just a girl, a woman, and that is all there was. Yet maybe she was not alone...maybe there were other people with her: Men. Violent? Desperate? Aggressive?

We had done a lot at home, and we were well organized. We were an enviable target for people looking for quick and easy gains. The world was full of con artists, swindlers ready to exploit our confidence and take advantage of us if we were naive. With no risks of facing any consequences, even murder could be a possible solution to ruthless people in our new world. I felt as if I had just found a stable base for us, and everything was collapsing again with unknown consequences.

Wait a second! This is exactly why we trained, to face dire situations should they come. Annah knew how to shoot and Mary did, too. She'd managed to handle and fire the Glock just fine, hadn't she? Yes, but against fixed targets, and maybe just to please me. It wasn't going to be the same, to shoot at another person. And the one who hesitates usually ends up horizontal. How would they react in front of a dangerous and menacing person? Would they hesitate? Probably.

I was torn and the tension in my muscles around the neck had become noticeable. But the opposite would also be true, right? "Do you think there will be others of my age?" Annah had asked, the first thing she hoped for and thought of at the store. Did I have any right to shut the door on that possibility? Did I have the right to protect my family so much as to become the cause of their ultimate loss?

We had an agitated conversation, especially after we managed to kiss Annah goodnight. Our daughter made me promise that I would find whoever had been at the mall because now we knew we were not alone anymore.

"You promise, Dad?" It hurt inside and gave me troubles at night.

"Dan, if there is even the slightest hope that Annah will not live her life waiting for us to die..." She did not finish the phrase. She started to cry softly and I didn't know whether she cried for us or for Annah. "Why are you so hesitant?" she asked.

"I'm scared, Mary! That's why! I *am* scared..."

I had not gone nuts, but I felt we were walking a very fine line. What I had managed to do so far would not be the solution of a lifetime, and I knew it. I remembered Albert Einstein once said, "We shall require a substantially new manner of thinking, if mankind is to survive," and I thought his words were perfectly applicable to our situation. I knew I had to find out who was out there. Was I adopting a new manner of thinking? Would it allow us to survive or ruin us?

An email from anyone alive in some distant location, unable to reach us, posed me no problem at all. That was safe knowledge, that others far away were struggling to survive the same way we did. Maybe we would exchange news and facts and nurture the hope that life, in some distant future, was going to be better. I was prepared for the possibility, dreamed about it even, that we'd be safe in our own bubble without external interferences. Already, a sense of stability and safety had crept in as what we did not know about the rest of the world could not harm us, could it? Now everything was different.

Mary had struck a chord. Why was I hesitating? Was that the vision I was preparing for Annah, for us? A life spent in a cocoon, pretending? For no matter how safe it was at the time, things could become worse at any moment or at least more difficult to cope with. We would surely have to adjust to the loss of electricity, of Internet, running water, etc. We already had very little use of the phones. Could we ever adjust to being alone? And what about Annah? We weren't going to be alive forever. One day will see our demise and what would become of Annah then? Living the rest of her life completely alone? Not the fate anyone ever had, even at the dawn of civilization. It would have been cruel. I hugged Mary and hid my face in her hair:

"I will find out who that was," I whispered in Mary's ear. "I only need to think about how and in what terms."

— o —

The next morning I explained what the night had told me in its wisdom. And I faced lots of disagreement, of course. Who am I kidding, disagreement? It was more of a fight. First, no, I was not going to show up at the mall and start to call out, nor was I going to drive around blowing the car's horn. Forget about that! And I was not going to bring them home with me either, or post notes with directions to our place and how to find us. No way! Instead, I would go alone with Taxi and wait, hide where I would have a clear view and able to survey the entrance without being noticed.

We knew they had been there; they didn't. I wasn't going to change my mind and lose our advantage, not immediately at least. Possibly I would be spending the night in town, if necessary, even a few nights. Gather all possible information before making contact. Where did I think I was? In a combat zone? And, after all, they might be struggling and need help. One can say we had a lively breakfast that morning.

I did not give up and, although the vote was two against one, the majority lost the case. No democracy to invoke. There was no case. They would not go by themselves, as I would have prevented that, and I would not go and look for anyone in town if not under my conditions. The only thing I agreed to was to come home before dark—at least for the first days—and to be in touch constantly. It was Sunday, the first of April, and it amused me to end my remark with, "And I'll go on Monday. Today is April Fool's Day and I am not going to play that role any time soon." That defused the tension a bit.

It was a bright day and I even managed to convince Mary, with help from Annah, to stick to our previously established plan to prepare for a picnic and hit the golf course. I profited from the support from Annah who had wanted to show Mary her progress in the game for days and it would have been just so good to spend some time together, as a family, leaving all the bad thoughts behind. I hoped nothing was about to ruin what we had managed to build.

The morning after, I set out at dawn for town. As agreed, I took Taxi with me, plus enough food and water to see us through the day. I wanted to arrive early to choose my location well and patiently prepare for a long wait and a boring task. I remembered to take the hoodie with me, well-sealed in the plastic bag.

"Be careful," warned Mary just before I got into the car. "And call as soon as possible. Don't dare make me wait, Mister."

We kissed and I left. During the entire trip, I could not help but think of what events I was about to trigger and who I was going to find. But the decision had been made and I hoped it would turn out to be the right one. I parked the car blocks away from the shopping center. Didn't want anyone to notice a "new" vehicle suddenly appearing nearby.

The town was dead. Not just because of the early hours; it was literally dead. It felt so weird to walk close to walls—armed, with a trained and tense dog beside me—down the same streets only months before I had shared with fellow citizens, leisurely walking in and out of a restaurant or going shopping. If I closed my eyes, I could see streets full of people and hear life noises, shoes and stilettos smacking the sidewalks in an excited crescendo. The vision didn't last, as if reality suffered from a mystical photoshop retouch stripped of every human presence in a click. I shivered.

Silence. Oppressive silence, if not for the birds. I glanced around for stray dogs; I remembered well the one who almost succeeded in attacking me when I filled the tank the first time at the mall near home, or the pack we had met in town only a few days before. Having Taxi with me was crucial and reassuring. Slowly, we reached the block where the mall stood.

The day before I had noticed two possible hiding places. One, the mom-and-pop restaurant facing the side of the building and the center alternate entry. I would have a clear line of sight to the car park that served the center, a bit down the sidewalk below, though the high street leading to the entrance to the grocery level remained out of sight. The other was a photographer's shop at the corner of another building, in front of the mall. From its window, I would have an unobstructed view of the entry and the streets at the crossing but only a partial of the car park entry. After considering the pros and cons of both, there remained nothing pointing to one location besting the other. I would have been well hidden in both so I opted for the photographer shop. I reasoned I would hear any approaching car with ease in the deadly silence Geneva had plunged into; it would be better then to be in front of the main entrance.

I realized the photographer's shop also had another advantage: an old wood-framed French door. With the help of my hunting knife and my 200-plus pounds, I could manage to open the door easily. Yet it took longer than I believed it would to get inside: a crowbar would be useful for future break-ins.

Once in, I rapidly inspected the place: empty picture frames on shelves, large photographs of old Geneva for sale, some portraits of past patrons, a small rear room with lamps and spotlights, and a chair against a light background. This must have been where the photographer took pictures of customers. The front windows were loaded with other decorations such as more pictures, large and framed old posters, fake plants and branches, and ornamental veils. Quite cheesy, but it helped a lot to see from inside without being seen easily from the outside.

I set myself up for a long wait and put down two bowls I brought with me for Taxi, one with water and another with some dry food. Taxi was the most critical asset I had, besides the Glocks and the Benelli shotgun.

I took the chair from the other room so to have a more comfortable view while we waited, then I called home. Just to say I was settled and all was fine. I would get in touch again later and not to worry too much; Taxi was with me and we were out of view.

"Don't try to call me, Mary. It might happen at a wrong moment."

"Don't play the hero, sweet pea."

Oh Mary, all her tenderness and ever-youthful love encased in those two little words, repeating themselves through the years like ripples in our pond of shared emotions. "It's not Fool's Day anymore," I tried to joke. "I love you."

After verifying everything was okay at home, I hung up. And so the morning passed. Taxi at my feet, half asleep, and I busy with constantly looking out the window.

Pigeons were coming and going. Was it only my imagination or were there many more of them around than before? Time oozed away, flowing like lava erupting lazily from a vent, slowly and impossible to stop, covering everything into oblivion under its dark layer of things that were and will never be again. And I had only to wait for the flow to reach me. Still, I almost dozed off.

Taxi suddenly stood up, nervous, and startled me. He went for the front door. Adrenaline woke me up rapidly and my heart accelerated: I quickly crouched and took up a better concealed position before even summoning a rational thought in my mind. I couldn't see what had got Taxi worried; I couldn't hear anything but the rumbling of my heartbeat. Then, I saw it: On the other sidewalk, a dog strolled down the street. Taxi moaned. Shit.

"Sshhhhh. Sshhhh." I reached and put my hand around his muzzle. "Quiet, Taxi."

Outside, the dog paused. Sniffed the air briefly, raising its nose at each scent, then resuming its walk only to stop shortly after once again. It too obviously had detected something but did not look too much interested or worried. I had to keep Taxi down and quiet. After a short while, the stray dog decided whatever it sensed was not his direct business and strolled away, turned left at the corner and we both lost sight of it. That was close. It was not the time to engage into another canine dominance episode.

Apart from the birds, the dog was the only sign of life in town that day. In the afternoon, a pigeon—or was it a dove?—and a crow chased each other in mid-air for a while. A crow can really produce strident calls in an empty town. The chase marked even more how deeply silent Geneva was and turned the scene into a surreal canyon of concrete and steel.

I called Mary again, this time to tell her I was coming home. Nothing had happened, saw no one, heard no one. At home, Annah had her school lessons with Mary. After lunch, they'd enjoyed the garden with Tarantula and then went for the usual walk with her. I protested, mildly; if anything happened I could not help them in any way. Mary sounded a bit hurt by my remark. Of course they had been careful, I should not worry so. Besides, I was the one to blame after all, why had I had her and Annah spend so much time shooting otherwise? They were able to defend themselves and did not need to stay home each time I wasn't there.

I had to apologize; I knew she had been careful and was fully capable of caring for herself and Annah, too. That was not the problem; I also had to adjust to this change. And, yes, they had checked the Internet: it was up still, but there was nothing showing any activity of any kind.

Since I was coming home, Mary said she would start preparing dinner.

"Come home in one piece and don't be late now. Don't make us come and look for you." Mary had found her cheerful mood again.

"Yes, ma'am. Not to worry."

They were definitely not the same people of a couple months before so I needed to start having a different perspective. I had told them exactly that: they had to learn to count on themselves. I could not be there all the time, every time, and it seemed I had reached my goal. With a pinch of regret, I was less indispensable. And it was good.

Before leaving the shop, I checked every visible area from there with the binoculars, one more time. Nothing.

"C'mon, boy, time to go home. Our ladies are waiting and a bit nervous."

We left and returned to the car as swiftly as possible. I decided to head back home right away, but not before Taxi stopped to empty his bladder against a tree. Actually, I did the same; both of us marking territory. Crows started to gather on trees for the evening to come. I did not remember having ever seen so many in one place before. Flying high, a hawk screeched.

Nature would not take long to reclaim Geneva. In a few years, things will deteriorate fast. Repeated cycles of freezing and warming will widen cracks between slabs of sidewalks, pipes will explode, and pavement separate and split with even more cracks. Weeds will be poking from the asphalt and building walls, and lichen seeds will sprout.

And fires will occur, maybe set by lightning to a wooden roof in the old town and move on to burn other buildings. Wild vegetation will cover streets and squares; the city sewage system will collapse and rain water collect into puddles. Small flows from the higher districts to the lowest will appear to then finally reach the lake. Cities will soon be a tough and harsh place to live or spend time.

For a moment, buildings became walls of stone; the streets, chasms and fissures in the earth; ravines and boulders, a crib for humanity. With all these images lingering in my mind, I put Taxi in the back seat and drove home.

— o —

When I arrived, I moved the UPS truck so as to open the gate, got the car in, parked the truck back in place again and closed the gate. Tedious and cumbersome, but safe. There was not much to tell Mary and Annah but that the wait had been long, and Taxi had warned me of the presence of a dog that I wouldn't have heard or noticed if it were not for him.

I did not feel the need to come back to the small discussion we had over the phone about venturing out without me. Chapter closed. Mary and Annah were no longer the helpless girls in need of their knight. Was I disappointed? No. I realized that it was exactly what I aimed for in all those weeks spent with them on the shooting range and patrolling with the dogs. We were reaching a substantial new way of being ourselves.

"How was it, Dad?" Annah wanted to know.

"The dog? Just a dog, sweetie. Can't say the breed but it was black." She raised her shoulders, quickly losing all interest.

We had dinner as usual and the day was then officially over. We stayed together on the couch, in front of the fireplace, reading books. Pretending, needing to spend time together as if nothing had changed. Without Skype, and unable to chat with friends over the iPod, Annah had discovered the pleasure of reading and Mary was extremely happy she had.

Annah was encouraged to read everything and discuss the story, the plot and its meaning afterward. It became part of her education program too. That evening Annah was reading "Pride and Prejudice," by Jane Austen and its issues of manners, upbringing, morality, education, and marriage in the society of early 19th-century England. The part Annah still did not like to do, however, was the book report that she was supposed to produce after each reading.

The next day, and the following for that matter, went similarly without much change or difference in the way I spent time. I got installed in the photographer shop early in the morning. The front door was as I had left it and, although the lock was broken, it still held the door firmly. The dog we had seen on Monday was nowhere around.

On one of the following days, I decided to fulfill my desire and indulge myself: I visited Davidoff on my way to our observation post. I silenced the alarm once in, looked for and chose the largest humidor they had on display and, lo and behold, the cigar room still was perfect as if nothing had ever occurred. The thought echoed repeatedly, and I could not chase it away: "as if nothing had ever occurred."

The world had all its reasons not to miss humanity much.

Could it be that I was becoming accustomed to it, or even enjoying the…freedom? I shivered entering the humidity-controlled room and I wasn't sure it was only due to the change in temperature.

The room was small, with a square central counter. All around, it had shelves full of cigars, cigars and more cigars, from floor to ceiling. The Davidoff brand reigned of course, with its "Chateaux" and "Mille" series, and "Cohiba" too, whose founder started rolling Cuban President Fidel Castro's own private cigars. Then cigars from Arturo Fuente, Augusto Reyes, Camacho, Cubita and many others which I have never heard of, all of them in alphabetical order.

I spent time in the room to look and read every single brand on each box, and kind, and cut of the cigars. I'd never had the occasion to do that before. Besides, I had not wanted to show the clerk that, in reality, I knew very little about the world of cigars.

I filled my new humidor with Cohiba's Esplendidos and, for good measure, I took two more sealed boxes of them. I left the place happy, knowing that I could come back whenever I wanted. Maybe that's the way billionaires feel about the world: Never needing to ask the price, knowing you can have as many as you want of everything, anytime, for how often you feel like it without ever thinking of cost.

On Friday, I called it off. I was tired of spending my days that way, waiting. Besides, it was Good Friday. We declared together it was a long weekend, and that Sunday was Easter. We would make some cakes to celebrate. And this Easter was going to have a special meaning for us all. It celebrated Christ's resurrection and we attached to it a significance for us as well—a resurrection, or our own struggle in order to achieve that.

On Saturday evening, we noticed some previously-lit areas in the distance were no longer. Annah noticed the difference first and rushed to warn us. Although a small spot on our visible horizon, it had gone dark.

Had the degradation started? Most probably, it was something minor like a blown bulb rather than street lamps no longer receiving power. Anyway, I would have not gone there just to check for the causes. It would have been another story if the opposite had happened: some new visible lights in previously dark areas. Then it would have been way different. So far, I believed we had been lucky thanks to the good season we'd had. When winter came, no doubt degradation would start for real.

The Click

It was Easter Sunday. For all Christian communities, it was a date to celebrate with family and friends. Easter Monday would be, too, and Annah enjoyed the holiday from lessons. Taxi and Tarantula profited aplenty from Annah's freedom. Mary and I also enjoyed our freedom from school plans. Dates, celebrations, and recurring events were vital to observe for, in a sense, they were all that was left having a tie with everything that was no more. Ephemeral things, days on the calendar, probably had more meaning for us now than they had before.

"*Dan!*" Mary yelled, opening the window in the home office that morning. Annah and I were in the yard taking care of—or playing with, to be honest—Taxi and Tarantula.

"Dan! Come upstairs, quick!" She sounded thrilled, not frightened.

"What the… Mary? Mary!" I shouted from down below. She was at the window, on the top floor, visibly excited.

"The Facebook ads!" She did not need to say more.

Both Annah and I rushed upstairs. When we arrived, Mary looked at us triumphantly, pointing at the iMac screen. It showed the dashboard for the campaigns we launched back in February, with all the data collected into graphs.

Of all the details about reach, target, and others statistics, only one really meant anything to us: the number of clicks...one. The enormity of the event is difficult to explain or describe in words now. One person; one concrete, unquestionably real and strikingly present survivor. Someone saw and had clicked on our message. One click. With one single click somewhere in the world, *our* world

167

had abruptly changed again.

We checked all our email accounts. The last messages received were only automatic emails acknowledging our initial attempts to post into moderated forums or subscribe to mailing lists. No human beings involved. But, now, it had to be just a matter of hours before we would be contacted and whoever had seen our message on his or her Facebook home page would surely not take long to do so.

The phones! I checked again to see if all were working. We had used them recently but they could die at any moment. Maybe we had a recorded message we had inexplicably missed. Nothing. Our voicemail inboxes were empty, as if they had never been used.

"It will happen, it will happen! Any moment now!" I told Mary, more to reassure myself than anything else. She and Annah watched as I verified again the campaign target details, and said, "Twenty-five countries. That one click could have come from anyone out of one of those. Could be as close as someone in Europe, or as far away as the US or Hong Kong."

The dashboard had no details as to when the connection happened, not the date or the time.

"Yesterday morning the click was not there. I am sure because I remembered I went through the campaign ad details. If it happened during the previous night…could that mean it is from someone in the US? No, wait, maybe someone in the Far East? So many time zones separate us. Mary, did you check the page yesterday?"

As I usually accessed the dashboard in the morning, it seemed impossible I had missed it! Wait a second; indeed the click could be from someone in Europe. Maybe someone *had* checked our message during the evening, and not necessarily that late at night, especially if no one among us had verified the page before going to bed.

"I don't remember." Mary noticed my anguished expression as I opened my hands questioning how could she not remember because she repeated, "I don't remember exactly. I think I did. Yes, I checked before dinner."

Admittedly, with time, we had started to believe we'd have no luck at all with the Facebook campaign. So, we were no longer systematically following the initial scheduled check routine. I believed the probability that someone could actually see our message, and react, depended on so many factors that the whole thing had started to have only an emotional value, a faint hope.

"It could've come from anywhere, Dad," Annah said.

"Yeah." I sighed.

— o —

Easter Monday passed spending time checking email and ensuring that all the phone lines were working properly. We all felt...pending. Here we had somewhat solid and undeniable proof that others were alive, too; one very close, living in or around Geneva; another in one of the countries covered in the Facebook ad campaign which miraculously had generated a click. One click, the most important click ever in the entire world digital history.

The truth was that, in all these weeks, I really did not expect to see any response from the ads campaign: I feared the entire world was disconnected. But I was excited so I checked the dashboard again and again—and all email accounts—almost maniacally. I did not want to go to town and hide in a photo shop waiting for someone to show up. Someone whom I'd waited for almost an entire week already. I wanted to stay with my family when we received a tangible sign, an email or a phone call, maybe both. Unfortunately, nothing happened. Almost 48 hours had passed since that click and still nothing. No signs. My mood changed completely. I remembered those tee-shirts sold at tourist locations: "My sister went to London and all I got is this lousy T-shirt!" I felt the same. All we got was that lousy click.

We did not know what to think. For all we knew, a glitch in the Facebook campaign could have been the cause. If it really was a person, why not get in touch with us right away? I needed to go back to Geneva and see whether whoever had been at the shopping mall was going to resurface again. I could not neglect the survivor who was surely living nearby, and trade that for an email or a phone call that could never come either.

I was disappointed, after all this waiting, the lost hopes, the renewed excitement, and then nothing. Nothing! Why? I urged Mary and Annah to keep a close eye on the dashboard and emails and immediately get in touch with me if...yeah, if. With a sense of betrayal from the entire human race, I left and resumed my sentinel watch at the shopping center.

— o —

Taxi probably enjoyed the stalking game more than I did. He was lying on the floor, resting and—at times— staring intently at me. He was alert all the time, probably because of me, but peaceful the same. I guess he knew we were there for something important: this was no time to sleep. Or maybe his master was going berserk and he could not fully relax.

Around midday, I enjoyed one of those treasured Esplendidos cigars Davidoff had graciously supplied me with. Taxi grunted at the smoke so I kept the fanlight above the entrance door fully open and air circulated freely. I gave no thought that maybe, outside, the smell of cigars could reach distant places. Not a single thought about that.

The back room also had a little oval window giving to the internal court of the building and providing some light to the back of the shop. With that one kept open as well, the entire place was not going to turn into a gas chamber. Anyway, it gave me something to do, in addition to chatting with Mary on the iPhone from time to time.

"Still nothing?" Mary asked.

"No. Not a sound, nothing in sight. Any email?"

"I would have told you right away…"

"I know. What are you doing?"

"Nothing, we miss you."

— o —

Another day passed. I came home feeling depressed a bit more every evening. The excitement of the previous days was now being replaced with frustration, and even anger. As if we did not have our truckload of emotional stress to deal with already. I did not know what to think and neither did Mary. That click, and the mess at the mall, both were crucially important, but they could not become a fixation

171

and engulf us all. We were fine as we were, right? But those were outrageously important, I kept repeating.

We had survived and we had no future. Annah especially had no future. Our only hope rested on us and other survivors to be numerous enough to become pioneers again in our own world. In that case, will we begin again as we once did? Eons ago? That's why it was vital to find other people.

We finally decided to leave a note at the shopping center. I had yet to decide to stay all night at the place and, frankly, I grew uneasy at doing so. Mary put together a meaningful text. She explained we, as a family, had survived that fatal February night. That in the past months we had fully organized ourselves at home and maybe others were doing the same. We hoped for them to be safe and sound as well. She did not add any details about our location or how many we were.

We agreed it was okay to leave our email, though no phone numbers, in case others could access existing online services to trace back to our home address. I had tried myself and did not succeed, but I did not want to risk anything, so no phone numbers this time. I guess I was becoming paranoid for real. We asked to leave an answer on a small billboard, left in the open, at the corner of Jargonnant-Terrasiere, stuck to the street sign pole.

I don't know whether in other situations, normal situations, we would have come out with such a plan. Maybe it sounds ridiculous now. It was the best we could think of then, short of camping 24/7 at the mall for who knows how long. Contacts with anyone might never happen; what we had found there could have been the result of a one time visit from someone on the move, never to return again. We were improvising on a stage no one had prepared us to deal with. A scenario we hadn't chosen for which there was no audience.

The next morning, Taxi and I went to the shopping center again. I was a bit tired of hiding and passively waiting without doing anything. Birds literally had started to conquer the spaces. They were very vocal, and their calls the only noises to hear when once it was only cars, and traffic, and people walking and chatting. The never-ending buzz of a living town had died. The difference with the present was striking: with all the reflecting surfaces in a town, every single and rare sound now bounced to reach far distances, and was cleanly distinguishable, giving birth to an eerie echo.

When we got inside the mall, the same unchanged and unwelcoming scene greeted us: decaying plants and rotten pastries. I let Taxi sniff the hoodie I had recovered almost two weeks before. He examined it and snorted, trying to find traces of the old scent. But it seemed no one with that odor had visited the place recently. With me close behind, Taxi wandered around seeking to find its track again, and I had the impression he did it only to please me.

We finally reached the aisle with the different cereal box brands, as many as one can imagine. In that, Switzerland was much like the US. Way more variety than truly needed of every product you could think of. The aisle was in the exact same state we found it the first time. I took Mary's paperboard where she had written our message, both in English and in French. I secured it in place with sticky tape and headed toward the upper level. Just in case. I again gave Taxi the hoodie, and once more he didn't find any new clue. He spent some time in the women's apparel and clothing area, but it seemed the odor had weakened and was nowhere for him to catch it again.

After a while, we left for my hideout to spend another day waiting. Taxi and I had just reached our surveillance post across the street and settled in when the iPhone buzzed. It was a message from Mary. Actually, an email, a straight email forward with no comments from her. I was speechless and watched the screen in awe:

From: Michael81_GG@hotmail.com Date: 13 April 2012 07:11:44 CET

"Hiya! Who the fuck are you? Not for nuttin' but the punks who whacked us are still here. If you're fucking with me, go see where you gotta go punk. M."

Who the fuck are we? If I was expecting alleluia, kumbayah, and "people of the world unite", forget it. I had to call home and talk to Mary.

"Dan? Have you read it?" Her voice trembled.

"Yep." I did not know what to say. The message was indeed troublesome.

"I don't know what to think, Mary. And what does 'the punks are still here' mean?"

"Dan, I'm scared. It feels so…harsh."

"Do you know anything about long headers in emails?" Silence.

"Never mind. I'll do it myself later. Maybe we can find where it comes from."

"Dan, please come home."

"Listen…" I started to disagree, but I changed my mind. I had spent enough time in town already and it was pointless to stay any longer. "I'm coming home."

That was not the message from someone eager to get in touch with anyone anytime soon. It showed distrust and suspicion. Well, I showed distrust and suspicion myself toward whoever I stalked for days there now. And still did. But this was different: I was just being careful and protecting my family. The guy must have searched for others too if he had seen our message on Facebook. So why that reply? And who was he referring to with that "still here." And the "us" in Michael81 email, who the hell was he talking about? Other survivors or the entire humanity?

If there were other people...could it be that groups of survivors became hostile to one another where Michael81 was? Possible. But why? Again the Mad Max movie scenes came to life in my mind. Probable scenario? Didn't know. Thus, I might've been right not coming out naively and looking around in the open, in full view for anyone who was still alive in Geneva.

This was no kumbayah world. Maybe criminals have had the same chances to survive as respectable and law abiding citizens. If Michael81—and his group?—got whacked...by whom? We could get whacked as well. Now I really wanted to go back home. Nothing better than some uncontrolled mental surge to trigger muscular movement: We left our hideout.

This time Taxi and I literally ran to the car, and I looked over my shoulder all the time in fear of some bullet or sudden attack at every corner. Taxi did not seem nervous, although he was aware of my tension. I knew I could count on Taxi at every moment, even at the cost of his life as dogs are that faithful. We rushed into the car—didn't even waste time to open the trunk—and reached home in a very short time.

So I was right to be paranoid, I repeated to myself. If anything, the message showed danger was still very present in our world and we had better treat any survivor as a potential threat. How silly I had been. "Homo hominis lupus," man is like a wolf to other men. The wisdom of the past and of our ancestors. I secured our entrance as usual with the truck. Mary and Annah rushed out of the door and hugged me, barely uttering a word. We got inside quickly. I locked the door.

"Dan, what do you make of it?" Mary frowned.

"There must be more survivors, and possibly they are organized into groups. I guess those groups fight for…what? Control of supplies?"

"But why, Dad? There's so much of everything for…" I think Annah was about to add 'for everyone', but she bit her tongue. I pretended not to notice.

"Yes, here we have everything for ourselves. And plenty of it. Maybe it is different elsewhere, where this Michael lives, and people are fighting for it? I cannot really say, sweetie."

"There must be many others then," Mary reasoned. *Yes, sure, and not welcoming*, I thought but kept my fears hidden.

"Maybe."

"And…in Geneva?" Mary went on.

"Maybe," I repeated.

"What did you do, did you place our message?"

"Yes, where the cereals are but now I need to go back to town."

"Why? What for?"

"Dad, no! Why?"

"The paperboard! We are saying we are in the surrounding area. Also, I am going to change our Facebook message, and remove our phone numbers; one could get to our address, too."

There, it came out. The possibility of finding a group of survivors who could turn hostile toward us was not quite what we needed, now or in the future. Nor what I expected to feel about other survivors. Moreover, we were not really hiding, and anyone determined to find people and provisions could easily get to and locate us. If a group of survivors was out there, in the Geneva surroundings, how long would it take before they'd find us? Mad Max, Mad Max...he truly haunted me.

The Valley mall was a well known location. How long before someone else, even if relatively far from there, would think about paying it a visit? There were many good places in town, and between Geneva and Lausanne, too...places to find food and supplies. That made our mall not the first in line for anyone in Geneva, but in the future? A gush of acid reflux burned my throat and almost choked me. I swallowed hard.

By all odds, it was better if we discovered them first, to have the advantage and be prepared. Suddenly, the idea of putting up the paperboard did not seem like such a great one anymore. I needed to calm down or I would shoot at anything moving without thinking. I thought I was rational and cool in most situations but, if I had reached this point, what could have happened to someone more inclined to violence than I?

Mary interrupted my thoughts. "Okay, then. But we're coming with you."

I realized there was little to discuss. Our world was not as peaceful and safe as we had naively concluded it to be. So we all got back in the car armed with loaded guns—as if going into battle—and with a strange light piercing our eyes. As if the warmth and fuzziness of a benevolent sun had been replaced by the cold reflection of an indifferent moon over a frozen land.

Our perspective became acutely different in those moments and all because of one single email that supposedly should have been an event received with celebration. I supposed we walked on the edge of a mental chasm. In its depths, violence, hatred, suspicion, and madness were all willing to embrace us to reach their ultimate climax.

We reached town without uttering a word and I had been careful to approach the mall via back roads, taking a long improbable detour. If our paperboard had already been found, maybe there would be a welcoming party waiting for us, the happy and naive family. Mary and Annah kept their weapons ready at all times. We parked on the sidewalk of a narrow street a few blocks away, got out, and crouched between the car and the building wall. We were ready to head off a confrontation.

Before moving forward, we scanned the surroundings with our binoculars. Nobody uttered a single word. The world had changed and it had changed us, more than I had imagined. I signaled Mary and Annah to stay behind and reached another safe spot with Taxi. After scanning the area, only then did I call the others to join us. Tired, we reached the corner in front of the shopping center entrance some 40 minutes later.

All was quiet and apparently safe. I pointed the binoculars to the photographer's shop which was exactly as I had left it. It looked as if nothing had changed, and that meant *nothing*! I kneeled down to Taxi and Tarantula and hugged them both. Then I took the hoodie from my rucksack.

Annah understood what I was about to do. "Dad! No!"

I looked at her and put my index finger to my lips. My sight was like a cold, transfixing spear. Annah blanched. That was not the moment for discussions. I loved those dogs, but they were our life insurance at that moment. Taxi and Tarantula sniffed the garment, sniffed the surrounding area, then raised their noses. I led them toward the shopping center and ordered, "Check." After a brief moment, they jumped forward into the open while I got the Benelli ready to shoot. I swear I would have shot whoever appeared if not with raised hands. Armed, Mary and Annah knelt behind a large concrete flower box at the corner of the restaurant.

We were extremely tense. Taxi and Tarantula dashed to cross the street and headed toward the automatic sliding doors. They had to stop there, undecided what to do as the doors did not open. T&T had to be below the fixed threshold for the motion detector trigger. They sniffed and looked around the entrance; a bit up and down the street, too. Meanwhile, we three in the back stayed put, ready for any reaction, movement or sound. Neither Taxi nor Tarantula seemed to sense anything out of the ordinary, or any danger. Taxi looked in our direction.

"Mary, cover me."

"Dan!" she protested trying to hold me but I had already started to run—half bent, strafing toward the dogs, scanning with the Benelli all around and ready to shoot at anything and at the first warning. Taxi and Tarantula were waiting for me, relaxed; they had done their job. I thought they would have perceived a danger or—I hoped—sensed if anyone was nearby.

As I slowly approached the entrance, the doors opened with their usual lamentation that would have signaled my arrival miles away. I quickly stepped inside, followed by the dogs, knelt down and glanced around. Nothing. I held my breath and listened. Silence. Only then did I retreat and, when outside, waved for Mary and Annah to join us, all the while scanning the streets around them.

Mary and Annah quickly covered the short distance from the restaurant to the mall and we were soon all together again. We gathered right inside at the florist shop and let the automatic doors close. We paused for a moment without moving or making a sound to let our eyes adjust to the light conditions inside and to listen for any unexpected noise. Then, with Taxi and Tarantula in front, we moved quietly, very quietly. The two German Shepherds kept sniffing for any abnormality. Watching our backs, and moving ever cautiously, we reached the produce store. The entry barriers opened.

Still using Taxi and Tarantula as reconnaissance—and as decoy—we reached the aisle where I had stuck the paperboard with our message. It was still there. Then John Lennon and his catchy phrase struck. Taxi and Tarantula got tense and alert even if we could not hear or see any reason why. Soon after, we startled at a fast approaching whooshing sound. We jumped forward to the main aisle, guns at hands, ready for the worst.

A muffled cry came from a figure on rollerblades who screeched to a halt as it saw us and started frantically to run away.

"*Stay!*" I cried to prevent Taxi and Tarantula from running after the skater, then "*Wait!*" to the figure already gaining speed and dashing toward the exit. It had been very fast, and the skater was damned good on those rollers. The way he moved, he seemed young but....it was a woman, in her twenties. She wore tight jeans, a black leather jacket and carried a large, empty backpack. She was wearing gloves and a black helmet that hid her hair entirely.

I started to run as fast as possible after the skating lady while Mary held Annah back.

"*Wait!*" Mary yelled. But the girl had already reached the exit and jumped outside onto the street. The sliding doors closed in front of Taxi and Tarantula, who had started to run with me and even passed me in the chase. I do not know what they would have done had they reached the girl in time. I got to the exit and the sliding doors opened slowly so I pushed them aside to make it faster, Mary and Annah catching up quickly. I dashed out, and together with Mary and Annah, we got a glimpse of the skater girl speeding down the street out of view. Rushing after her, I whistled for Taxi and Tarantula to come back.

We stopped, panting in the middle of the street. Well, there were absolutely no more doubts; we were not the only survivors.

"What do we do now?" Mary broke the silence. It made little difference now as the die had been cast. We all knew of the existence of each other yet I had lost the advantage.

"Give me a pen."

"I don't have it with me! What do you wanna do?"

"Come, quickly."

I ran back to the mall. The level above the grocery had a stationery shop near to where we had found the skating-girl's hoodie, as I was sure it was hers. Everyone followed me, crossing the grocery and then to the upper level. Still running, I reached the store full of writing tools of every possible kind and for any writing surface. I got a black marker. Now to the paperboard.

"What are you doing?" Mary asked while grabbing my arm. I stopped.

"Mary, the only one sensible thing to do with a woman I just met. Asking for a date." I said, smiling.

"What?" She almost cried. I left Mary standing there, rather upset, already running toward the sliding sidewalk and back to the grocery level.

Taxi and Tarantula were bemused and kept following me undecided whether to be worried, excited, afraid or angry at me for all that senseless running.

"Dad!" I guess Annah was not much amused. When they finally reached me at the cereal aisle, I had already written my message on the paperboard.

"No! You are crazy!" said Mary as she read what I had just written.

"Mary, it is the only thing to do," I said, taking the paperboard with me. I went for the entrance.

I stuck our message next to the automatic doors and it very visibly covered the entire metal panel that showed the mall's opening hours. That girl seemed terrified when she saw us. She was not expecting to see our group there and it must have been quite a shock. If she had come back to the mall, though, it meant she probably got her food and anything else she needed there. As we did.

She went around on rollerblades so she probably didn't own a car, and she must not have lived too far away either. Undoubtedly, not in the blocks around the mall. Hence, I kept reasoning, she might not have the leisure, as we did, to go too far for supplies nor have the choice—or the need—of multiple places because she must be able to reach the mall easily. She would be back there again, sooner or later. Maybe a bit later now that she was scared, but back nevertheless.

On the paperboard, I added that our intentions were good, we would not harm her or anyone who was with her. I gave her a daily appointment, alone and with no dogs, as proof of our trustworthiness. I would wait for her one hour every day. She had to show up on Jargonnant Street, near the car park entrance. And I would come out to talk. From afar. No physical contacts. No harm.

"Mary, I have to do it!" I nodded toward Annah. "You know I have to, right?" I turned and grabbed Annah, pressed her against me. She curled up close to me like a baby.

"Dan, please don't do it," said Mary, holding both hands to her face as if she was praying.

I did not reply; I did not know what to reply. We got back to the car. Mary held my hand all the way home. Our world was changing rapidly, and there was still Michael81's pending message to deal with.

Part Three

Epiphany

Michael, if that was truly his name, might have had valid reasons to mistrust our message. So far, we had it rather easy around here. Ours had been more of an emotional struggle, overcoming the initial fears and getting ourselves organized. We had not faced any menace or dangers…so far. Maybe not everyone had gone through the same? "Who the fuck are you?" was not a good start for a friendly conversation, but we didn't have many options in selecting future relationships.

We replied to him in the best and most transparent way we could, and we started with a "Dear Michael." That alone quickened my pulse. We chose not to ask any questions, leaving the decision entirely to Michael whether or not to disclose any details of his situation or where he was writing from. We continued describing how we went through that morning in February, how we discovered things. And about the dead people; how they apparently all died for the same reasons and roughly at the same time.

Mary and Annah were watching over my shoulder while I typed, rewriting things over and over with palms sweating as if they were runners in a relay race in the effort of putting down the right words. Sharing emotions and passing Michael the baton with enough reasons to read our words and reply back. I had the impression we were under examination and that every word was wrong and in the wrong place.

Because of all the dead commuters, their demise had most likely occurred between 5:30-6:30am and everyone seemed to have died in the same way. We were in CET, or GMT+1, so he could use that if he lived in a different time zone than ours. He would then be able to verify whether there were any coincidences in timing. We shared we had proof of at least another person alive in town though we could not say if there were more.

Funny, while writing those things, my brain felt as if it floated in a cold bath, detached. Repelling emotions as poisonous spores bogged down rationality with their sticky ooze. I wondered whether my wife and daughter felt the same but I could not raise my eyes off the screen.

I told Michael that I didn't believe the causes to be poison or a plague of some sort. We had no symptoms of anything; we felt healthy, at least physically. Unless, for some mysterious quirks of our genes, we were immune to an external agent but I doubt that was what happened. Everything had been so sudden, with people dying in their vehicles, in their beds, or waiting for the first bus in the morning. Something or someone had access to the switch of human lives on Earth and decided to pull it.

For the first time since that February morning, I formulated a thought which lingered unexpressed and which I repelled, because it frightened me. As when as a child, I lay in bed at night, head under the covers and not daring to move a muscle. Almost holding my breath, certain there was a malignant presence in the room that waited for me to move before it struck. Pretending to be dead to avoid death...

I wrote Michael that, as crazy as it sounded, I believed we could have suffered a preordained attack, and on such a large scale that everyone was dead or incapacitated. By whom or by what we had absolutely no clues, nor evidence. Maybe *we* were just crazy. Mary squeezed my shoulder when I wrote those lines. I raised my hand to meet hers and we clung to each other; my emotions had been able to breach the steel barrier the brain raised so eagerly before. I turned to glance up at her face, and her eyes were swollen and wet. There was no fear when she met mine.

We described our experiences with TV, radio channels, our searches on the Internet and our inability to get any information beyond that fatal day. Nothing or no one was contributing with news or broadcasting anything, on any channel. Twitter didn't work anymore for our accounts, was his still on? Or did he even have one? Utility services were still up and running where we lived on the outskirts of a major Swiss city. He did not need to provide us details of his location in case he felt in danger, or unless he happened to be so close to us that we could eventually meet. We concluded, hoping he could survive, hold on, and stay safe. I signed it, "Dan and family. God Bless."

My hands collapsed, aching. I realized how tense my entire body was; my neck and shoulders were burning. I sighed and turned in the chair. Annah sat on the couch, her legs raised to her chin. She was crying and making no sound. Only mute and silent tears ran down her face, marking time in a metronome maintaining a consistent tempo with despair and defeat.

A lump formed in my throat. Could we have done things differently? Obviously. More? Could not think of anything more then, could not think of anything more now. I would give my life and concede to death to give hope and a future to my daughter. Even though I thought death would have laughed at my proposition.

I turned around and hit "send". Hoping Michael81 would receive and read it, and be willing to reply to us. We knew we might never get an answer from him. Likewise, we might not ever again see the girl with the rollerblades but in that case we had more things to do than writing a message. The steel barrier my brain set up as a last defense had collapsed.

"Mary, you and Annah are the reasons why I did not break down. We cannot live in fear, hiding like hunted animals or running away from the dangers and difficulties that arise from our situation, which is scary and unreal. The truth can be dangerous to know but, more than death, we should fear living in a cage behind bars until old age reaches us and all hope of a future is gone."

I looked into Mary's eyes. "Our future is to work toward Annah's future. I will not hide anymore. I'll wait for the girl in rollers on the street, alone."

"No, you're not. After all you have written now...how could you do that? Risk your life and ours, too? What is it now? You are willing to risk everything on a bet, an intuition?"

Mary continued, "You have assured us so far, and amazingly well, but we only have each other. If anything happened to any of us now, the others will not survive. Don't you understand that? Do you want to risk it? Do you really love us?" She looked away from me and took few deep breaths. I wasn't prepared to answer such a question. I watched in awe as she turned her back on me, her head lowered in resignation. For all our lives together, no one has ever questioned or doubted the love we had for each other.

I glanced hopelessly toward Annah, but she didn't look at us as she'd shrunk even more on the couch, sobbing. She was not used to these bursts of emotion or to any of our disputes, which we never had in front of her. I believe Annah wanted to say something, anything to stop what she believed was splitting her parents. Her lips moved and her mouth opened to a void; she started to shake. Mary turned toward me again and my heart sunk as I expected the worst. My mouth was dry and, despite all my strength—physical and emotional—there I was, my legs suddenly feeling like rubber bands.

"Why Dan?" My heart rushed and I felt the warmth of a blood surge rising to my cheeks. I loved her so much that I realized she had the power to crush me if she wanted to.

"I know you love us, so why? Why are you even thinking of exposing yourself to anything or anyone out there? You know nothing about who we will meet. You have no right to do that!" She marked it with a punch to my chest with her open hand.

I didn't know how long she'd kept all that inside. Trying not to let it go; trying to rationalize, always supporting my decisions. She couldn't do it anymore. She could not hold everything back any longer. It all came out, and I felt it like a turbulent flood. All her temper, fears, angers, and love. A rainbow of emotions slammed against me, but there was a golden pot at its end: she was still by my side. Yet I was scared.

Mary vented all her frustration; I bent under the abrupt storm of her feelings. Exhausted, she collapsed on the couch near our daughter. Annah had witnessed the scene and was still crying softly, silently. Mary hugged her and whispered into her ear. I couldn't hear Mary's words, but I recognized the rhythm of an ancient lullaby she used to sing to soothe Annah after a nightmare. I looked at them, and I wasn't sure what to say.

"I cannot lose you; *we* cannot lose you." Mary said with a welling up of threatened sobs. I knelt in front of them, relieving my legs from the effort of keeping me standing, opened my arms and embraced my girls: they were the reasons I kept going and I was the only firm and steady ground they had. We stayed there, together, never feeling so alone and delicate than in those moments. We were a fragile knot of life, a blimp made of love, floating in a universe ever more indifferent and refusing to get involved. I was unable to imagine our future. That night, Mary and I expressed with love our rights to live and desire, and to nurture hope.

— o —

I had been married to Mary for twenty-two years. Maybe I should have known that she would never let me go alone as I planned. The next morning, Mary's words still echoed in my mind, and against all reason, we all went together—dogs included—to the possible meeting with the girl. We took a totally different route this time, with many small detours in between. In the end, we reached the Natural History Museum, on the tipping point of a hill. From there, Mary and Annah would be on the lookout for anything suspicious and, at the very least, send Taxi and Tarantula for help.

I did not want my wife and daughter to come trying to rescue me if I was about to be truly in danger. If the worst case, I preferred they'd actually run or stay hidden. They could not help me against a fatal threat and, if odds were truly against me, I did not want them to be threatened or risk their lives. That one had been the most difficult negotiation for me, to allow them to come with me. In our favor, the Swiss society was not a violent one. "Mad Max", a realistic movie scenario for most of the US, would have not been credible if that story was to unfold in Switzerland, Geneva even more so. Mary had used my own reassuring terms as their reasons to accompany me.

"Ok, I agree with you, it is improbable that there will be people there waiting to kill you or harm you. Fine! Then there is no reason at all for us to stay home and wait, right?" Annah gave me *her look* as if to say, "She got you one more time, Dad."

Before starting the walk toward the shopping center, I called Mary on her mobile. This way, we would be in constant contact. Instead of walking straight toward the mall, I took a little detour and talked on and off to Mary to make sure she could still hear me well. I arrived at the photographer's shop from a lateral street. The mall was at the corner, to my right. I crossed the street and paused in the middle of the intersection.

"See me?"

"Yes." Mary confirmed, and that lonely whisper— uttered as in a last breath—made me shiver. I felt her love in one single word, and alone in the deserted city, I felt the ache of the world.

"Okay. I am reaching the shop." I rubbed my face to hide I was talking. There could have been more onlookers than just Mary and Annah that morning, but I also needed to wipe off my eyes, swollen and wet. All theories about a non-violent society were going to be put to the test and I was the specimen for the experiment. I kept walking, thinking only about the next step to take, the tension cramping my body from shoulders to belly. As on a mine field, I feared every move I made could have been my last one.

I reached the shop and went to open the door. *I am getting into a trap*, I thought, and my hand hovered, undecided. Sweat trickled down my back. I closed my eyes and rested my hand on the knob for a split second. I sighed and opened the door slowly, peeking inside. Everything seemed untouched. Apparently, no one had been there since the last time I had. I stepped in and, with a trembling hand, I reached for the phone.

"Mary, I am here. Nothing to do now but wait." I do not know whether I had been able to hide from Mary the lump I had in my throat.

"Dan...I love you." Mary's reply came as a reminder of everything I risked and all my assurance melted away like a jellyfish abandoned on a shore, pierced by the hostile light of a deadly sun.

An hour later and no one showed up. I verified with the binoculars that the paperboard was still sticking up fine, left the shop, and walked back the same way I had before. There were fewer reasons then to believe my life was in danger but still my back was rigid as if I had swallowed a broom stick. Mary and Annah waited near the car. Mary hugged me.

"You look tired, hon. We've seen nothing unusual from up here. Maybe there's no one."

"Dad, I checked all nearby buildings and the neighborhood with the binoculars. And Taxi and Tarantula have been calm. So can we go home now?"

Faking a smile, I nodded. We went home.

— o —

It had become tedious, to say the least. Rollerblade-girl was a 'no show' and Michael had not cared to reply yet. Or could not. I tried to perform an IP reverse lookup, but the process did not provide much information either.

So our lives went on as usual. Annah kept studying with Mary; I went around with the dogs, checking on our neighborhood and other nearby villages, or fixing things in the house and getting even more prepared for the next winter. Everyone tended to the garden and the first lettuces were starting to be visible. Tomatoes, cabbages and eggplants seemed fine, too. We also cultivated sprouts of various kinds to add to our diet and soon, during summer, I would go hunting for fruits. One of the advantages of living in a rural area, orchards were not far and everything was at our disposal.

Days passed uneventfully until one morning, approaching the shopping mall entrance for the usual appointment with Rollerblade-girl, I noticed someone had finally written back on our paperboard: "You were not alone!" I called Mary right away.

"Rollerblade-girl wrote back! She must have seen you. Come over here and pick me up. I think we can go home for today."

In the few minutes waiting for Mary and Annah to drive the short distance to the shopping center, I started to write down a reply on the paperboard. Who knows, maybe Rollerblade-girl was watching at that very moment. "I will be alone next time. You can count on me!" The noise of our Volvo grew louder and, a few seconds later, Mary and Annah were at the corner.

"What happened?" Mary asked.

"She must have checked the surroundings these last few days and noticed you and Annah. She wrote 'You were not alone!' with the exclamation mark included as if that upset her."

Mary kept silent for a moment, her hands gripping the steering wheel with force.

"You plan to go by yourself now, right?" She definitely knew me. I didn't answer immediately and searched for words.

"Mary, I don't think I'm facing a danger anymore," I said. She nodded. There was nothing more to say.

During the drive back home, the three of us stayed silent. Taxi and Tarantula, sensible dogs that they were, kept quiet too.

Mary drove particularly slowly, and the desolation and solitude around us were palpable. Especially that day. I didn't know what my wife and daughter were thinking about but I could not chase away the thought that, in Geneva, and the large area that I had been able to explore and visit in the last weeks, there were only four people alive. Four!

I spent the day without having a specific goal; there was so much at stake, for everyone. My mind seemed unable to formulate one thought and bring it to a close. Thoughts jumped at me and flew away before I could grab them and understand their implications.

We were holding on so much to our previous life; I had clung to that and created a cocoon around us. But the new life was there, so tangible and manifest, that the cocoon could not last much longer. I didn't know it then but the past was catching up with me.

That evening, Michael81 resurfaced: "Youz guys seem kosher," he wrote.

We learned that he came from the East Coast and lived in New York City. There were other survivors with him, gathered little by little in the past weeks, and they'd started to get organized, also little by little. In March, they had seen heavy raining and the rivers, forced underground by Manhattan construction through pipes and through the years, had invaded practically all subway tunnels.

Water was flowing freely in some streets now, bursting through sewers and the same subway stations. There had not been enough sunny weather for water to evaporate and building shades did not help either. In many areas, water had collected into large and smelly puddles. It had been, all in all, a quite chilly month.

Electrical power was still pretty much available around the city though some areas were in the dark and, when night came, street lights were not functioning. Water reached higher than the curbs in most places and flooding the ground levels. Freezing nights had widened cracks of the asphalt and sidewalks slabs were popping up, turning them into packs of domino tiles, slanted and piled atop each other. Especially in the Lexington area, where pipes had actually exploded, adding to the water flow. Weeds and cockroaches were everywhere.

In the early days, they saw Central Park horse-drawn carriages riding alone, at times with their dead driver still perched on the bench. The scene still gave them all goose bumps. "How can you ever get used to that?" Michael asked. Some zoo animals must have managed to escape as he swore he'd heard some kind of a lion roaring. He and others never went out unarmed and never alone. They have been in and out of apartment buildings, to look for others, or for any clue of what had happened.

They had found a girl that way one day, going around with air horns and blowing them to attract people. To their astonishment, she came screaming out of a building, and ran to them in panic. Michael and his group had almost left the area when she ran down the stairs because the elevators in her building were not working anymore. The poor thing was breathless and he said, "She burst into tears in our arms."

They'd also spotted strange auras at night. "Did you see them where you are?" Michael asked in his email. "Sure you did. They must wear a suit that glows, that's what it must be. They whacked us, man," he said. "They are the cause for all that happened and they are after God knows what. They cleaned NYC of the dead. Were they there in the daylight, too, but we couldn't see them? Who knows?"

He had seen our messages a good couple of weeks before he decided to finally make contact. He thought us to be a trap. He wrote, "But them, they don't seem to care, they were not after survivors, they were more after the corpses. At least for now. Where we have spotted them, the area is clean afterwards."

He kept saying they did not have Internet connection where they are staying so, "I am writing this from an Internet café we broke into recently. You should not expect an answer right away if you write back. We check online for others, but not daily."

Michael went on with a most noteworthy fact: He shot at them once one evening, from afar, with a 7mm Dakota rifle. He swears he got the guy. His head should have exploded and instead he simply turned toward his direction, unhurt: "He looked right at me, man, from that distance and right into my scope. It freaked the hell out of me and I ran." He did not try a second time; he stayed put now, especially at night, when it seemed the 'aliens' preferred to go around. "So, take care, be careful and watch out!"

I had to read the whole thing again. Had we seen "them"? Seen who? At first, I could not make much sense of what Michael wrote: "them," "spotted at night," "aura." I read that part again and it gave me a cold chill, a sudden numbing dread in a fearful anticipation. Internally, and unaware still, a dot from the past had started to connect.

We had not seen anyone ourselves, apart from the rapidly disappearing Rollerblade-girl. And she disappeared behind a corner, not out of some Harry Potter trick. We hadn't seen anything or anyone glowing in the dark. I didn't want to alarm Mary, so I edited Michael's message, removed all the parts referring to 'them' and printed it. I brought the copy downstairs. Mary was preparing dinner and Annah was reading a book in her room. I paused. It seemed at home we were in some sort of denial, acting as if everything was as normal as ever. Mary had even made a list of books for Annah to read. So that "memories will not disappear," she told her, and Annah could cultivate those memories in her own time and share further. *With whom?* I thought cynically.

"Michael, from New York," I said, handing Mary the email. She shook her head, without even looking at the paper.

"Read it to me," she said.

I did and finished the whole story with the Central Park carriages strolling around by themselves, and that he was typing the email from an Internet café. Then the good wishes, and that survivors there were starting to get organized.

"New York is much larger than Geneva, and this proves there could be others. With time, maybe, many others."

Mary nodded. She was somber and stared at the stove.

Without raising her eyes from the dinner she was preparing, she asked: "How many, Dan? Can you tell me? Maybe it is just that girl we saw…and we might not see her ever again." She paused then, looking straight into my eyes: "I love you, Dan. And I love Annah. Sometimes I wonder whether all this makes sense. What will be our life next winter, or a year or more from now? Can you tell me?"

"Mary…" I started, but Mary raised her hand to silence me.

"I will carry on, for you and Annah. But I cannot promise you for how long, Dan. Not this way. Why didn't we die, too? Why, Dan? It would have been so much easier now." Her body seemed to implode, as if something broke internally. Resting both stiff arms on the counter, here head collapsed between her shoulders.

"Now? Mary, what are you talking about? We would be dead, now. You would be dead, Annah would be dead. Is that what you wanted? You have seen those rotting remains. Mary, don't do this…"

"Just hold me, Dan. Please."

I held her tightly in my arms. I cried without making any sound. Mary wasn't, and that made me cry even more. Warm tears, heavy and coming from the depths. I could not lose her. I could simply not. As if she was reading my mind, Mary whispered in my ear, "I don't have any more tears, Dan…"

I wanted to answer Michael soon; instead I stayed there and hugged my wife, hoping she would not crumble further. That night, the whole night, I kept searching for her, continuously pressing my body against her, breathing her.

Mary complained a few times she was cold during the

197

night, inviting me to lay next to her even closer and put my arms around her. I prayed to God that I could be the fire that kept her alive, that kept her away from that cold that grows from the inside. It rises like a shivering fever and consumes you inexorably, eating up all your strengths and leaving you emptied, hopeless, and ready to give up.

— o —

The morning after, I did not want to leave Mary alone. Instead, she looked at me in her special way, that one look she used so many times in all the years we'd been together, to tell me "You can let go, it's okay." That released all tensions. I knew she was not lying and I needed to foster hope.

"I'm fine, don't worry." Then to our daughter. "Annah, tell your dad that we will be fine."

"Come back home soon, Dad. You promise?"

"I promise." I hoped I was not going to disappoint her.

Devotees said that praying to the Lord only when you are in need is hypocritical. Instead, they say, you should pray always, and especially when things go well. I think the Lord knows better and can see better than anyone into everyone's heart. He knows whether we are sincere or not. He does not need to judge a soul from the number of prayers He receives, even more so when those become, with time, a mere ritual.

There are others who have mandatory scheduled daily prayers. Does that make them better or does God prefer them to all His other creatures? Is His love measured by prayer hours? In my heart, I was sure He knew, if He had time to listen, that I was sincere that morning. Besides, I did not pray for myself. I prayed for my wife; I prayed for Mary.

— o —

I arrived where I was supposed to be to meet with Rollerblade-girl. This time, I did everything in plain view. I stopped the car in the middle of the street. I lowered the windows, stepped out and even opened the trunk. Nothing to hide. Then I sat cross-legged, well in front of the car. I had a Glock tucked at my back, under my vest, and one under the driver seat. My hands rested on my knees. I waited.

The sun started to warm the air and the asphalt, too. The hot bitumen smell and the petroleum vapors soaked my senses. I felt its taste in my mouth and it was intoxicating. About to get dizzy, the odor was somehow pleasant. *I am getting high*, I thought, lightheaded. A few crows gathered as casual spectators, perched on the tree in the middle of the traffic island at the end of the street. Unless I imagined them.

There I was, sitting like a duck with a wobbling head like those figurines in the back window of cars. Good thing Geneva didn't have zoos in town as in New York. In that position, and the way I felt, I would have been easy prey for the "kind of a lion" Michael believed roamed freely in Manhattan. Almost an hour had passed and I could not stand to sit much longer. My joints hurt and sleepiness crept in as the body oxygen level was replaced by the aromatic tar vapors.

At that moment, I heard the swishing sound of the rollerblades from behind and the adrenaline rush heightened all my senses as my body released glucose directly into my bloodstream. My breathing and heart rate jumped. Everything happened very fast: My blood pressure shot up and a hot flush erupted like a fever making me sweat as if I was taking a shower from within. A screeching sound made me shiver as the wheels came to a halt and, although it was somewhere to my left and out of my field of vision, I didn't have to turn my head. I saw her vividly in my mind, menacing. A cold chill slid up my spine as a pair of eyes stared at me intensely, carving holes into my back; the burning sensation of a bullseye glued to my neck. Rollerblade-girl was breathing hard behind me.

"Thanks for coming," I said, still seated and about to change position. I had the impression Rollerblade-girl jolted when I opened my mouth.

"Who are you? And stay as you are, don't turn to look at me! You didn't trust me, I do not trust you."

The voice was pleasant, that of a young woman. Not exactly afraid, not calm either. I tried to combine the few images I glimpsed the first time we saw her with this voice and tried to imagine even more details about her. My God! I was hearing another voice, a different voice than mine, Mary's or Annah's after such a long time!

We lived a world deprived of laughter, children cries, chatters, the always present human murmuring that we took for granted everywhere in the world. One can never feel the presence of something as strongly as when it is no more; the void replaces what once gave us reassurance, continuity, fulfillment. Don't people talk about the deafening sound of silence? I experienced in a flash the unbearable weight of emptiness.

She had a charming voice, with a pleasant Italian accent. The kind of voice which makes you look for its owner in a bar or at a restaurant. When the charm of the voice marries with the charm of the person then one is gratified with the pleasure of having discovered harmony in human incarnation. She sounded determined. I didn't move.

"Well, I do trust you now. I would not be here sitting like this otherwise. The people you saw are my wife and daughter. And they were worried for me. They still are. They…I…we wouldn't have hurt you."

"Where are you coming from? Do you know what happened? Is everyone dead? How can that be true?"

"From out of town, in the countryside, and could you stop shooting questions like darts?"

She paused for a second.

"Funny you are saying that…"

I didn't make out the meaning of her last remark.

"Don't stand up. Turn around slowly."

With the help of both hands, I twisted around, slowly, as she requested. Rollerblade-girl was firmly standing her ground. She was fit, a rather athletic body, dressed entirely in black if not for a peach-colored top that I could perceive more than see from her semi-opened zipped black leather jacket, hiding a full breast. Her recent "shopping" from the mall, no doubt. She wore jeans, tight and low-waisted that perfectly sculpted her figure. A rebellious lock of black hair refused to be constrained by the helmet she wore. Her eyes were invisible behind dark sunglasses. She was very attractive and she kept a crossbow pointed right at me.

"Well, I am at your mercy it seems. I assure you, I am totally alone." I noticed she was glancing around for the presence of others.

"Okay, mister. What do we do now?"

"Honestly? May I stretch my legs? They are starting to hurt."

Rollerblade-girl nodded and I did it with a grunt of satisfaction which raised a hint of a smile. While massaging my knees, I went on. "My name is Dan, Daniel Amenta." I pointed to a bulge near my groin. "And that is an iPhone in my pocket. I would like to call my family."

Her lips briefly raised into a smile again. She must have liked my funny contortions and then considered whether I could be faster than her dart in the remote case I wanted to try anything. The crossbow made a short upward jerky motion that I took for agreement so I slowly and carefully took the phone out and showed it to the girl, raising my eyebrows.

"Put the speaker on."

I did as she commanded and called home.

"Mary?"

"Dan! What happened? How are you? Did you see the girl?"

"All's fine. Why are you asking multiple questions?"

"What?" Mary said and Rollerblade-girl smiled more openly, evidently getting more relaxed. I could not see her eyes through her glasses, but the crossbow was no longer pointing straight at my chest and I noticed her hands were less tense on the grip.

"Never mind. I'm okay and I'm with..." I looked up at Rollerblade-girl. She hesitated. I raised my eyebrows again and gestured with the phone.

"Laura," she replied.

"I am with Laura."

"Laura? That's the girl's name? Can she hear me?"

"I bet she can, hon…"

"Laura? This is Mary, Dan's wife. If he introduced himself that is. I am sorry if we scared you last time. We meant no harm. You are the first one we have seen in months. Alive I mean…" She paused, then with a firm voice she continued, "If you are alone, you are welcome to come home with Dan…and stay."

I looked at the phone, then at Laura whose expression I could not decipher. I didn't expect that, or to come so soon. Mary was still capable of surprising me after all these years.

"Mary? I don't know what's on Laura's mind," I said while looking at Laura. "We just met so maybe that's premature. I only wanted to reassure you…"

Mary cut me short, ignoring what I said. "Laura, I love this stupid man. Let him come home…please!"

What the…! Why and how had Mary taken for granted that I was not in control of the situation, that instead Laura was in charge? Laura lowered her crossbow and interrupted my mental rumination.

"Tell her not to worry."

"Thank you, Laura. Thank you!" Mary's voice burst from the speaker before I could speak.

"If you ladies will allow, may I intervene?" I was simply ignored again.

"No, I thank *you*, Mary. I do not want to be alone anymore. I am frightened and I want to get out of Geneva, too." Laura kept looking around as if she still expected to see someone suddenly coming out of nowhere.

"Mary, I love you. I believe I'll be home soon…maybe with Laura." I glanced at the girl, who leaned now carelessly on the car. "I'll call you again."

"Come home with Laura, Dan," was the terse reply.

Ever so cautiously, I began to stand up. Laura did not react, watching calmly. I stepped forward and stretched out my hand.

"Shall we start again? Dan…"

She put the crossbow on the hood, took her helmet and glasses off, and gave me her hand to shake.

"Laura," she said with a smile.

She had beautiful light blue eyes with a dark blue outer ring. The contrast with her dark hair was striking. She was undeniably attractive, but what I noticed most was that those eyes were frightened. And not because of me.

"Looks like, if the world before had let women do the talking, we men would have had much less occasion to fight." I smiled and pointed at her crossbow. "Do you really know how to use that thing?" Laura smiled back.

"You would be surprised. I am less afraid to venture out during the day but I spend the night hiding and sometimes I'm too scared to fall asleep. For all this time, I thought I was the only one alive." She paused. "Instead, you seem…cool and relaxed?" I gazed at her.

"Well, we were scared too the first days. We didn't know what to expect. Then we fell back to a sort of normality in our lives. We aren't in need of anything, but we are prepared for the worst. I am ashamed to say that we practically go along with our lives as we did before…after adjustments, that is. I am lucky, with wife and daughter both doing well."

Laura stared at me as if I came from another planet. Unsure whether I was pretending or that was all there was to say. I saw she had a burning question, but maybe she was too afraid to ask it right then.

"By the way," I added, "we are not alone indeed. Ah, are you coming with me?"

She began to take off her rollerblades and pulled a pair of sneakers from her backpack, gazing at me for a long moment.

"The little girl I saw…your daughter?"

"Yes, her name is Annah. She's twelve. Almost thirteen, she would want me to add."

"I don't know if my little brother is still alive. I am…I was in Geneva to study toward a Master's degree. I have not been able to reach anyone from my family." Her voice broke a little before she regained some composure, straightening up her figure despite the weight of her losses.

I got busy with rolling up the car windows and closing the trunk. Laura took off her rollerblades and was about to put on her sneakers. I watched her for a moment; she moved graciously and…shaking my head, I laid her crossbow on the back seat and forced my eyes away from her.

"Listen," I said. "You don't need to come right now if you're not sure...maybe some other day." I finally glanced up at her.

She gave me a long, level look as if I'd said something really weird. I couldn't tell what she was thinking; there was no emotion in her eyes that I could discern. Then fear appeared again.

"No! I am coming!" The words erupted as if they were darts from her crossbow; fast, direct, piercing. Laura's face paled and her lips tightened like the string of her weapon, ready to fire more darts. She paused and her eyes wandered around, again as if to make sure we were indeed alone. Then, more calmly, in an almost apologetic tone, she said, "I need to get some stuff from my place. I don't own much, mostly clothing. Maybe we can go back to my apartment another day too? But before it gets dark!" She hesitated. "I also have some food left."

It sounded as if she tried to give me more reasons to take her there. She was no longer the resolute girl who'd kept me under the threat of a deadly dart and I wondered why.

"Food is not a problem, yet. What is with the dark? What exactly are you afraid of?"

Laura did not reply; she simply got in the car. I went to the driver seat, puzzled by that abrupt change.

"So, where are you staying?" I asked while starting the car.

"Champel. It is not far from here. Maybe a couple of miles. Turn around and go toward the Cantonal Hospital."

"Alright, I will."

Before reaching the hospital, Laura made me stop in front of an old apartment building. One of those beautiful old Geneva buildings with marble and stone decorations and with steep old shingled roofs. Six floors, but as tall as a ten-story modern building. She noticed my surprise and explained she rented a studio there. That her family paid the rent directly to the landlord, an old lady she only met once.

I didn't bother to park, just stopped the car in the middle

of the street, blocking non-existing traffic. We got out. The slamming of the doors sounded particularly loud in the deafening silence that surrounded us. Silence that always struck me every time a sudden noise broke it. Like smashing a perfect glass pane, invisible until the precise moment it explodes in thousands of fragments instants later.

"It's on the third floor. I'll get some clothes and be right back."

I looked up and tried to single out a window or a balcony, but they all looked the same. We covered the short distance from the sidewalk to the entrance of the building. The hallway was elegant, with marble and a beautiful iron balustrade in the staircase surrounding the elevator cage. In that moment, the scene seemed blatantly normal, as if I was taking a date back home. She stopped on the first step of the flight of stairs, turned and stared wide-eyed at me.

"There are two women in the elevator. Sophie and Monique. They were nurses at the hospital. I found them both, that morning when leaving for my classes."

Then she started to climb the stairs to reach her floor. I didn't call the elevator to verify her story. I imagined well what waited for me. Rotten corpses, mouths agape, darkened dry blood. No need to add those images to those I fought against on a daily basis. Like shingles flying toward me, blown off by that powerful night wind that started everything. Dodging them all, one by one and, some, still splatting hurtfully on my face.

While Laura was busy getting her stuff, I called Mary and briefly told her about the last twenty minutes or so. Something in Laura worried me. Above, I heard a door closing and steps coming down the stairs. I hung up and, a few seconds later, Laura appeared. She had changed and put on a dress and flat shoes, and she handed me a large bag. Again, I couldn't help but notice how beautiful she was.

"Ladies things." She paused. "And I want to make a good impression if I can," she said, smiling.

Well, she did. I held the doorway open for her. She stepped out. "Thank you!"

"Where do you live, Dan?" She asked as we got back in the car.

"Near a little village in France. Some fifteen miles from here."

A somber expression appeared on her face and, again, the veil of fright in her eyes. She looked even younger than she was.

"You…you are not with them, are you?"

I was about to turn the ignition key, and I froze a second. I stopped, straightened back in my seat, and met her eyes.

"Them?! Them who? Another one told me about *them* just yesterday. He is another survivor, we exchanged emails. In his last message, he refers to some *people* and used the same expression: *Them*! He lives in New York. Actually, I still have to get back to him. Who are these people, Laura?"

She hesitated before answering. Then, looking straight into my eyes, she said, "I don't think they are…people."

The past got busy catching up and connecting dots. Laura started to tell me what she saw. She was shaken, and while she talked, scenes from my youth burst in front of my eyes with a kind of superimposed vision. What Michael hinted at, and what Laura now described in better terms, I had seen it already, years before. Maybe some thirty-five years before. Shocking. I was ready to imagine every possible scenario but that one.

Laura went on. "I have seen them only during evening time, though. Three or four times. The first time it happened, I spent the whole night hidden and too afraid to move from where I was," she said. "During the day, I guess they are not here. They always start to leave just before dawn, when their luminescence begins to fade."

The biggest differences between Michael's recounting, Laura's encounters, and my experience were that they saw them from a distance, and for both of them, it had been frightening. I *saw* them. Only one of them to be precise, next to me for what seemed a long time but I didn't get scared at all. On the contrary. I wasn't ready to share that with Laura.

"You will need to tell Mary this, too. Where we are, and nearby, we haven't seen anyone of the sort you describe."

I only half-lied. We hadn't seen them where we lived in the last couple of months. In that sense, I told the truth. Haven't seen anymore of them in the last thirty years or more, though physical evidence of that encounter was vividly present in every moment of my life since.

Laura noticed I was troubled. Anyone would have been by what she said. She did not question me then. In any case, she had no way to imagine the real reason why her recount troubled me so much. So, all that happened was not the fault of humans. Or maybe it was...but not directly.

I was probably ten or eleven years old. We lived in an apartment on the top floor of a seven-story building. Today it would be called the penthouse. My family was no different from every other middle-class family of that period. We lacked nothing of anything essential but what we had was not always of the best quality, and we could not afford the latest and greatest. Superfluous expenses did not have a place in our single-salary budget.

Mom once had a stable nursing position which she quit under pressure from both my father and his family when my older brother was born. She stopped dreaming about returning to a job she truly loved when I was born. She regretted that decision all her life, putting the blame on a husband she discovered was not Prince Charming only weeks after they got married. Father had squandered a good education. For lack of ambition, or just laziness, he resolved to work at the family business.

Though Mother was raised in a working class family who came from the middle of Italy, my father's family had a small enterprise that allowed my grandparents to live a wealthy life...and they spent a fortune. By the time my parents got married, the business only allowed an average life, just above struggling. Father must have cultivated an inner frustration and made sure his wife was there to pay the price, too. He felt superior due to her humble origins. I discovered the anguish and the sadness of my mother only later when, still young, I became her confidante.

She was sorry she had no one to talk about her pains but me. She knew it was not right to open up the way she did with her son, but she could not do without: she had no family members close by, having moved hundreds of miles away from home to follow her work aspirations. In the fifties, that was no meager accomplishment for a young woman. Her family, too, made her pay the price.

I always believed she just managed to keep everything to herself for years and then decided to release it all on me before exploding or committing suicide. She tried a few times, as she once painfully admitted, stepping back from the balcony barrier at the last minute. She told me the void almost talked to her in an assuaging voice..."a few seconds and it will all be over." She said what prevented her from taking her own life was the crude and painful image of my father getting remarried, her children raised by a stepmother who didn't care about them. Or, worse, her children neglected and sent to a foster institution.

My mother had been raised Catholic and for years after the marriage she had been fully observant. My father had his own ideas about God and spirituality, and he kept searching obsessively for a path of faith that could provide answers to his unrest and tormented soul. My mother stuck to her Catholicism and it was a reason for fights and cruel criticisms from my father. It made him exceedingly bitter toward his wife, whose only blame was that she didn't need to follow him on his anguished spiritual quests.

In different periods of his life, my father followed and experienced the Mennonites, Mormons and the Latter Days Saints Church, the Lutherans, and then Freemasonry and Rosicrucians. He ended up in outright esotericism when he finally decided confessions were all wrong in one way or another, or swarming with fanatics. Heretics who didn't understand the true message of Jesus Christ or whatever Master he was involved with at the moment, or coming from a spiritual dimension readily accessible if one truly wanted to.

He had beat my mother once, the one time I know of, when she vehemently opposed that we children were to be raised as anything but Catholics, especially after seeing my father changing churches and faith so often. If it were up to him, I would have been baptized multiple times, with multiple confessions, and introduced to different rituals because the previous ones had to be "erased" and amended for with the new ones.

When he got into esoteric practices, he scared my mom by conducting séances at home. He befriended various mediums who came and went, sometimes without warning. Of course, he had planned for those visits but he didn't care to communicate or share those plans with his wife. Once, my mother told me after so many years, she came out of the shower dressed only in a babydoll nightie and was faced with a total stranger in the house, invited by my father who didn't care to mention the fact to her. It was the scare of her life, not to talk about the humiliation of being seen practically naked.

My mother protested only once about what went on in the family and at home. The result was that she had to wear dark glasses for weeks so neighbors would not notice the bruises and the black eye.

She had been able to keep we children from witnessing her struggles, unaffected by the ordeal she lived in her marriage. Alone, pretending everything was just fine. While my older brother had always been confrontational with Father, I was instead intrigued by this man who was never at rest, intellectually speaking.

Mentally, he communicated an internal turmoil that often

erupted in verbal violence and abuse against whoever dared to contradict him. He was not a man to accept rebuttals to his sayings or listen calmly to refutations. He would have talked and talked, more and more vehemently until the other person had to quit discussing or decide to punch him to make him stop. I think he was shrewd enough to sense whether the other side would have capitulated before going to those extremes.

Thinking of it, I am not sure whether it was my father who quit the various religious groups, sects, or esoteric congregations he was involved with at each time. Most probably, they instead resolved to get rid of a disturbing and unmanageable member. Father freely talked to me about these things and he called me "the one who listens," while avoiding my older brother who had an aversion for everything my father dug into. His interest in me increased the moment he discovered I was able to sense when he held séances at home, or any of his "spiritual enhancement experiments" as he called them.

He even tried and tested me to prove whether I could truly have this...capability. He started to organize sessions while casually telling everyone in the family that he had a totally different plan. He made sure I was to spend the day, for example, with my grandparents. Mom was of course terrified by all this, and although she could not make him stop, she succeeded in preventing him from having me participate directly in his rituals.

After he had practiced séances at home, most times I felt discomfort for a couple of days. A hostile aura hovered at home, and I sensed it in this or that other room where he had recently conducted his spiritual enhancement sessions, alone or with other members. Sometimes I felt repulsion even at approaching objects that had a direct role in his practices. He was fascinated by this sensibility of mine, and discussed the facts with his medium friends who invariably wanted to spend time alone with me, hypnotize me, or work with me to see whether I had some manifest inner power.

Mom would have rather died at the idea that I could be involved in all that. She showed to have a strong resolve to oppose Dad's plans, more than for any other things she disliked in her marriage. I think my father understood and resented that: he could manipulate her and bend her will, whenever and however, in almost everything. But when it was her children's safety at stake, Mom never flinched. The only option he had was to kill her rather than convince her.

Who knows, he might have caressed the idea in some wild dream, especially when he was suspected to entertain a mistress. He must have reasoned that the risks and possible consequences were too high for his liking. He always calculated. Besides, in part, I think he was afraid that I would steal his spotlight in his communities if truly I had spiritual powers, so he kept my participation to a minimum or limited to only his personal tests.

Once, I remember, I became unable to enter into the living room for days, the aversion was so extreme. I screamed when he forced me into the room, and I pulled and struggled till I escaped his grip and left the room, running. He confessed later that he had to "dismantle" an esoteric protection he had put in place to test me. Something to do with summoning a Guardian; he specifically called it "Guardian of the Threshold." Whatever he was doing with those esoteric experiences, they had a clear impact on me. Over the years, I became convinced that not everything is charlatanism.

In certain circumstances of my life, I had a strange infancy; otherwise normal and rather a common one under many others. In my late teens, I tried esotericism myself, just because. It was familiar, even if I did not like the weirdness and the uneasiness that those early experiences had provoked in me. Once, during a séance, a medium announced that I held an opening and that spiritual energy kept flowing through me to him. I didn't like the idea of anything flowing from me to him. I did not like him much in the first place, and never went back. The séances though were...interesting, and I had seen ectoplasms in a few of them. Maybe they were real, or maybe just cunning tricks. I honestly could not say.

I am one of those individuals who had gone through out of body experiences. All of them were a kind of lucid-dream: The sensation of being fully awake and yet, floating into this bright world which kept a resemblance with the physical one, as if seen through a sort of a force field, distorting shapes and colors. One night, the out of body event happened all by itself, without me trying to induce it via learned practices. I stopped venturing along that path.

The experience had been tremendously physical. Something violently grabbed and pulled my legs up, and jerked my whole "me" away from my physical body. Only my spiritual head still overlapped with the physical one and held me in place. I was shaken relentlessly. My heartbeat raced like crazy, and when everything stopped suddenly, I was drenched in sweat. It never happened again after that night, and I never tried to provoke it myself anymore. I don't like it when I evidently can't control a situation, or am not fully aware of all possible outcomes. But I digress...

— o —

So, I have seen *them*, well before Michael and Laura. I do not recall any abnormal events in the days before the visit, any change from the routine that I could take as a possible explanation. No fever or food poisoning as possible causes for hallucinations, nor Father playing with his esoteric tricks. Besides, though I never doubted what happened, the things I read and heard from Michael and Laura came as confirmation, if I actually needed one. What I saw when a child was real, not a lucid dream.

That evening, we had dinner as a family. We watched some TV, then my brother and I were sent to bed. We shared the same room as my parents could not afford a bigger apartment. Our bedroom gave into a room acting those days as a living room; a double French door with opaque glass panes separated the two. That room also had its own independent access from the entry hall.

We used our room to study and play, too. During the day, the French doors were kept open, merging the two spaces. From my bed, to the left, there was a large window and a glass door that led directly to a wide balcony. To the right, a door led into a corridor which itself gave access to additional rooms. The last one, down at the end, was my parent's bedroom. We had moved to this new room the year before and—for the occasion—we got fold-away beds to make it even larger. We went to bed rather early that evening as we had school the next morning.

I was about to fall asleep when I started to hear whistling sounds, and whispers and hisses. Intermittently and with both ears. I called my parents, crying because the noises scared me and I couldn't sleep. I told them I heard whistles inside my head. Dad thought I had bugs in my ears so he took me to the kitchen and tried to attract a possible insect out with the help of a flashlight, telling me in his commanding voice to stay still. But there were no insects. "What's wrong with you, Dan!" I felt guilty for not having bugs in my ears.

The noises came and went. It was stressful for me and for my parents, too. Mom was worried, Dad annoyed. Then, after a last intermittence, they entirely stopped. Parents were relieved, each for their own reasons. Mom decided I needed to go see a doctor the next day. At least for the moment, I finally was able to go back to bed and get some rest. Mom stayed at my bedside, caressing my head, and she held my hand until I fell asleep.

That night—of course, I have no idea how much time had passed—I awoke suddenly, perfectly lucid. The faint light from city streets entered through the thin veil at the window that acted as our curtain. The house was silent, everyone was sleeping. I sat on my bed, turned to my left and saw my brother sound asleep. A faint white glow came from the entry hall. The glow was steady and cold, as if coming from neon lights. While its source was clearly in the hall, the glow gave light to the living room and to the corridor itself. I could distinguish detail of our bedroom, normally hidden in the darkness at night.

Still curious about what lit the hallway, the living room got slightly darker as the light intensity grew toward the corridor: the source of the glow started to move. I remember all this as if it just happened and can relive it now as vividly as then. A total and unnatural calm engulfed me, sweeping over my senses as a high tide of warm waters. I called my brother in a whisper, raising my voice at every attempt but he kept sleeping, breathing hard.

The glow left the hall. The living room plunged into darkness as the light moved into the corridor. Then it appeared, standing at the door, occupying its whole space. Obviously tall, it must have been around 6.5 feet and with large shoulders. He stood there for few seconds—in that moment I sensed the entity was a male—and, turning his head slowly, he scanned the room as if examining the place.

The glow prevented me from clearly distinguishing his facial traits and the entity lacked sharp contours—it looked fuzzy to me. Our bedroom was flooded with his light and his head turned toward me. I stared at him, motionless, and with the strange sensation that everything was perfectly fine. I was calm, and in peace.

The entity stepped forward and entered the room. He stopped and stood in front of my bed. His body continued backwards, with a large and thick protrusion, from the lumbosacral area in his back. No, it didn't seem to be anything like a tail. The protrusion was as big as a grown man's thigh, and long, maybe four to five feet, getting thinner toward the end. As with the rest of the body, the end was fuzzy with no sharp edges inside the glow. It was definitely part of him, and at the same time, it wasn't. I don't know how to explain it better than that.

He turned slowly and faced me, still sitting peacefully on my bed while watching the whole scene as if I had no part in it. I had the feeling he was there analyzing the situation and wondered about me, asking himself whether I was as he expected.

After a while, he stepped to the side, then moved forward to come to a halt at the left side of my bed. I could reach for him if I wanted to. This surprises me even today. Why that profound serenity? Wouldn't it have been natural for me to panic, to scream for help? Why nothing? Yet I had no fear or anxiety, just an internal peace like one I have never felt again.

The entity sat. On my bed, next to me! I did not move. I do not know how long he sat there. Time froze and we were still silhouettes in a black and white picture. Even that close, I wasn't able to clearly see his facial details. Still, he seemed wise and profound. I clearly felt his piercing stares within his opaque glowing face. He was benevolent, with kindly feelings. I sensed all that, and that he was there to do something good for me. He raised his left arm and, ever slowly, he approached his hand toward my face. He kept raising it and finally rested it on my forehead. There, the hissing noises started again, abruptly, as if he had switched them on. The renewed influx of noises in my ears did not startle me though. They've never left me since.

He kept his hand there, and slightly lowered his head, closing his eyes. Like that we sat, together. My head itched from the inside. I closed my eyes; colors and shapes danced in my vision. After a while, he pulled back his hand, the colors faded, and I opened my eyes. He rested his arm on his lap, or at least so it seemed to me. He raised his head again and stared at me. I touched my forehead, as it had started to give me a tingling sensation.

I then had an impulse, and did the same: I raised my arm and stretched my hand toward his chest. I started to feel a prickling sensation to my fingertips. I was about to press his chest with my opened hand, and it did not find a firm and solid obstacle. Exerting some pressure, my hand penetrated inside the glow. And there it disappeared. My hand and wrist got inside the entity and could feel nothing but a growing stinging sensation and warmth. I was not harmed, nor was my hand hurting.

After a short while, I pulled my hand back; it tingled as did my forehead. What happened next is hard to believe: The entity stood up and made a gesture with his right hand, as when one opens his own hand to show he does not hold or hide anything. I lay back down on my bed and went under the cover, up to my head. The glow rapidly diminished in intensity and retreated. The entity had gone, the room plunged back into darkness. I fell asleep. I never told this story to anyone. No one. Ever.

The loud hissing noises have stayed with me since that night, and I hear them all the time. Initially, it was difficult to fall asleep, but soon I got used to them. Sometimes, I even profited from their presence, using the noise to achieve a trance-like state, focusing from one tone and hiss to another.

Often, while doing that, I enter a lucid dream where I hear music, beautiful and enchanting, and then the tinnitus disappears altogether. The music only lasts a few seconds, and I sort of awaken again to start the cycle over until I finally go to sleep. I regret that I do not know how to write music to transcribe those melodies.

Other times it is voices, words spoken here and there, never a full statement though. My name is called, or I hear words of warnings, or reassuring short phrases. It does not happen when awake, only during this transitional phase before falling asleep, triggered when I concentrate on my tinnitus. If I am crazy, then it must be a well-conceived madness as it is limited in time and I have never received orders to do anything from those callings in my head. So far.

My tinnitus is exceptionally loud, I heard it even in airplanes when flying for business. Even the inflight noise in the cabin is not stronger. Doctors say tinnitus usually is the result of a hearing trauma but my hearing has been tested and examined multiple times and with increasing technologies over the years. It is just perfect, actually, much better than the average: I hear pure tones in a large spectrum of frequencies and at an extremely low intensity. Doctors said over 98% of the entire population does not hear the way I do.

— o —

Laura, without possibly having any knowledge of this, described—though in less detail—the entity who visited me when I was a child. She said she saw a few of them on different occasions. Together, in groups of three to four at a time, and always from a distance. She never tried to approach them and rushed to hide when she crossed them in town. She was terrified by all that implied. I was shocked by her story and not for the reasons she might have guessed then.

"I can't believe you've never seen them." Laura eyebrows raised, and she slightly tilted her head. I avoided her glance.

"Yeah, me neither." I started the engine, which hummed softly as we drove toward the lake. Laura was watching a spot between her legs, her hand clenching the folds of her dress.

"They did it, right?" She asked without raising her head.

I did not reply. What other possible explanation could I provide? Mentally, I took note that maybe I had better chase them around for a special reunion. Our survival—even more than that, our future—was not entirely up to us after all. My hand reached for hers to free up that tension. She resisted my touch only briefly then she took my hand between hers and slowly brought it closer to her hip.

I called home, announcing that indeed I was bringing someone with me. That generated cheerful reactions, especially from Annah who probably longed to be with somebody else than just her parents. Smiling, I turned toward Laura, and I saw her eyes wet with tears she tried to hide from me. Crying and smiling at the same time. That was good; it spoke well of her personality and brought hopes for the first step of a growing community. Maybe.

When we arrived, Annah was already opening the gate: in our world one could hear a car coming from miles away. Laura marveled at the UPS truck, and the barbed-wired fence. She recognized T&T, our two German Shepherds next to Annah. She got out of the car and watched me operate the truck with a question clearly spelled out on her face. Smiling, I invited her to step forward to meet Annah and Mary standing in the driveway.

Laura caressed Annah's hair and fell into an emotional hug within Mary's opened arms. Taxi and Tarantula recognized Laura, too; her scent was still fresh in their memory. Their welcoming was singularly vocal, and I had to calm them down a little. Laura and Mary were both crying and sobbing, hugging like old friends finally reunited, amazed to see each other after having lost all hopes to meet again one day.

"Thank you, thank you…" Laura kept repeating to Mary who kept reassuring Laura that the worst, her worst, was a thing of the past now.

"It's over, you'll be fine here, it's over…"

What had we done to deserve all this pain, all those

deaths, all the losses? Apocalypse theories and scriptures have always been a regular presence in all mental ejaculations about the future of the human race. God's judgment, the final days, ultimate justice taking place in some near or remote time. Christian eschatology is full of those things. Were we fully into it? Apocalypse also stood for the process of disclosure of a truth hidden to the majority of mankind, in an era dominated by falsehood and misconception. What was the truth we were yet to discover? Were Saint John's Riders of the Apocalypse glowing too?

I am sure those who were very informed and had studied the Rapture, Tribulation, the Book of Revelation or John's Apocalypse, and similar, would explain everything and point to proof everywhere around us. Each of them would affirm proudly that they were right. But they were not here, and they were probably dead. Who knows, perhaps rightfully dead? Maybe somewhere, someone can tell everybody, "I told you, I told you." Meager solace now.

"Dad?" Annah grabbed my attention as I was lost in my thoughts and she pointed to the gate still open. I went to attend the complicated procedure to lock us safely in, UPS truck first. The three women started to walk toward the house; Taxi and Tarantula had taken their share of hugs and were trotting alongside. Mary turned briefly, glanced at me and smiled openly. I was sure she had something in mind, but what?

Mary and Annah showed Laura around: the vegetable garden, the basement with our provisions, the preparations I had ready for when electricity abandoned us, the generators, the stock of fuel, our food storage, our home, and how Laura could fit in with all that. I judged I was one too many if I joined the show so, after checking everything was sound and fine, including Taxi and Tarantula's food and water, I went upstairs. I wanted to get back in touch with Michael and describe what Laura had told me; tell him about Laura, too. Maybe there will be others joining us some day.

Our property included an adjacent cottage that we used for visiting family and friends. Mary suggested that Laura stay there as we were not expecting company anytime soon. Laura could decide later on if she wanted to move in with us, in the main residence. It did not take long for Laura to make up her mind:

"I would never go back to Geneva. You will never regret you opened your heart so much to me. You rescued me. I think I would have gone mad soon."

Annah was so happy to have Laura at home with us, and cheered even more when she said that and rushed to hug her. Laura returned the embrace and closed her eyes when she did so. Although there was not less than ten years difference, at least, the two girls hit it off quickly. Annah was fascinated by the young woman and Laura? Probably thinking of her brother who would have been about the same age as our daughter. Regardless, having Laura with us seemed to have a great and positive influence on Annah who became more cheerful every day and less troubled than in the past weeks.

After dinner that evening, we struggled to send Annah to bed. She agreed only after Laura promised she would be there the next morning, and for the days to come.

"You will be my little sister and I will be your big sister if you want." Annah was so happy I felt a sweeping sense of gratitude toward Laura.

"And would you teach me roller skating?"

"Of course, I'd love that. We need to make sure you get the proper equipment, then we will hit the roads. You'll learn in no time. You'll see."

When Annah fell asleep, the three of us went to sit downstairs on the couch and I lit the fire. Mary wanted to know about Laura: Her past, her ideas, what triggered her and what gave her pleasure. Laura glanced first at Mary, then at me. She lowered her eyes and, with a sigh, she opened up.

"I was raised in Italy. My mother is French and she met Dad in front of a fuming dish of spaghetti all'amatriciana. 'Hot as a volcano and as spicy as our love,' Dad used to say." I exchanged a smile with Mary as I took my place on the couch.

"My infancy was nothing but ordinary, surrounded by love, care, and family values. I was an only child for twelve years, then my little brother was born, somewhat unexpectedly." She paused. "I miss him."

Mary reached for her hand. "You do not need to continue."

"No, I want to." Laura reassured us.

"My Dad is…was a university professor of philosophy." Laura eyes got bright with tears, reflecting the dancing colors of the cracking fire. Tears that were like the dew on our blue iris on late summer mornings. She changed to past tense as if talking about dead people.

"Mom was a midwife. In high school, I became passionate about Marx, Nietzsche, and Freud in particular. There was a time when I almost only read Freud."

Mary started to get interested. I wasn't particularly into humanistic studies. Only math and physics. But Mary loved the arts, philosophy and literature. She changed position to get more comfortable and more apt to listen carefully, as if she needed to shut out body signals to focus on what Laura was saying.

"Together with philosophy, art history was my favorite subject and, in high school, I learned to truly *look*. I've always liked the whole history of art, in any period: ancient, medieval, Renaissance, Baroque…a certain taste for surrealism that was accompanied by philosophical interest. I think I made my dad proud. Paul, my brother, was Mom's darling, and he looked up to me for everything. He always asked me to explain what Dad meant when he was talking philosophy." Laura paused for a long moment, then she smiled.

"The very first time he asked me what '*fisolopy*' was…" She sighed, fighting some inner demons and her hands trembled. Before we could say anything, she abruptly changed the subject.

"Over the past three years, I've come to know about the great music and composers thanks to some friends…one in particular. He liked haute cuisine, too, of which I might have become even more passionate than him, or at least we're even." She paused again, and her eyes lost the inner brightness they had before, as when a dark cloud hides the sun, promising rain and cold and shivering.

"I could go on, but I prefer not to bore you any longer. I don't have any news from him, back in Italy. He hasn't replied to my calls or emails. I haven't seen him since the time I left to come study here, last July. I do not believe in God now. Now I have even more reasons to believe I am right not to." Laura's voice broke with those last words and she couldn't hold back her emotions anymore.

She cried, big tears tracing her face. It hurt us too. Her pain flowed into us and with us, melting our agonies together. Laura collapsed into Mary's arms. In that moment, our grievances became one. We felt the intensity of the hardship, and the misery, and maybe we started then the mourning of billions of lives.

"Why did it happen, Mary? I am sorry, I didn't want to cry. I miss them so much, so much. Oh, Mary… I didn't have time to tell them anything. My brother, he was so young. Why wasn't I there with him? I always weep, inside, even when I do not have any more tears to shed."

We all cried, weeping like kids who had lost their best friend. Fused into one single, miserable, aching heart. Feeling the crushing weight of merciless avalanches of the souls of everyone we lost, and whom we would never see, hear, feel, or touch again.

"Laura, Laura, you're not alone. Don't cry, Laura, you're with us now." Mary managed to say while sobbing. My throat was a knot, unable to utter a word. Mary continued to soothe Laura's ache, then she started to speak in a voice full of love, almost whispering, and it was as if she poured an ointment on our wounds.

"Laura…darling. Life has not given us the opportunity to share moments of joy. We meet in times of grief. Each of us must deal with deep wounds, the loss of family and be strong to cherish what remains. We have been deeply wounded by all that has occurred. Time will never heal this pain but we have to turn the page. We will not have the chance to forget."

She told how it had been for us, and how we discovered what happened when I took Annah to school that morning. Our initial searches for others, the fears, the vanishing hopes, the burial of Joe and Beth. With all that had happened since then, I almost forgot the sadness of those moments. We mourned.

Laura told us about her first days and weeks. How she woke up one day, got ready for her lessons, and left home. She called for the elevator and then the horror started. The doors opened and she screamed and could not stop.

"Monique and Sophie lived together on the fifth floor. They had collapsed in the elevator, crammed together in the tiny space. Their faces were swollen, and blood came out of their nose and ears. Their lips were bluish and their eyes were almost out of their sockets, everything sprayed with blood."

Laura continued, "I screamed for help, ringing all the door bells on my floor and others as well. No one came out to help. I could not understand why everyone was ignoring me, why no one came. I screamed so much."

She told us she had collapsed when no one answered at the first-floor corner apartment where a young couple from Italy, with their baby girl, had just moved in only weeks before.

"She was so cute, their baby, Stella. I kept banging on their door, calling their names. I kept hitting that door until my hands hurt. I was in terror." She called out for Antonella, Stella's mother, until her voice faltered and she fell against their door, sobbing. She realized then how everything was oppressively silent.

Laura finally ran out of the building, still calling for help, and the terror grew even more after she started to see the first corpses. In a car, or a bicycle rider, a weird, unnatural, contorted figure, forever framed within his bicycle. She panicked even more when she started to realize how quiet Geneva was that early morning in February…and why.

She reached the place where some of her friends lived. A renovated old villa hosting fifteen students, not far from the Cantonal Hospital. She tried the intercom of her colleagues first, then everyone else: no one answered. She didn't know what to do at that point. So she wandered around most of the day, afraid to go back home. She reached the old town almost without realizing it, meeting no one alive. She thought she had almost lost her mind and does not remember much of those first hours. She was only fully aware of where she was or what she was doing in the evening. Maybe because she started to be cold. Inside.

In fear of everything, and in the unnatural silence of a dead town, she returned to her apartment at dark. She remembered, shivering, not to approach the elevator. Got into her apartment, crashed into bed and fell asleep...a heavy dreamless sleep until she awoke because someone was screaming. It took her a while to realize it was her and then she started to cry until dawn, when she fell asleep again as if losing consciousness.

The next morning, she was more rational and tried to call everyone she knew, starting with her family. The more numbers she dialed, the more desperate she got. "I could not continue. I could not distinguish the numbers anymore because of my tears. I threw the cell phone against the wall and broke it."

None of her family answered, neither her friends nor any colleagues. She never tried to call the police.

"Why not?"

Laura had no answer. She didn't, that's all. She did not have Internet at home, only connected at the free wireless service of the University. It was too expensive to get a connection at home, on her student budget.

"I didn't want to be even more of a financial burden for my family."

They weren't rich, and it was an effort for her parents to allow her to get a higher education in Geneva. Her leisure had been the rollerblades and her crossbow; she practiced shooting with it at the Archers Association of Geneva. She looked at me mockingly.

"I could have pierced your heart in a blink."

"I am glad I didn't give you any reason to even think about it."

Laura paused and grinned, "I thought about it…"

I then told Mary how I had been waiting for Laura to show up. When I called her at home, Laura was actually pointing her crossbow at me.

"You are out of your mind," she said. And then to Laura, "And you? Would you really have shot this idiot here?"

"No, I don't think I would have been able to do that."

Laura added she thought about what to do next after she almost bumped into us at the mall.

"I got the scare of my life. You were not that reassuring with your guns, and the dogs. I could think of only one thing: Run!"

She did, and as fast as she was able to. She was about to fall right out of the mall but managed to regain her balance at the last instant and dash down the street, profiting from the descent to gain speed.

"I was afraid you would've launched the dogs after me. I did not dare to approach the mall for days. Actually, I didn't dare to leave home for days."

She understood we were a family; she had seen Mary and Annah and, in those split seconds, noticed how Mary reacted to protect Annah, hiding her behind her body. We could not be bad people and she convinced herself that we did not have evil intentions. She needed to believe that.

"How did you manage to see us? We thought we were well hidden."

"I was just lucky I guess. The day after, I left a message on your paperboard, the rest… it is now our common story."

She went back to tell us about her first days, alone in the city. She left the apartment each time she emptied the fridge, and only then. The shopping center, Eaux Vives 2000, was the largest and closest to her place, and she found the automatic doors worked. She started to visit it regularly. The first days, she only got enough for one meal. She was afraid to be caught, even against all evidence that no one was going to complain or stop her, ever.

She soon started to replenish her fridge like it had never been before. From then on, she went once or twice every week. At the beginning, just for food, then she started looking for other stuff as well. She went everywhere on her skates, visiting all the places she knew when she felt a bit safer. Eventually she did, sort of bringing the mourning to a closure.

"I was emptied and devastated. I resisted the urge to jump off the Mont Blanc bridge each time I crossed it. Get it over with and the water was hypnotizing. The idea of being alone, where everyone was dead, terrified me."

She was glad she didn't, now that she had met us. When it happened, she was not prepared. Not prepared at all. She had given up all hope of finding other survivors.

"That's why I ran. It was so unexpected."

She was always scared since she saw...*them*. One evening in late February, she went too far to be back home in time, during daylight. She was still half an hour away from her place, and it was sunset already. She skated fast, with an alerted urgency, even if she knew no one could hurt her simply because no one was alive in town. Streetlights went on, as usual. She rushed anyway. She did not want to be out at dark.

She was coming down fast from the rail station toward the Mont Blanc bridge. As she reached it at full speed, she noticed something that looked like flashes of light. They were around the old "Batiment des Forces Motrices" and I remembered the building she referred to. Laura kept talking from memory.

She stopped on a dime and rapidly crouched behind the first pillar of the bridge. Then she peeked, and peed herself immediately after; a diffusing warmth between her legs she at first did not recognize. From the bridge, she saw strange figures with thick tails coming out of their backs. They were glowing. From afar, they looked like sideway capital "T"s. She froze for a second then pressed her back against the pillar, gasping for air, her heart pounding. She could not breathe properly and started to sweat, a cold sweat that made her shiver. It was her first ever panic attack.

"I was petrified. On all fours, I forced myself to reach the Four Seasons Hotel across the street because I couldn't stand up anymore, my legs were not responding."

She advanced slowly, moaning with the effort. The sliding doors opened and she got into the elegant hall. She hid there all night, scared to death to the thought that, at any time, one of those glowing figures could appear and find her.

233

"The next morning I ventured out only when the sun was high, and dashed home."

From that day, she always had the crossbow with her. In March, she saw *them* two more times, and always when the night set in. Never during the day, thank God. She would have been too scared to leave her apartment even in search for food.

I held Mary encircled in my arms, sitting with her back against me. I couldn't see her expression, though it was evident she was moved by Laura's story. When she mentioned the glowing figures, Mary became very tense. Her fingernails hurt my arm.

"Mary, you are hurting me."

She turned and gazed at me. She was dazed. "Did you know all that?"

"No. I was shocked myself when Laura told me," I lied.

"Dan, this means…"

"Probably." There was no need for her to finish the sentence, I knew exactly what she meant. "Laura," I asked, "did they ever notice you?"

"I don't know, though once I believe they must have seen me. I was completely out of view, and still one of them looked right at me for a few seconds. Then he turned around, as if uninterested in my presence."

I asked that question more for Mary's benefit than for myself. I remembered Michael had practically said the same thing: the entity did not even react to Michael shooting at him. And they let him go.

"See, it does not seem they are after the few of us who are left." I realized immediately that maybe I said a bit too much because I gave the impression I already knew enough to be able to say that.

"What do you mean, and how could you say that?" Mary stared. She was scrutinizing me.

"I can only imagine. Also, because we haven't seen them scavenging around, have we?"

"We haven't had romantic walks in the moonlight either, honey!"

Laura must have sensed Mary felt I wasn't telling the entire story so she, gladly, came to the rescue.

"I believe that too, Mary. They seemed to be just observing things, like when visiting...," she hesitated, "...ruins."

"Laura, if I were visiting the archeological site of Pompei and discovered one of the original inhabitants still alive, I would be *very* interested in him," Mary said.

"Maybe they already know about us." I again regretted that as soon as I muttered it. This time both women gazed at me. I was walking over egg shells.

"I mean, enough to cull us the way they must have done. What interest would one or two weaklings inferior to them provide? Did the Spaniards show interest in the Incas after they massacred them? And Incas were much closer to Spaniards than we are to... *them.*"

They listened to me, but their faces revealed the doubts I had raised in their minds. Either I was talking bullshit or I wasn't kosher. "I'm pretty sure, if they wanted, they would have found any of us in no time."

This appeared to be more plausible to both Mary and Laura, but not enough to close the deal, at least with Mary.

"It has been an intense day, emotionally intense for everyone." Mary stood up.

The lady of the house decided the evening was over. She took Laura's hand and offered to take her to the cottage but Laura begged to stay with us, in the house, and sleep on the couch, if possible. She would feel safer, at least for the first night, and talking about the past weeks affected her deeply. She was still shaken and Mary did not argue. On the contrary.

"Of course, Laura. Don't worry."

I brought down covers and a spare pillow. When Laura was set for the night, we left and went upstairs to our bedroom.

"Are you okay if she sleeps here in the house with us?"

"Sure, if it is fine with you...oh, you mean for good?" I replied. I did not want to start any discussion, just in case Mary had her mind set on what I said before. But I should have guessed better.

"So, when did you see these entities before, Dan?"

If Mary were a dog, she would be a hound dog. She felt there was something behind my phrases and would not let it go.

"You've never kept anything secret from me..." She paused. "Until now."

"Mary, it is something I kept buried for years. I never have been tempted to let it out and mostly, it simply rested, buried deep down."

"This is not anything recent, right?"

"No."

In all those years, keeping it secret had not been that difficult. What would I have done anyway? Telling everyone, even people I knew quite well, that I saw a ghost? A spirit? "I see dead people" only worked for Hollywood blockbusters. In real life, that doesn't do any good. At best, people would wonder what was wrong with me; at worst, people would not wonder at all and would instead be sure there *was* something wrong with me. Soon, I would have become the subject of conversations. When I was not there, that is.

Mary waited for me to go on. She put one loving hand on my arm and squeezed it gently as if to say, "I am with you. Don't be afraid."

"Also, Michael in New York saw them." I blurted out.

"You didn't tell me that! Why?"

I turned around to face my wife, totally on the defensive. My voice rose without control and flooded Mary with words, as if not daring to give her time to reply.

"Why? Why, Mary? Because! What about preserving what we have managed until now. What about giving hope and nurturing it? Why make you worry for no reason. Why? Why? Because I am still shocked that they do exist, and am still nerve-wracked. Besides, also from what Michael said, I believe they are not interested in us and I need to figure out what is in it now for us, all of us."

Mary kept silent.

"Michael shot at them. Didn't seem to do any harm, they just looked at him and he ran away."

"When did you see them, Dan?" Mary insisted, looking straight into my eyes.

I resigned. There was no point in keeping everything to myself any longer. I told my wife everything. She knew about my tinnitus because of medical records and check-ups I went through even after I married her. I added the part about the music and the uttered words I heard. I told Mary these glowing beings must have been on Earth at least for thirty years or so by now. Maybe even longer, much longer. Who could tell? Maybe all the crazy fellas blabbering about aliens and abductions, and all the tin-foil cap buddies were not so crazy, after all. Maybe, just maybe, that is why we were alive and many others weren't.

"Laura didn't see them before in her life. And she's still alive."

"Yes, and all her family are dead. Mine is not. Oh, c'mon, Mary, I don't know! I don't know, okay? I wish I knew." I turned my gaze away from her, looking out the window. Inside, an inner voice kept telling me: *You need to know, you need to know!*

"You are out of your mind."

I startled and turned to face her, to understand what she was talking about. "What?"

"After all these years, I can read you better than yourself. I see what happens in your mind. You are not going anywhere! You're not going out to find them!"

"I was not…"

"Yes, you were!"

"Mary! What should I do now, Mary? Now that I know that it was not a hallucination, even with the tinnitus. Now that I know that whatever it was, it was not a moment of lucid craziness. I doubted for years."

"I don't know, Dan. I don't know."

That didn't sound exactly right. It did not sound like the Mary I knew: Strong, resolute, with her 'there are more solutions than problems' attitude.

It was difficult for Mary and I to have a good night's sleep after all that. At times, I was awake; at others, she was. A few times we were awake together and our hands searched for each other. We fell asleep from exhaustion in the early hours of the morning.

When we woke up a bit later, the smell of coffee and cooking had miraculously reached our bedroom. A soft chatter came from downstairs. We looked at each other. Mary put on a robe and we both went down to the kitchen. Annah and Laura were talking and preparing a large breakfast for us all. Grilled slices of white bread, scrambled eggs and bacon, orange juice, butter, jams and marmalade.

"I didn't know whether you preferred a salty or sweet breakfast. Annah suggested we do both." Laura greeted us with a glorious smile and sparkling eyes.

"Well, that is definitely a good start for the day. And it comes truly welcomed." I was already hungry!

Annah smiled and ran to hug her mother. "You're not angry, are you, Mama?"

"Of course not, honey!" Mary smiled too as Laura's presence seemed to have given Annah back the happy look she had lost recently.

"We discussed a lot, Annah and I." Laura said, then she smiled at our daughter: "I now know everything about her, the school, her friends, and she knows everything about me and my university life. It has been good for both of us."

I looked at Laura, knowingly. Ironically, it had been easier for Annah to open up to Laura, sharing her pain and fear, than to us. Mary understood that, too, and I was sure she would ask Laura about it later. At least, generally, in case Laura promised Annah to keep everything secret.

It was difficult to think clearly for me in those moments. I looked out the window and wondered whether *they* were there. Glowing entities, invisible during the day maybe but definitely there, and very much real now. Why on Earth should I trust them and expose myself to that risk? Because they paid a visit to me in my childhood? Hadn't they eradicated the human race from the planet? And very easily, too; rapidly, and so efficiently. How long did it take for them to put an end to billions of lives on Earth? Hours, at most, it seemed. Why? This question burned and stung like a drop of acid, burning the flesh, and leaving toxic fumes that burnt the eyes.

My mind was filling up with questions like an unstoppable flood into a chasm in the earth. I knew where that would have brought me. For now, it was time to enjoy the moment and the rich breakfast. And start to get to know the new member of the family. For now, it was only laughter and smiles in the kitchen, and I felt better pushing all those torments away.

— o —

Laura started to fit well into our lives, with a lot of help and encouragement from Mary. Laura participated in Annah's teaching, joined me in my patrol routines, preferring her crossbow to any guns, and took it upon herself to plan for a better search for others, too...she wanted to print leaflets to leave around in case someone out there was alive.

"If it were not for the paperboard you left at the shopping center, I would not be here now," she answered my doubts about the validity of that method.

She moved into our cottage after a few days. Annah spent quite some time there, too, together with Laura. They became very good friends; the 'big sister, little sister' they'd promised to become the very first night. Mary started to stay home more often and dedicate more time to what she loved best: gardening. She encouraged Laura to join my sorties at every occasion and we were now a steady patrolling duo. I think Laura enjoyed it and I did, too. There was another good reason for it, at least in my mind: To have Taxi and Tarantula add Laura to their human pack.

In our patrols around nearby villages, we often split into two human-canine teams, keeping in touch with the walkie-talkies. Laura was meticulous, and she wanted to give others the opportunity and the new hope she'd received from us. She kept track of every spot we had been to and marked on a map all visited villages, and planned for the others. She had established a rallying location for any survivor to give signs of their presence in the region. Just a lingering hope. The controlled area grew quickly, even too quickly for me, but I didn't want to dampen her enthusiasm.

Laura was also well-educated and Mary enjoyed discussing disparate issues with her. For myself, I just loved the intellectual fencing match between two beautiful women. Very engaging and entertaining, and better than TV, especially when all TV channels were dead. One evening, Laura and Mary engaged in a lively discussion about beauty and art. Laura talked fast, waving her hands all around.

They could go on for hours and the beauty of it all was

that I didn't need to participate. Only listening, and saying, "Yeah, that is an interesting concept. What do you think?" to keep the discussion alive. I enjoyed it. One evening, spent among adults, with Annah sound asleep in her bedroom, we ended up talking about love and couples. At one point, while looking straight into our eyes, Laura told us, "I love that feeling of triumph that life is and... I love sex. I like to consider sexuality in all other aspects of life. I think I am a bit of a... *fauve*: the colors of my sexuality are the bright colors of Matisse, the 'Sacre du Printemps', Positano."

She told us about the short-lived and loose group of early twentieth-century modern artists whose works emphasized painterly qualities and strong colors over the representational or realistic values retained by Impressionism. That sparked another discussion with Mary about Cezanne and Van Gogh post-impressionism, fused with the pointillism of Seurat.

Laura brought the discussion back to couples and their role in society.

"A responsible procreation requires consideration for the rights of the unborn. Rights including those set forth in theory by the Constitution: health, education, freedom. Even those claimed virtually by everyone, well-being, happiness, self-realization. I think you aimed at those with Annah. I envy what you have..."

The more Laura opened herself to us, the more it pushed us to do the same. After a while, Laura was part of everything we did.

It was roughly three weeks since Laura had moved in with us when the Internet stopped working. Initially, I tried to solve the issue hoping it was a local problem: restarted the wireless, checked all configurations, reset to factory default the ADSL router unit, then reconfigured it. Nothing. Either the synchronization of the signal was lost for good and could not be regained, or the signal simply had gone cold. The only alternative was to check at the laboratory to see whether it was still up and running, as I believed it would be.

"I need to go to CERN," I announced one evening after dinner. "I don't know if the Internet went cold today or days before since I haven't checked lately. Anyway, it is dead."

With Laura slowly integrating into our life routines, the Internet had taken a back seat as Laura stole the spotlight. She was way more concrete and present than Michael or any other hypothetical click on the Facebook ad campaign could ever be. If they were ever to show up, that is.

"Don't go alone. Take Laura with you," Mary suggested. Laura was just about to get up but I disagreed.

"No, it will be alright. I won't be long." Laura sat back down and looked away from me. I could tell she was disappointed. She said nothing but she turned and her wet eyes begged me...in vain.

CERN laboratory was practically a small town, services included. Actually, not even that small as it habitually consisted of an eight-thousand large community, much larger than many of the little villages around, both in the French and Swiss territories. The main lab site expands across the national border, part in Switzerland and part in France.

Quite a few villages are inside the circle of its accelerators complex, the largest one built inside a 27 kilometers tunnel, or some 18 miles, 100 meters underground, and hosting the most powerful hadrons collider in the world. Protons or lead ions smash together at the site of its major experiments detectors, deep down below the surface. That infrastructure was now bound to be the ultimate one, unmatched by any other lab in the world. Competition was over.

I reached the entrance in the French territory, at the doorstep of the village closest to our house. I didn't take the expressway; I wanted to avoid going through the car wrecks...a multitude of open air tombs with their macabre display of long-gone owners.

The laboratory was a 24/7 institution, with its few access barrier gates operated by the guard on duty while all buildings, inside the compound, had access open all the time. I stopped right in front of the guard booth with its tinted glass and got out. The barrier, of course, remained lowered and blocked the entrance. But the door of the booth wasn't locked though some obstructions inside blocked it from fully opening.

The lights of the car didn't allow me to see clearly

inside, even when pressing my face against the glass pane of the door. Inside, the booth was immersed in the dark. I went back to the car to get a flashlight from the glove compartment, returned to the booth and forced the door. It opened a bit so I pushed harder and with all my weight. Something ceded and got crushed on the floor. The old stench of a decomposed body greeted me.

Covering my mouth, I entered the booth. The flashlight beam was clearly visible, the air inside was dusty. Particulate matter, those particles which can be seen floating in the air on sunbeams. So fascinating when I was a child, playing with tiny little movements of my hand to create swirls in the air and watching how that translated into dancing dust.

Behind the door was the crushed skeletal mummy of the last guard who had been on duty and the particulate in the air mostly came from his corpse. I coughed in repulsion. The flashlight showed me the location of the command box of the barrier: two large buttons—one green, the other red—on the left wall below the windowsill. I pushed the green one and the bar raised only to stop with a grind just before reaching the vertical. Another damage that no one will ever repair. Entropy at work, the gentle degradation of a dead civilization.

The barrier raised just enough to let the car pass without getting scratched. The lab was a familiar place for me: I had worked there for almost a decade. I knew very well where to go so my first stop was the main building—or the "500"—which hosted an area where a few computers were devoted for general access. It was a quick and easy plan with high chances for success.

Before that moment, I never seriously gave much

245

thought to all of the people who had died at CERN that February. Technicians, Ph.D. students and fellows, researchers, all either in the lab early or about to finish a very long night of work. All gone...all ideas, effort, passion and imagination obliterated by someone's decision. By then I had stopped thinking Mother Nature had betrayed us in some mysterious way.

From the entrance, I went straight, keeping to the right at every intersection and following the perimetric road to reach the "main" building hosting facilities like the bank, one of the restaurants, a small shop, the post office, the auditorium, the library, and offices. The main building was in front of Building 2, separated from Building 1 by Building 52. Obviously, you either knew where a building was, or you searched for it on the map.

I stopped the car right in front of the stairs leading to the building entrance where CERN shuttles made one of their stops. None was parked there nor would any appear later. Everywhere was now a perfect spot to leave a car, anywhere in the world. Someone had solved for us, once and for all, every traffic congestion problem but it was meager consolation.

The building was mostly in the dark. I switched on my flashlight and opened the doors. Going in, a familiar scene greeted me and I followed the corridor leading to the User's Office that hosted some ten PCs for public use. I went straight for it; I would have liked to wander around a bit but not now, maybe later.

The PCs were on and, thankfully, there were no corpses in the area. Touching the spacebar on the keyboard of the first one made the screen come alive. After a little while, the Alt-Ctrl-Delete pop-up to log onto the Windows environment showed up. Alt-Ctrl-Delete: I always wondered under the influence of what substance a Microsoft software engineer had conceived that peculiar sequence. The feeling of sloppiness and mediocrity struck me then as it always did. Long live the Mac. Nope, that is gone too. Long live nothing! There was no chance to wish a long life to anything. No one but us, Laura, Michael and probably a few other survivors scattered on the planet.

Windows PCs at CERN were the slowest of all to come alive because of the myriad of security checks in place. After a few minutes, the desktop was finally ready and responding. I launched Internet Explorer and waited still more. In addition to the inherent speed of the operating system, or lack thereof, these were public PCs. Old models and not particularly powerful so I had to be patient. Besides, I had all the time in the world, so I relaxed a bit. No one was going to disturb me or hurry me up to finish my tasks.

Finally, after a small eternity, I was able to check all three of my email accounts and there it was...a message from Michael! It was a few days old and I realized how much I had recently neglected checking the Internet.

———

"Sorry for the radio silence. Lots of things. We have been fucking invaded, man! INVADED, that's for sure. But they do not care about us. I do not know what these bastards are up to. We are leaving the City. We are a small group. Three men, four women and a couple children. No relations.

One of the girls here comes from Danville, Pennsylvania. We'll go there first, then we will see. There is no future in large cities now. Here, things have become much worse. Many blocks have no power anymore so we are leaving while we can. I think we will do better on a farm or sumthin. Who knows, we'll all become Amish. We will be the new Pilgrims, Dan. We will rebuild. They did it, and with much less. We will do it again! With the help of each other and our Lord.

Take care! I don't have time for more now. Maybe one day we will be in touch again. God Bless."

—

Well, there goes Michael and contact with others. At least, we did not need to leave a big city and try to survive in the country. Roughly, we had that already. I checked the Facebook campaign; it was still going on but with no additional clicks. It was literally like a message in a bottle and sent to the good will of the ocean. Who knows who was going to pick that up, or when. Was I truly expecting to get another result like Michael's? That had already been amazing luck. Whoever was left alive in the world most probably has more urgent things to do than going to a Facebook page…if they even had Internet access.

Almost four months had passed and—slowly but surely—the world's technical prowess had started to regress, apart from some bubbles where things were kept alive with effort and continuous care...as we were doing at our place, getting ready for when we could only count on ourselves. Nonetheless, I planned to visit CERN for as long as everything there worked and keep checking for even the slimmest probability of finding evidence of more survivors.

I got back to the car and drove through the exit, on the Swiss side this time. There, the gate barrier was already raised for outgoing traffic. I slowed down. Right in front of the exit, on the other side of the road, there was the building complex hosting the control room and the main access to the underground facilities of the Atlas experiment. More out of an impulse than actual reasoning, I drove straight toward the compound. The barrier blocked the way. A single red and white bar that needed to be activated using a badge, which I did not have. Well, security was not an issue anymore. I drove slowly forward and made contact with the front of the SUV. The bar bulged, bent, then broke with a loud snapping noise.

I moved forward and reached the space in front of the underground access. A bit further down, an external metal staircase led to the control room in the main building that had the entire Atlas experiment frescoed on its wall in a geometrical perspective. From the road, it gave the illusion of a 3D representation of the entire huge detector. I got out. This time, I took the Benelli shotgun with me in addition to the Glock.

The moon was waxing crescent, and the crescent shape would continue to grow in the following days. The buildings casted a neat shadow but inside I would need a flashlight; especially if lights were not working for any reason. I advanced toward the metal staircase that goes all the way up to the control room at the very top. Even with all my care, every step resonated in the complete, pervasive silence.

I briefly stopped midway, then continued to the top. The door was closed; another badge lock. So I took my 'universal' badge, the Benelli, and stepped back as far as I could and aimed at the lock. I fired. It was the first time I had fired the Benelli in the dark and the effect had been powerful. The door must have felt the same as it slammed opened, almost kicked off its hinges. I pumped and reloaded the shotgun.

Inside, pitch dark. I pointed the flashlight into the corridor behind the door. Empty. With the flashlight in my left hand, I balanced the Benelli comfortably and walked in. I stopped: All was silent. I remembered that the door to the right led to the control room. I opened it and put the flashlight away. All monitors and computers screens were on and diffused enough light for my eyes to distinguish things clearly.

The room was quiet, and I realized it was because there were no computers inside. Just silent monitors relayed to computers located far away in a dedicated and separate clean room. That was the first time I'd seen this final setup. There was no one in the room that I could see so I lowered the Benelli and adjusted it at my back with its shoulder strap. I took the Glock, nonetheless.

I stepped further inside and discovered I wasn't truly alone as I thought. Should have realized it before. For, however faint, the slightly sweet and pungent smell of long-dead rotten bodies lingered in the room. I think my brain, when I got in, simply shunned and ignored things like smell, and even sound, to concentrate on everything visual. I was only now calming down a bit, after assessing the environment.

On the floor, behind the desks, were the dried remains of three technicians, or physicists, that had been on duty at the time. They were a little better preserved than the guard in the booth although they were pretty much just a bunch of bones, cartilage and dried skins on a skeletal support. Who knows, maybe I would have even recognized them if they were not at this stage of decomposition. Every corpse was far beyond visual identification.

Some of the monitors showed internal webcams down in the experimental areas. On one, I recognized details of the wire-chambers of the muon detector spectrometer in the underground area and those did not show the presence of any corpses. I had nothing more to see or to do there for the moment. I looked at my wristwatch; it was time to go home instead, postponing further exploration of the lab for other days.

Outside, my flashlight was of little use. My eyes were more than accustomed to the low light and the moon was a bit brighter, or so it seemed to me. I started to climb down slowly when my tinnitus grew louder and less chaotic at the same time. Similar to what happened to me when I had been woken up abruptly during the night because of a ringing phone, or when younger Annah screamed because of a nightmare.

On those occasions, the tinnitus volume increased, louder for a few seconds and with an additional lower frequency humming, only to subside again until the mostly incoherent hisses, whispered noises, and tunes became predominant again. Like the crushing of a single gigantic ocean wave on a sandy beach, the thump, the roar and the shock wave, the surf subsiding soon after, and the noise of millions of grains of sand and pebbles rolling against each other and screeching all along. Then, steady and regular as always, the violence before forgotten as if it had never occurred.

This time, though, it lasted and there were some regular modulations in both pitches and tunes that I never heard before. At the midway landing of the staircase, I turned around, instinctively, looking toward the car. I froze. There was a glow coming from the area giving access to the underground experimental area. I had parked right in front, and that was a glow I recognized. There was no possible mistake and I didn't know what to do. The glow pulsated irregularly.

I continued to climb down as quietly as I could and it took me some time to reach the last step. Right from the stairs, it wasn't possible to glance directly toward the access area. Side-stepping gave me a better view and then I saw them. There were four, similar to the entity who visited me when I was a child. From where I was, I could not distinguish any difference between them: clones of each other, each one glowing almost exactly as the others, although differently. Maybe it was their equivalent of human fingerprints? They were looking straight at me. Motionless. As if they were expecting me to come forward.

I knew, there and then, they had been waiting for me to come out. As many years before in my child bedroom, there we stood, not moving, with the additional discomfort of my now almost deafening tinnitus. Though that too was not exactly true; I could hear perfectly well. As if I had two separate hearing systems at work, with one not excluding the other. I was calm, unnaturally calm, and I recognized that old feeling. My rationality did not fight against it.

It was a stalemate situation unless I did something. The four entities were simply standing there, aware of my presence but not doing anything. No gestures or actions. Just standing and watching. Not exactly what I would call an encouraging reunion after so many years. Then it happened.

I startled. As if I got punched directly to my brain, I felt them. I say "felt" because I cannot use the term "heard", my physical ears did not perceive anything. Instead, my tinnitus almost disappeared and I received—yes, better word than *heard*—their superimposed messages: "Not now", "Later", "Too Soon", all forming in the 3D space around my head, a space the tinnitus had filled for so many years.

I stepped toward the car slowly, and I felt a wave of unspoken approval. Was I doing what I was expected to do in that moment? Was I receiving the approval for my behavior in the past months? Still staring at the four entities, I approached the car and opened the door. Under constant attentive and watchful scrutiny from them, I stepped in, started the engine, and drove away in a state of trance. The unnatural serenity slowly disappeared as I got farther away and an uncontrollable tremor engulfed me. I stopped the car at the border and watched in the rear mirror to see if any glowing entity followed behind. The only light came from the moon and the lamp posts.

My hands hurt; I was gripping the steering wheel so hard that my knuckles were all white. I let it go. Meanwhile, my tinnitus got back to its normal noise level and regular incoherence. I sweated. I had not been killed, I had not been abducted. I had been told it was too early. Too early for what? My shaking was under control again. I was elated and excited, yet at the same time troubled and scared: Maybe—finally—I had communicated with them! Or at least they knew how to communicate with me!

More dots from the past got connected, providing further explanations. Things fell into place, slowly, revealing a larger portion of our new reality. The entities were for real, and I did not have just a weird childhood dream. They were real. I stepped on the gas pedal and accelerated into the night. By the time I reached home, I grew resolute in keeping the whole incident to myself. "Not now," "Later," "Too Soon," were resonating and spinning around, helping in supporting that decision. I thought I would have received their approval for that decision, too.

Mary and Laura were waiting for me at the door; Annah

must have already been in bed. Taxi and Tarantula greeted me with their pure canine effusions; joy that allowed me to spend a moment alone and pretend I was relaxed.

"We were worried. Mary was about to call you but you left your phone at home. Next time I'll go with you…you're sweating, aren't you?"

Laura was sincerely worried, but I was married to another woman and Mary hadn't said anything yet. Then she asked, "So. How was it at CERN?"

She didn't sound that interested. The impression that it was just for her to say something, anything, struck me as a slap to an innocent kid. As soon as she said it, Mary's expression changed to a quizzical frown as her tone must have felt odd to her, too. I glanced at her but she did not look back at me.

I told both about the room full of old public access PCs but that they still worked. Then about Michael's last message and most probably his last one; that he and his group had decided to go to Pennsylvania, trying to found a new rural community, helping each other rebuild…whatever that meant. Things in New York had deteriorated, and faster than here apparently. We were not in the same hurry to leave and find a new place, we were rural enough where we were. Even if more people were to join us, probably the best short-term solution would have been to occupy Joe and Beth's house rather than going anywhere else.

I was not so keen about leaving what we had already achieved, unless it was for something certain to be better. Even if power were to disappear, we still had the generators, and the basement was packed with supplies of all kinds. We could even continue to run fridges and freezers down there. Besides…"Not Now," "Later," "Too Soon." What did they mean?

"I am sure there are others alive somewhere," Laura said. "But for now we should think of our world as if we were the only ones, and adapt!"

She stressed that last word and looked at Mary. Something happened while I was away, but I couldn't figure out or guess what. Later, when Laura left, and I was alone with Mary, I tried to understand the subtle change I felt when I got back home. I didn't get anything specific from Mary, just that they were worried because I was there, at the lab alone, and they had nothing to do but wait. Nor could they reach me:

"Why did you leave the phone at home?"

"I'm sorry. I guess because I left in a hurry. I didn't think it would take that long."

"Doesn't matter. The important thing is you're here now...Do you like Laura?"

That came unexpectedly as she asked the question abruptly and out of context. Her eyes were fixed on me, trying to read the answer from my face rather than hearing it from my voice.

"Why, yes...of course. I think we have been lucky with her. Besides, she goes fantastically well with Annah. And not just Annah, to tell the truth. I think she is bringing a lot to everyone here."

Mary kept looking intensely at me. I straightened up and ran a hand through my hair. She followed my gesture with her eyes.

"Indeed I like her too," she said. "She is bright and full of energy. She is young...and she likes you, too."

Now I was sure there was something I wasn't at all aware of. Uncomfortable, as when at school I knew the teacher was about to ask me something I hadn't revised, waiting for the blow to strike and be sent back to my seat with a bad note.

"What do you mean? What's going on?"

"Nothing, nothing!" Mary replied, too rapidly to be true. "I agree with you, she is bringing a lot to everyone. I meant nothing else."

I couldn't get more from Mary that night, maybe another day. I knew I was turning around a crucial point but Mary erected a wall of avoidance and resorted to reply with banalities of everyday tasks. That was not like her.

"Mary, I love you. I do love you. Never forget that."

"I know. And I love you, too…in this different world, even more." Mary caressed me, lovingly and with nostalgia, as if I was about to leave forever…or she was.

I was troubled, too troubled to go to bed and sleep. I told Mary and went downstairs where I grabbed an Esplendidos that had come from the Davidoff shop in town. Now, my practically infinite personal supply of cigars. I filled a glass with Caol Ila Islay whiskey, one of my favorites, and went outside.

Taxi and Tarantula laid in their kennels, half asleep. They raised their heads, alerted when I went out. I shushed them gently but firmly, and patted their heads. No, it wasn't time for an impromptu stroll. "Be good guys, lay down and stay still!" They yawned and drifted back to sleep.

I sat comfortably on the terrace, lit my cigar, and gulped a mouthful of whiskey. My mind was spinning fast, though no clearly formulated thoughts were queuing up at my brain's door. I was confused.

Honestly, the confusion had set in months ago. The world had changed and it was changing still. And now I saw *them* again, too. We needed to adapt, Laura had said. Hadn't we adapted already? Wasn't it enough? What was she really saying? Sure it was in relation to Mary.

I looked around, mentally noting all the things that were not visible from my lawn chair: our supplies in the basement, the shooting range we built, the nearby hardware store, our gas storage in Joe's tool shed. We did adapt, didn't we? *We did adapt!* I shouted mentally, as if someone was indeed able to hear my thoughts.

Laura was still awake. I could see the light in her cottage. Her door opened and she peeked outside. Just before I could say anything, she saw me and stepped back inside. She closed the door, gently. I stayed there with my hand half-raised in a missed greeting and feeling odd. A few seconds later, I heard the door being locked. The window shades were open and only a transparent veil impeded a clear view of her bedroom inside.

Her silhouette appeared at the window and she began to undress...slowly. It was impossible she didn't realize I could see her. She was suggestive in her movements, a sensuous disrobing that Laura prolonged with carefully chosen delays. A teasing show put on just for me. Laura covered her breasts with her hands when she took off her top, then began to caress herself between her legs. Though I only imagined this last part as I could not see below her belly from where I sat, I didn't dare stand up for a better view. I held my breath multiple times. Left alone in the ashtray, the cigar consumed itself and released dancing spirals of smoke sinuously seducing the moonlight.

Pliny the Elder wrote that a nude woman can lull a storm out at sea by stripping. I knew exactly what he meant. The light went off in the cottage and, shortly after, I could hear Laura moaning. She was…masturbating, leaving me with my galloping and fervid imagination. I swallowed my whiskey. I was excited, too.

The sun shone bright that day. Summer had definitely set in, even if it was only late May. In the distance, the Alps were perfectly visible, the air crystal clear. Even the weather seemed to be following a different pattern than the usual one. That morning, I had a bit of trouble looking Laura in her eyes. Instead, she gazed at me quite thoroughly, and intensely. Annah was happy; summer and school holidays would soon come. She complained Mom made her study even more than when she was at school for real, and Mary was cheerful because her yearly spring allergy was abating.

"Annah, get ready for our lessons. I'll join you upstairs in a second," urged Mary—"and you two, leave us alone. Go for your patrolling and we'll see you at lunch. If you have no preferences, I'm planning to have lasagna today."

"Wonderful." I could not contain myself. Mary had always been great in the kitchen.

"You sure you don't want any help with that?" added Laura as I left to get Taxi ready.

"I am sure," I heard Mary reply. Then she said, "No, Dan. Please leave Taxi home. Yesterday, Tarantula was very nervous and today we have a lot of new stuff to study. It was difficult for Annah to pay attention with all that whining. Maybe Tarantula will behave better if Taxi is home with her."

I turned to look at Mary with a quizzical expression stamped on my face. Was about to reply when Laura grabbed my hand and pulled me.

"C'mon, big boy. Don't delay the school schedule. Don't worry, I'll be there to protect you."

She laughed and exchanged a mocking glance with Mary who gestured me to hurry up and, then, gave me a long kiss. Her eyes beaming into mine, glued, as if she were seeing me for the last time.

— o —

We had three rally points in Geneva, in addition to nearby villages. Laura always hoped that, with time, others would come across her messages. She regularly kept increasing the radius we covered, arguing that the only reason we did not find other people yet was because I limited myself to just a few miles away from home: "Imagine if everyone were doing as you did," she once said laughing. "No one would ever know of the existence of others!"

She probably had a point but I did not intend to discourage her, or be accused of negative thinking and defeatism by discussing the theory of a discrete uniform distribution. We were not a known, finite number of equally spaced survivors equally likely to have been spared. I had little hopes of finding anyone nearby, especially after such a long time. By then, it was hard to visit all rally points in a same week. Hope is what keeps you going, even when all the odds are against you. Besides, I liked the passion Laura put into everything she did, and also enjoyed her presence around me.

"Let's go to Geneva first," she said once in the car. Radiant and gleaming, eager to leave, as if we were about to go to a party.

I was amused and bemused, and her enthusiasm was contagious. I smiled. She was alarmingly beautiful that morning. Especially after the evening before whose images still teased me. If she wore mini-shorts, I would have said I was riding with Lara Croft next to me. She had on tight, low-waisted workout pants, and a tee-shirt. Both as revealing as they could be. Between her legs, she kept the bag she used to carry the leaflets she edited for the "people out there" along with the heavy duty staple gun. That thing was able to shoot a big staple into anything. We crossed the border quickly and reached Meyrin.

"Did you ever drive a Ferrari, Dan?"

"Huh?" Where did that come from? "A Ferrari? Nope. Never had the chance. Why?"

"What prevents us now?" She said, smiling with the naughty expression of a very bad girl. Teaser, again!

Geneva was a wealthy city and luxury cars never lacked in town. Right there, a Ferrari and Maserati dealership had its showroom just five minutes from the airport.

"Turn there," she said swiftly. Too surprised to reply, I did instinctively as she said.

"Keep going and, at the next crossing, turn right again."

I knew where she was taking me. In no time, we were in front of Modenas, one of the official Ferrari dealers in Geneva, probably the largest one. In its parking lot, right in front of the showroom, there were two Bentley Continental GTC 6.0 convertibles, plus enough Ferraris to make any male drool in awe. We got out and Laura seized my hand, pulling me toward the showroom windows.

"Look!"

I didn't need any encouragement.

There were a number of Ferrari 612s, a 599 GTB

Fiorano, a GTO, and the new Ferrari Four. I could not take my eyes off those beauties and I wondered about the sensations I'd get from driving those mechanical jewels.

Unbelievably, I felt like a kid in front of a candy store, hands pressed against the glass. Laura profited from my trance to disappear, unseen, into a red-walled cubic tunnel next to us that acted as the entrance to the showroom. Suddenly, I heard a couple of shots that awoke me from my daydreaming. Laura was missing. I ran toward the tunnel and, expecting the worst, my hand reached for the Glock.

Laura had already stepped into the showroom, doors wide open, glass shattered on the floor. She was sparkling and waiting for me.

"Laura!" My heart resumed beating.

"What?" Laura smiled in excitement. I went to join her but she left to search for the dealer's office. I noticed mute alarm devices blinking furiously because of our intrusion. I ignored them: No one would be coming to check what we were doing.

The showroom was large, boasting a sleek design along with an impressive display of cars. An open bar area was ready to welcome wealthy customers; I guess one must deserve a flute of champagne while waiting for such a brand new baby.

A panel informed the visitors that they were at the largest showroom in Europe, with 6,600 square meters exposition surface and a permanent show of the most exceptional cars from the Maranello brand. A rapid calculation gave me 71,000 square feet. Wow, huge indeed! The panel also explained that customers were able to configure any car to their liking on a multitude of touch terminal displays and a member of the staff would love to accompany them for a test drive.

"Dan!" Laura called from an adjoining workshop area. Pulled reluctantly away from my car dreams and dream cars, I followed her voice. I found her in the back garage area with a few keys in her hand and the sexiest posture one could ever imagine. My memory saw her in front of her window, naked. I sighed. She already had the workshop's large barrier open into the private parking lot.

"We just need to check which key opens which car. Come!" She threw a bunch at me and ran to try the rest on the nearest Ferraris. I thought we were out of our minds, but it was fun and thrilling.

Triumphantly, she turned the key on a roofless red Ferrari SA Aperta. While I watched in awe, she pushed the start button on the steering wheel and the four-valve V12 engine came alive. Pure mechanical ecstasy. And the sound... the perfect sonic expression of its powerful 670 hp engine.

"In the standard configuration, that is."

Laura corrected me. I had thought out loud without realizing it. I got in the passenger seat and watched Laura setting the switch on the right to the 'race' setting.

"How do you know this?"

"Ferrari's? I love them and this is the most powerful roadster they make. A 6-gear, V12 takes you from zero to 100 km/h in about three and a half seconds."

I must have showed incredulity, or my mouth simply must have remained open. I was speechless. Laura laughed, then she smiled knowingly:

"One of my ex's was crazy about Ferraris."

"One of your ex..." *Lucky guy.* The thought rushed through my mind like an avalanche and it wasn't about the Ferrari.

She handled the gear paddle, shifted gear, and we were off.

"Hold tight now!" She warned as she drove out of the parking lot and back to the street.

I was in awe about the car, in awe about her, in awe about everything. We reached the straight four-laned main road that connected Geneva to Meyrin and to the airport. There she stopped, right in the middle. The engine had the most beautiful sound ever and the exhaust note was pitch perfect. She pumped the gas pedal a few times and the engine roared. It seemed we were in pole position for a race.

"Look at this." She pointed at something on the left of the steering column. A silver plate with an F1 silhouette Ferrari camped with the inscription "31 Formula 1 World Titles" and the matricula number of the car itself. I nodded, *Pretty cool*, I thought.

"Ready?" Before I could even reply she launched the car. Oh my... Jeez! I was literally in a bullet. The Ferrari roared, and the acceleration slammed me against the seat. Laura was gleaming and screamed in pure joy. We reached 100 km/h in no time and got to 240 soon after while I held tight to the middle handle bar. Now I know why engineers put it there. It was a pure magical moment. I screamed in turn.

An epic wail emanated from the exhaust pipes. Fantastic! The wind roared and my vision tunneled narrowly with the increasing speed. The road shrunk to a slim tape of asphalt.

My soul got possessed by the gods of speed.

In a few seconds, the possession was over. We covered the straight mile stretch and fast approached the interchange. Laura geared down and slowed the car. We reached the end of the strip and my heart was pumping hard. She stopped the car and jumped off like a fauve, a breathtaking wild animal.

"Your turn now!" she said defiantly.

I jumped out, excited, and started toward the driver's side. Laura walked the opposite way and blocked me in front of the car, her hand on my chest. Without a word, she pulled me to her inviting lips and kissed me furiously. No, she was eating me, and pressed her body hard against me. I lost my balance from the surprise, the excitement, the loss of breathing. We landed on the hood of the Ferrari, warm and vibrant under me. I gasped.

"Laura. Oh my God, Laura…Wait!"

"Now, Dan, now. Please now." Her hands got busy with my belt. My brain erupted in flames and I started to hyperventilate.

"Laura! Mary!" I grabbed her arms and managed to hold her over me and, for a second, stop her frenzied lust to which, I knew, I was about to succumb at any moment. She looked at me with her dazzling blue eyes, wide open in her fevered assault.

"Idiot…she already knows." My grip weakened and she took advantage, forcing herself down and kissing me again with passion and paroxysm.

"She knows, she knows." Those two words hit me and crushed all reluctance while my body screamed, "Yes, yes!" Laura took off her tee-shirt, revealing her breasts. Her nipples were hard and aroused. She unzipped my trousers and helped me pull them down; Laura pulled down her workout pants, too. Naked underneath, she grabbed me and guided me inside her.

"Oh God, oh God."

She was so warm and tight, and she was so beautiful. Inside her, nothing mattered anymore. Her perfect breasts filled my vision. Her face was in ecstasy as I was. She kissed me in wild excitement and moaned. That excited me even more, if that was possible. Every muscle ached, and I gripped her whole body with strength. I feared I was going faster than the damned Ferrari, like a kid at his first time and got worried I would soon miss a beat. We were both terribly excited and frightened and hopeful and doubtful. Everything mixed and at the same time. Laced together, beaded with sweat, swallowing her tongue and getting lost in her warm sweetness.

"Oh…slower, but don't stop, don't stop!"

Laura reached down with one hand and images of what happened the night before filled my mind.

She was pulsating hard around me and brought me rapidly to paroxysm with the last few powerful moments. I tightened my arms around her and bit her neck. Laura screamed and pulled herself aside. She grabbed me and, before I could protest, she gave me the most intimate kiss until I couldn't resist anymore.

Laura then crawled up to me and rested her beautiful body over my chest, panting. She was breathless and I was still gasping. My head was spinning and dizzy. I was emptied and drained—physically and emotionally—and my mind was invaded with mixed feelings and a burning sense of guilt about Mary. The conscience hurt while everything else floated in nirvana.

"Oh my God, Dan. You can't imagine how I feel. It has been so long…"

I caressed her. Laura was truly beautiful and I had developed a sincere affection for her. I guess it was more than I admitted myself as I wasn't prepared for this. I began to understand recent events. How Mary and Laura's complicity had grown over the last month…and last night. I kissed her tenderly. "She knows!" echoed in my mind.

"You planned all this, right? I mean, both of you."

"Mary knew you wouldn't notice anything until the last minute. You are such a nice boy." She chuckled. "It is a different world, Dan. I think I love you, and I love Mary and Annah, too. And you are probably the only man around, and will be for who knows how long."

"And Mary accepts all this?"

"Not at first. Then she understood. I told her, I would have never ever tried anything with you, or seduced you." She paused. "I would have left, Dan. One day, I would have left you all."

I listened to her and so I understood why Mary seemed to have changed. Her questions and her glances, the brief looks at me and Laura, the allusions I refused to consider or take into account, and her sober mood at times. It must have been around the time Mary decided or when Laura told her. All started to coalesce into a meaningful structure. Like when you see the hundreds of pieces of a do-it-yourself furniture kit: It is a mess until you get your hands on the instructions. Then, the sequential order makes sense, and you can see the final product through the thousands of pieces scattered on the floor.

"She is a fantastic woman, Dan."

"That she is. Before, you said she knows? About today?"

"Yes, keeping Taxi at home, the Ferrari." She chuckled again. "We have planned everything."

"And yesterday?"

"Yesterday…sort of. It was a lucky coincidence. I saw you on the terrace so I improvised. Mary told me you are a good man and that I would have to really seduce you. Otherwise, you would have resisted, or forced yourself not to notice anything."

She laughed gently and cheerfully. "Would you have resisted, Dan?"

"Laura…" I had no words. I didn't know whether to feel outraged, happy, flattered, or what.

"By the way, the Ferrari is our gift. From Mary and I with love."

"The Ferrari…part of the plan too, huh?" I felt like an idiot talking about all that with a beautiful and naked young woman, languidly resting over me and caressing me.

"Weren't you surprised by how fast I got in, found the right keys, had the workshop garage door open and all the rest?"

"What if I had found a working key before you?"

"You couldn't." She said, chuckling and smiling knowingly.

"Okay, I give up." This time I chuckled, too.

Then, Laura continued more seriously. "Ah, yes. If we

go back home with the Ferrari, Mary will know and there will be no urgent need for you to talk or discuss anything. She loves you, Dan, and she doesn't want you to feel guilty. Neither do I."

I knew all this had been done with the best possible intentions but...

"Maybe I don't feel guilty. I mean, why was I not part of this…process? After all, I had to have an active role in it. Or am I wrong?"

Laura said nothing.

"I feel a bit used, Laura. So…Mary essentially gave you the permission to seduce me? What am I? A sex toy? To you both?"

"You are taking it all wrong now, Dan."

"Fine. Then explain it to me, Laura."

"What do you think? That it is just about sex? Mary loves you profoundly. And selflessly. You said many times we all have a duty to survive. Well, open up your ears and clean out your eyes, Dan. Mary is surviving, I am surviving and, if you do not understand this, maybe Mary was wrong in holding you in such high esteem."

She said that without taking a breath and she wasn't finished. Her face turned red when she filled her lungs.

"What are you talking about, permission? What Mary has done is the greatest proof of love she could give you, and to me, to us all. What do you think I am? A slut looking for sex? I saw you, and Mary, and your love. And started to love you as well, for who you are, not for what you have between your legs! Any other man—"

"There isn't any other man, Laura!"

She burst into tears and punched me on my chest and face and slapped me, waving her arms hysterically and screaming at a high pitch. I struggled to stop her and managed to grab her arms before she hurt herself. Laura resisted forcefully, fiery and hot like the fauve she compared herself to.

"Wowowow, Laura! Stop, stop, calm down... shhhh... calm down... "

I succeeded in containing the fury and held her tight until she relinquished. My voice lowered to a whisper in her ear.

"It's alright, Laura. I know of all the suffering. I know of the void and the pain, and I know of Mary's tears and imagine yours, too."

I kissed her hair and her cheeks. Laura started to sob and shake—and finally—she totally and gently abandoned herself into my arms, letting me fully embrace her.

"Laura, Laura. Young and lovely, Laura. I am sorry, I am sorry..." I raised her chin to look into her swollen, beautiful and so vulnerable eyes:

"I am just scared, Laura. I am scared I will not be able to love you both and that I would lose you both! I forced myself not to think about you. Because I love Mary and because there is Annah. That is a role I know how to fulfill. Now, I don't know where I am going to..."

She seemed to me even younger than she actually was. Laura was tearful. "Can't you love us both? Mary and me?" She seemed lost and afraid of my answer.

Lovely Laura...so strong and so fragile, too. And Mary, how has she been able to keep all this to herself? I couldn't imagine the struggle and the inner strength that required. I am not sure I would have been able to do the same if the situation were reversed.

The old world clashed with the new world and the old order made no sense in the new. What was right before was not necessarily the right thing to do now. Laura asked for love; to love and to be loved. And Mary, hers was the ultimate act of love and selflessness. I understood that. Who was I to elect myself judge, armed with old norms and morality and condemn what these two women had been capable of doing.

Laura had confessed her feelings to Mary and offered to leave us, preferring to put her life at risk, being alone, rather than hurting Mary and Annah. Yet Mary had changed and accepted the challenge, adapting to a new world and new needs. Better than I had done, and better than I would have imagined. She judged Laura worthy of love, worthy of her love even before mine, and spared me from all the grief and the hurting she instead must have been enduring on her own.

"I am only a man, Laura, and I will need your help. Yours and Mary's. Help me never to become a jerk, never to hurt any of you."

She hugged me and kissed me and cried even more, but those were different tears. She was radiant, like any woman who finally finds love.

"So, shall we go get the Volvo?" she said, drying her tears and giggling like a young girl. "I'll drive that one home." Before I could reply, she said, "And I love you, Dan." She kissed me. "Now drive this Ferrari. She is waiting for you."

I didn't know whether she referred to Mary or the car. I smiled. We quickly put our clothes back on, and soon I was behind the steering wheel of a Ferrari SA Aperta. My own Ferrari! I smiled at Laura, sitting next to me. So beautiful and, yes—in this new world—I could love and care for two women, and there was a chance it would be alright. The Ferrari responded forcefully to my commands; the steering was incredible and the sensation of power, incomparable. I didn't want to but it was irresistible: We screamed again, together.

We got home, as planned, Ferrari and all. Mary waited alone at the door when we pulled in, first the Ferrari then the Volvo. Mary smiled, knowingly. I felt a bit embarrassed, as a child who had been caught after some naughty tricks. I attempted a smile, too. Mary's widened and her eyes got misty. In my hesitation, Laura got out of the Volvo and preceded me. She and Mary hugged.

"Thank you," I heard Laura saying. "I love you, Mary." Timidly, I walked toward them; Laura moved aside and Mary hugged me.

"Mary…"

"Shhh…don't say anything. You love me, remember? And I love you, Dan. Only this counts."

Laura smiled and her beautiful, loving blue eyes were wet with tears, too.

"Wooooh!" Annah finally appeared at the front door. She ran out toward the Ferrari, ignoring everything and everyone. Now, we needed to think how to explain everything to Annah: Our family was evolving and changing...and adapting.

Part Four

New Paths

The dictionary says "deviant" is someone who "does not fit the conventions, ethical or behavioral, or social expectations of the group or the society in which he lives." Did we reach the point where our conventions and beliefs faltered? Which were our social expectations?

Ethics, right and wrong behaviors, social good and wisdom, its acceptance and refusal, all come from interacting with others. One has to confer with others on these things. How do we understand, know about them? How do we judge when we talk about what is right and what is wrong? Can moral judgments be capable of being objectively true? Do they depend on historical ages, or is it because they describe some evident feature of the world? Were the Romans righteous yet, when disabled, flung from the Tarpeian cliff to their death?

Which were now the evident features of the world, those of our historical age? Human population had practically disappeared, culled and purged by external entities who appeared to our senses as humanoid figures, glowing in nature and difficult to distinguish from one another. Most probably, humans were now so few and scattered that small groups would need to grow significantly from within before the chance to interact with other communities could ever materialize in the future.

If admitting our primary objective and duty was not to give up and disappear, like a blink in the planet's existence, then we needed to reinvent ourselves from the ground up. Were these not God's holy words: "That in blessing I will bless thee, and in multiplying, I will multiply thy seed as the stars of the heaven." Was there a new start? Was this the age to come? If so, what would be our role and destiny?

As for the entities—apart from the seemingly obvious role of being our executioners—what was their role in the future, and what did we need to wait for? Had I understood them correctly? Was I coming too early, was it too soon for them to deal with me, with us? Did they have expectations from us, and were we fulfilling them? And what if we weren't...

Whatever our choices, did we deviate from the expected path? Deviance is far from being synonymous with freedom. I have always wondered mercilessly if I was ever free in my choices, or was I simply reactive and a mere slave to my reactions? This is even more crucial an issue for younger ones, like Annah and Laura, because youth is the age of choices. Important choices that may give a direction to one's life or lead to another, terribly different one. Will they be given the time to make their own choices?

We thought about the directions our lives might take and the bubble of "normality" that I strived to maintain around us. What was normal or abnormal could not be derived from absolute ethics only or from the behavioral conventions of a society which was no more. We had the freedom to choose anew what was normal and ethical. Didn't we? Could we?

What was freedom now, really? Was it, for example, not to be influenced by the education we had received? By the conventions and morals of the previous world? Certainly not. If that is the case, we shall never start to read our first book or learn from the experiences of others.

Instead, we can and must talk about freedom as coming from the multiplicity, variety, and quality of different influences which can break the chains of our own beliefs and convictions. Freedom is for the curious ones. Free is the one not influenced by taboos. Free is the one who reasons and evolves continuously, and refuses to accept anything without thinking.

Freedom is that which comes from knowledge, the freedom that comes from curiosity, the freedom that comes from the times when the first man did not refuse to look into a telescope and discovered other planets, the freedom that comes from those who tried relentlessly when all others said it was impossible. It is in this freedom that deviance has its roots.

Long live the freedom of those who have been derided or insulted. Those who first thought photography was art, who first thought humans could fly—or even walk on the moon...those who dreamed about the future and made it the present. Freedom had always had an impact on the world. What happened with Laura certainly had an impact on me if my head was now filled with all these confused ideas and thoughts.

— o —

Annah accepted our enlarged family as soon as she understood it would not undermine her parent's relationship. Much later, the announcement that Laura was pregnant and Annah was going to have a little sister or brother made things even easier. Our family would grow. For me, that was also the trigger for not wanting to passively wait anymore for signals or events that might harshly affect our world as we knew it...survive and adapt.

During those weeks, I hadn't tried to get back in touch

with the entities, or to contact them. Yes, I saw them a few other times and always at CERN. On every occasion, I had the sensation that I should not approach them any further. Again, the unspoken messages were received that it was too early and I obeyed. Retreating every time, yet feeling increasingly distressed and finding it a more difficult thing to do.

I didn't share those encounters with the family, which now fully included Laura. I could not think of us all as 'free' when we could be just entertaining specimens of a disappearing species, part of a short-term experiment soon to be concluded when *they* grew tired of thinking about us. Specimens that could be discarded on a whim. So, whether or not it was the right time for those entities, it soon became the right time for me.

"I have seen them, Mary. Again," I said one afternoon.

Astonished stares greeted my words. Laura didn't know yet about my childhood experience with one of the entities; it was time to tell her, too.

She turned toward Mary. "Did you know that?"

"I was told only very recently and I was as shocked as you are. Dan is probably right. This is not something that happened or was decided abruptly."

"And what do you think?"

One of the problems of polygyny, I learned from direct experience, is that "wives" tend to talk to each other and to support each other in all moments. Sometimes it was a bit irritating but I never expressed my feelings or complained about it directly.

"I believe we must be part of something bigger. A larger

plan. Besides, you are pregnant, and in a few months we will need to get ready for your delivery. Maybe it is better to know now than later."

"What do we do if…" Laura did not finish the phrase, we all understood what she meant.

"I don't think they will harm me." I replied quickly. "They've had plenty of occasions to do that. Laura, we cannot continue pretending they are not here." I reminded them about Michael and his group in New York and that, as far as we knew, they too had not been bothered at all.

"As far as we know…" Laura stressed.

We reached a status quo where our lives were rather stable and secure. It was tempting, being ignored to continue ignoring. Very tempting. Living our lives undisturbed. At the same time, the knowledge that I could communicate with them, in some way, was paramount. From all that had happened, in the past and in the recent encounters, it seemed that it was not a hazard either. What became the most disturbing was the rather passive attitude I had adopted lately.

Sure, I had in mind first and foremost everyone's safety and, so far, everything had been just phenomenal for us. I was scared to lose what we had. Life surely would become more difficult for us in the near future, but for now…

Nature had gained ground and everything looked more primeval. Vegetation and weeds were growing where they had never been allowed to. Little wild animals had conquered more spaces. But apart from this? Nothing yet dangerous or disturbing. It was actually astonishing to see how a few months with no human activities had turned everything into a more rugged and rough scenario, and a more natural one, too. Taxi and Tarantula enjoyed that more than any of us. In the explorations of our vast territory, they loved hunting hares and rabbits found in our own neighborhood. No need to go into the woods anymore; the woods were coming to us.

But we were not alone and that was the strident note. It was not just us and the planet, us learning to share our space with the rest of all familiar living things. *They*, either visible or invisible, were a burden. A fearfully heavy presence. I could not ignore the fact they existed, we could not ignore them. And they were the only ones from whom we could receive answers and hope one day to understand what had been our fate and why.

Okay, I admit it. Although when near them I experienced a surreal calm, I was scared afterwards and left scarred. If they wanted to, I was sure they could end my life in no time as they had with all the others. I could be just a nuisance or soon become one: Who did I think I was to believe I was important to them? Maybe there were thousands like me in the world right now, some even better than I was in their eyes. I had no clue. All was supposition, a rough guess that I was somehow needed. I had nothing really to support that, apart from the fact they had paid a visit to me when I was a child. I had no directions. Stalemate.

Even when I used to play chess, I hated stalemate situations. I preferred to risk losing a game rather than aiming for or accepting a stalemate. I had the impression that the game was a failure if it ended as such. It had been years since I played my last chess game with a human being. The people I knew didn't play chess and my games were mostly against computers, rarely with players in chess forums. For all I knew, they could have used a computer, too, to play against me. I wasn't particularly good but I wasn't particularly bad either as I was able to provide enjoyable chess games. However, the one I played with our glowing wardens was not particularly enjoyable, at least for me. It was a stalemate I had to break.

— o —

From what Michael wrote about the entities, we could not hide from them. Somehow, no matter how concealed a human would be, it seemed impossible to stay out of their sight. That made the initial idea of having Mary come with me out of the question. I would have exposed her to an unnecessary risk. And Laura was pregnant so she was excluded, too.

Besides, Michael fired at them without any discernible and tangible result. What could Mary do then? No, better to confront them alone, and hope they had no reason to get rid of me, an annoying lower life form. I knew it had to be done, but how and when? Yes, we got scared just thinking of it. Scared to do it, scared not to do it. A stalemate to be broken. We spent days pretending everything was fine, and as soon as Annah was not around, we could see from each other's eyes that we thought about it all the time.

No doubts, I felt like the luckiest man on Earth and I probably was. We had reasonable prospects to live a comfortable life. I had the love of two women, my daughter, and a new child coming. Enviable, but we kept forgetting one factor. A fundamental one that urged me to break the stalemate rapidly: Annah.

Annah had started to hit some limits of her life. Growing up, it was inevitable. What chance did she have to live her life to its fullest? Very small. These were her concerns, and they took root in her and sapped her spirit. She was thirteen then, and she pictured a lonely future for herself. Living long enough to see us all dying and, in the end, taking care of the new child Laura carried. In Annah's teen-aged eyes, we were already old and our death was imminent and impending in her mind.

Regardless—to her—she was heading inexorably toward loneliness. A future she started to fear as worthless and scary. I took care to spend time alone with her, whenever possible, even just for a leisurely stroll together with the dogs. That day we were talking about the baby. Possible names, which of her toys she could give him or her...then, her mood suddenly and abruptly worsened.

"Dad, do you think I'm pretty?" she asked, and immediately added, "Never mind, I will never be in love anyway."

In a normal world, I would know what to say to reassure her. I would talk about the fears of first loves and first discoveries, when a single look is strong enough to make you blush or bring you joy and hope. When a smile is large enough to promise all mysteries will be revealed, the pains and the strong emotions, the warm fuzzes of first loves. But there and then? How could I tell my daughter about falling in love, finding a young man who would cherish her more than his own life, that she will feel the same immense happiness I felt when she was born? Annah's words—*I will never be in love*—hit me with extraordinary strength.

"Sweetheart, I don't know and you don't know. I can't tell when it will happen, but it will happen." My heartbeat accelerated. "I know we are not the only ones alive, but your life will follow other paths than mine or your mom's. I would be lying to you if I told you any differently."

"There is no one, Dad. You tried, Laura is trying, there is no one. Or too far away as Michael is. Mom has you, even Laura now has you. There is no one for me."

"Annah. We will always be here for you."

I regretted saying it immediately when she cried out, "Dad! Don't treat me like a baby. I am thirteen! It is not that! I am talking about being together, having my own life one day. I will never have what you have...you, Mom, Laura. And she even said she wanted to be my big sister!"

Annah burst into tears and walked away from me. I knew even too well what she meant, and that it would be more and more hurtful growing up. She did not deserve that.

"Annah! Annah...Laura loves you, and you know it. This is not the end of it. There are others, and I will find them! We will find others. There must be others. It will take time but I will find them."

"How can you know for sure, Dad? How?"

"It has to be, Annah. It has to be..." But it was impossible for me to look at my daughter and say that.

There was no way to know unless I confronted them. If I met them years before, as I had, who knows how long they'd already been among us. Watching, testing us, getting ready for what happened. Maybe, I was not the only one they had visited in the past; maybe, we were part of something much bigger. It had to be, I truly believed it had to be. I needed to hope it was. Otherwise, everything would have been meaningless, cruel, and mindless.

What I hadn't considered was that sparing us could've arisen from a mere lack of concern. As when a boy stomps on an ant nest and destroys everything, just because, to see what happens. Kills most of the ants, disregarding those still alive. Digging up the underground lair to discover the inner chambers, smashing the larvae. Interested for a while, then leaving behind havoc and destruction without any additional thoughts about the struggling few left.

Were we like ants to them? It couldn't be! They had spoken to me, they appeared in front of me when I was a child. *I was no ant! I was no ant!* I repeated in the attempt to convince myself that there was going to be continuity, a new start. For Annah, even for us as a race. I returned home with a sober Annah, but with a firm resolution.

I took Mary and Laura aside. They did not like the idea of having me out there at night, chasing those entities, but they could not think of any different plan or how to make me change plans.

"So you would rather stay put and wait, living in doubt? We have found our golden cage, is that it?" I asked.

"But aren't you thinking about Laura? She is pregnant, Dan. What if something happens to you?"

"Mary, what if anything happens to you, or Laura, and Annah? What if anything happens to any of us? Then it is over! The end of everything. Everything, Mary! Is that what you are wishing for us? I don't. I cannot believe you could envisage that for us. And then? They have no future: We will not live forever, Mary. What will happen to Annah and the baby? Mary, it cannot go on this way!"

Then, I said it. "I think they did something to my brain when I was a child. A preparation for these times."

"What do you mean?"

"I think I can talk to them. Communicate, rather."

"What?" Both Mary and Laura responded at almost the same time.

I told them what happened to my tinnitus in their presence; that I felt thoughts forming in my head. Not like real voices, but they were patently not my thoughts.

"Maybe it is deeper than that. I can't explain it any better. I never experienced telepathy, but I think that's probably what it is. My senses are not involved, something else is at play!" I took a deep breath. "I mean, this is beyond everything imaginable, Mary. I am not scared about myself, you know me. I hesitated because of you all, but there is no more time to waste!"

I told them about the discussion I had with Annah. She was the future; the baby Laura was carrying was the future; and we had to know, for them, what future we were going to send them to. Maybe to no future at all, but at least we would try to do something about it. I would chase those entities and, this time, I would not back off quietly like an obedient and scared puppy.

We spent the whole night together, something that had never happened before. I could not leave either of my women alone. The next day, no one mentioned what we had talked about even as I prepared myself to spend the following nights away. I didn't know how long it would take, and the entities were not at CERN on a regular basis.

If not CERN, maybe they were attracted by other technology sites, too? There were a couple electrical plants not too far from the lab and bio-med firms were established in the region. There was also a reactor facility at the EPFL, the technology institute in Lausanne, and there was the

Superphenix reactor in nearby France. It was shut down then but the nearby Bugey nuclear plant was probably still active, and only some 25 miles away from Geneva. I would travel there, too. I only had to hope that, now that I wanted to find them, they would not hide from me. After CERN and Lausanne, and other nearby sites, my best bet would have to be Bugey.

That same evening I kissed all my girls goodbye, ensured they were safe, and left. Not that easy to leave though as there were unanswered questions in their eyes. Annah did not know all the details but knew or understood I was leaving to keep my promise to her, to find other people, and that was enough. Mary and Laura listened to all my reasons and reassurances and tried to show they were strong, but their eyes betrayed them. They looked at me as if it was going to be our last time. Taxi and Tarantula would stay home with them, of course.

"I will be back. I am only spending the night out, then tomorrow I will be home. Don't worry."

Their smiles were forced. And, in my heart, I knew it would have been too much to hope for, that all I needed was to spend one more night at CERN. I actually thought it was useless, that *they* would rather show up when they decided to. But the stalemate had to be broken, one way or another.

— o —

I reached CERN and spent the night there, visiting all experimental areas and workshops...waiting. Thinking, *I am here*, yet feeling stupid all the same. Nothing happened; I saw no one, no glowing, no lights. While exploring the site more thoroughly, I found more corpses than anywhere else in town or in the nearby villages. Proof that the laboratory was indeed a 24/7 facility as there were always people on duty in the various stations.

Judging from their clothing and general appearance, some must have been young Ph.D. students working on their thesis. What a waste of lives and talents. With some distress, I fought away images of an enormous foot stomping on the human ant lair we were. As with everyone else, they had been caught while busy at their own duties at the lab. Death had come suddenly and struck all at the same time.

People had died at their desks, in front of still lit instruments, working at some detector prototype, or monitoring cryogenics. No one had time to run or hide. It had been so sudden. How? I wandered as a ghost among ghosts, all of them screaming at me, asking me to find out why they had to disappear. Their voices, myriads of voices, assaulted me like a swarm of angry bees: "Why?!"

Worn out from a sleepless night, I got back home at the first light of day. Mary and Laura greeted me as if I had come back from war. I had little to share but the desolation and the emptiness I felt all night. I needed to rest, at least for a few hours. I took a shower that was unable to wake me up and crashed into bed. Laura came to get me; lunch was ready. She sat on the bed and held me in her arms lovingly and, for a moment, she lulled me. Without knowing it, she repeated the same urging words Mary had told me before.

"I cannot lose you. What would I do, Dan? We would not survive," she said, placing one hand on her belly.

"It won't happen. I can't explain it, but I am sure it won't happen."

"Dan, we didn't have time to say goodbye to anyone. To

anyone, you understand?"

I nodded, and I had no words to console her.

I wasn't yet accustomed to our situation. I loved both Mary and Laura, and I couldn't prevent myself from thinking about Laura when I was with Mary, and about Mary when I was with Laura. I had to tune my feelings properly so as to be fully with Laura when Laura was with me, and fully with Mary when alone with Mary. No matter how odd it seemed, to be entirely with Laura and Mary when I was with both, everyday, in every situation. Change, adapt, survive.

It was a warm June day and we planned to spend a restful afternoon together. I wanted to stay with all of them. Breathing them, playing with Annah and the dogs, caressing Laura's womb and kissing Mary, and everything at the same time. I was hungry, and wanted to taste everything as if I had not much time left. "Oh Lord, if you are there, make it so that nothing will be lost." I didn't know whether I had to say instead, "Oh gods, since you are there…" I wasn't sure of Him alone anymore.

Evening came again, and again I got ready to spend one more sleepless night out. I headed back to the lab, for the third time now. And then, if unsuccessful as with the previous nights, the next day I would make the trip to the EPFL facility. The night would be very long, immeasurably so. It was not yet time to find sleep, and I could still hold out until the bright dawn. If only they could hear me speak, there or wherever I would be, about the human suffering they had caused. If only there was a chance for me to ward off this disgraceful devastation and have hope for a future.

I reached the lab, entering from the main gate. There was no way to favor a single building over any other. First, I again visited the places where I had seen them previously.

There were no glowing lights, anywhere. I wandered from one area to another in the faint luminosity of the sparse electric light poles. I never felt so much grief as during that particular night. There was possibly one thing worse than hostility: indifference. Had they left and returned to where they'd come from? Not now, not when it was time for everything to start over.

The entities didn't show up and dawn came as an insult, a statement to our own insignificance. My heart was pounding and I felt as if they had killed us all again because of their indifference! "Not now," resonated in my mind. But if not now, when? What had to happen before we were judged worthy again of consideration? When dawn came, I wept. I wept because of our fate in the hands of those who had already decided our destiny, and had decided to kill billions of us. I found myself on my knees, tasting my own warm and salty tears.

The sky was clear, and I watched the sun rise over the mountains where a golden light had lingered before it appeared. In ancient times, it was the Sun god that granted another day to the mortals, renewing its promises. Now, who were the gods ruling our lives? I had deceived myself about surviving and changing. There was no adaptation in my efforts to continue...I was only delaying our demise.

Annah's grief was a grief for us all. We had no future staying, we had no future leaving. One man, two women, a girl, and—soon—a newborn baby. These were not enough seeds for mankind's second chance.

I think I learned the true meaning of desperation that morning in June. I felt we had no hopes, and that we were without options. Around us, the world was beautiful; it, too, indifferent to the fate of men. The valley was resplendent.

Birds singing more than ever now that their songs were not interrupted by the harsh and inappropriate noises people arrogantly produced. And the birds sounded so happy.

It was hard to accept what had happened, and it always will be. I felt numb and had trouble believing that the massive loss of human life had really happened on a global scale. What if all that was left were literally a few small groups, like ours and Michael's, on the entire planet? If that were so, then everything would be accomplished and done in a few more years. The fate of men sealed under the watch of indifferent gods after having vented their rage on us. Emptiness, despair, yearning, and deep loneliness grabbed my heart and squeezed it.

The morning haze disappeared fast, and I had lost track of time. The sun was high in the sky so Mary and the others were surely awake by then. With a mourning soul I stood up, aching like a very old man, and returned home.

— o —

Opening the gate, I felt guilt and anger over things I did or didn't do. Guilt for whoever did nothing to prevent the deaths, even if there was nothing anyone could have done. Could I have imagined all this when I saw *them* as a child? Had anyone else seen them, too? Did someone know more? Even if the devastation was nobody's fault directly, I was angry and resentful. Angry at myself, and at God...and at Joe and Beth. At all who had died so easily and abandoned us. But I had no one to blame for what was done to us. I had no one to ask except the glowing gods that were not appearing anymore. I feared our own mortality: Of having to endure life without Mary, or Laura and Annah, and about the responsibilities we now faced alone.

The ladies had prepared for my return, setting up breakfast on the patio. How normal everything seemed. As if nothing had ever happened, they struggled to make everything cheerful. This was a catastrophe without any of the connotations of a catastrophe. I felt Mephistopheles wrap his arm around my shoulders. Mary and Laura saw my distress and came to me, angst in their eyes. I stopped their questioning.

"I am fine. There is no one, I saw no one, and I…"

I didn't know how to continue. I must have looked dreadful. Laura took my hand and Mary surrounded my face with hers. She looked straight in my eyes, as she always did.

"Dan, it is not your fault. Maybe they'll show up again."

"Yes, Dan, don't lose faith. If you do…"

I knew what Laura meant. If I gave up, what would happen to them? There were more ways for them to lose me than just physically. Probably more cruel ways than if anything fatal happened to me.

"You are both right, but I am tired. Maybe it's just that."

"Come now, rest a bit. You are not alone, Dan. This is not a weight you need to carry on your shoulders alone."

They both pulled me to a lawn chair and lovingly took care of me. I didn't want to go inside. I wanted to have them and Annah around me; seeing them and listening to their chatting. Yes, I longed for noises, for things that broke the silence, a silence as heavy as lead. Tension and grief started to disappear, my tears became their tears, and they took my pain on them and dissolved it. Taxi and Tarantula approached and rested their heads on my laps. After that, I fell asleep.

The weather changed in the next few days, and it rained a light but persistent rain. I gave up my forced schedule of visiting technology sites as the hope to meet with the entities there was slim. After all, nothing supported the hypothesis that they favored those places rather than others. In the end, the plan was just a wild shot in the dark. It could—or it could not—bring any results. Mary and Laura agreed that, if everything was as I told them, it was more probable for the entities to get back in touch with me rather than the opposite.

Spending those nights at home was good for the morale, especially when daily visits to CERN and checking for contacts via email or via the Facebook ad campaign had produced nothing. Life at home had a pleasant and regular flow made up of looking after daily chores, caring for the vegetable garden, and maintaining our efforts and commitment to create occasions for whoever could still be alive in the region to get in touch with us. And staying together. Pure and simple.

Laura's pregnancy had been uneventful so far, and she was able to keep up with the regular pace of our scouting activities. Sometimes, it was a casual outing, just to stay together. We visited places we didn't know before and took lunch with us to spend the day outside. The world was magnificent that summer. Daylight at our latitude lasted quite long so, often, bed time came when it was still bright outside. We didn't mention the entities at all those days. The grief and the sadness were almost forgotten: We had all we needed, and more than anything else, we had each other.

It was only after the end of June that I resolved to go to Lausanne and visit the EPFL. Maybe it was simply due to a full recovery of my moral strength. Everyone kind of agreed with the decision: In everyone's mind, the belief that the entities were not a danger had grown somewhat stronger.

On the evening chosen for the plan, I left home around 9:30pm so as to arrive about an hour later at the laboratories when the lazy night had yet to fall and I would still have a bit of lingering twilight before dusk. I drove toward the highway, not knowing what I would find there; so far, we had only traveled on local roads from one village to the other. Yet, I didn't expect the Lausanne area to be any different from that around Geneva.

Five months of urban and road management neglect had started to leave a trace. On the highway, the vegetation separating the lanes invaded part of the asphalt, and the shoulder had become a growing culture of weeds, low plants, and shrubs. Untreated asphalt cracks widened, and green timidly spotted an otherwise dark gray cut in the countryside scenery.

There were not so many vehicle wrecks on the highway, which I welcomed. But I got almost halfway though my journey when, in the distance, the lanes seemed to be entirely blocked by what soon appeared to be a rolled over double-trailer truck. Slowing down, I couldn't help but realize that there was no way to go any further. I stopped the car and got out cautiously to have a closer look. Around me everything was calm. I switched off the engine. The world of silence made every natural sound prominent. Not a noise interrupted the monotonous song of the crickets and the gentle breeze among the branches. The foliage had never been so chatty...before.

The trailer was loaded with what at first seemed to be large bags or casings jammed and piled onto each other.

After a few more steps, though, I clearly saw the contents and stepped back from the sad scene. It was a cattle transport and all had died in the accident, or soon after. The decaying process of the bodies had taken place thoroughly and their skeletons were covered with mere rawhide and skin, hung on bones like an old coat. The pain for those animals must have been excruciating and surviving the accident made them suffer further, only to meet an even more terrible death. It was a good thing I was alone as this wasn't a scene for my ladies, no matter the age.

The cabin smashed in the accident, crumpled when the truck rolled over, and was now stuck against the guardrail. I realized then that we would never be able to get rid of obstacles such as that one without proper machines. Whenever and if ever we were to move somewhere else, we had to be ready to travel on alternative routes and be able to take those at any moment and from any location. Probably that also meant avoiding any route that didn't provide us with multiple options to reach a destination, any destination.

I returned to the car, u-turned and drove on the highway in the opposite direction. Extremely dangerous in another world, but not in the one I lived in. Dusk came, and the highway was dark. The countryside was deserted and there was no sign of human life. As expected of course, but disturbing as ever.

After driving a few miles on the highway, a faint light appeared in the distance. It meant only one thing. I slowed down and unknowingly held my breath until I gasped for air. Getting closer, the distant glowing came from separate sources. I had not been followed; I would have noticed.

I stopped the car and got out. At that moment, I had a brief glimpse of a luminescent circular shape with spikes similar to a wheel quickly disappearing into the starry sky. But even today I could not be sure of what I saw in that brief moment. I hesitated. I had never seen anything like that before. I took a deep breath. Back in the car, I kept driving slowly until I clearly distinguished five entities standing in the middle of the lane as if they always had been there.

The tinnitus again rumbled in my head but, as before, it started to get less chaotic. I prepared myself to hear something, though I didn't know what 'prepare' meant. *They* did not move. Maybe they had all the time in the world. I didn't. My head felt like it was burning and buzzing inside. Not just from the strong tinnitus but from the many questions, too...all ending with a big "Why?"

I advanced the car until I got about fifty yards away from the standing figures. The night was upon us by then. A clear night with bright stars, brighter than ever in a world where no man was present but me. *This time it has to be different,* I thought. I was resolved not to be chased away and I did not receive any negative feeling as I approached. On the contrary, I felt I was being encouraged. Again, an unnatural serenity captured me, more imposingly than ever before. As if they had desensitized me to any fear and anxiety when in their presence.

The tinnitus became a multi-toned, randomly-fluctuating pitch sound, and the hissing white noise totally disappeared. I slowly walked forward a few more steps until I was no more than ten yards from them. There, I stopped. They were distinguishable after all. Similar but different. One in particular was shorter and thinner than the others.

The tinnitus changed now into a reduced group of pure notes, their pitch fluctuating high and low in unison. In my head, I heard "It is time." I didn't or couldn't react physically but—emotionally—it was if the eye of the storm had finally reached me, revealing the sun and the blue sky when all around was dark devastation. The wind roared furiously. It was like one of those vivid dreams of mine, in the transitional phase just before falling asleep. It was happening for real, though, and it felt perfectly natural.

The five entities approached. I had the time to look at them carefully while they slowly advanced toward me. They seemed to be wearing a sort of tunic dress which hid their legs and feet. It touched the ground. The glow was rather intense, forcing me to squint my eyes. Their faces were old. Nope, bar that: They were wise, not old. They kept approaching until they encircled me and I was then flooded with light from all directions. I could not see anything but them now, and barely. Beyond, pitch black. I had the impression they were smiling. They each raised one arm to the level of my head and kept advancing.

I was in a trance-like state that I knew was induced. I did not move; on the contrary, I longed for their touch. *If it has to be the end, so be it,* I thought. Did everyone actually die this way?

"No, Dan." The voice was clear and loud in my head and I startled. Their hands fused together, clasping onto each other around my head and face. In that instant, I lost consciousness of my own body. My ever-lasting tinnitus turned into one long melodic note. At the same time, it was all possible notes even though the sensation was of perfect unity. The purest note which had the potential of all sounds, pitch and frequencies. The mother of all sounds.

My eyelids were shut and I saw a myriad of colors, vast plains stretching to the horizon. I was standing on the highway, and I was somewhere else at the same time. My vision didn't change whether I kept my eyes open or closed. Around me, the five entities stood like the spokes of a wheel and I was its hub. I could swear they were smiling. The pervasive calm allowed me to keep my rationality intact, unless that was a sign that I had actually lost my mind.

"Greetings, Dan."

"Where am I? And who are you?"

"First, you are safe. You have no fear, have you?" But it wasn't really a question. They lowered their arms.

"We are known as Moîrai, but we have had other names in your past. Krataimenês, Daimones…." I recognized that name. "No, that is not 'demons' in your language although some judged our actions as evil on certain occasions. So, in those cases, we could have been demons too. Those are names from the times when humans were aware of our presence. Not anymore. Apart from a few like you, no one is aware anymore."

"Is that your name, Mourrais? Krata…?"

"Moîrai? No, what you call names…I am known as Alaston, and here with me are Mênis, Algea, Akhos and Kratos. I met you before. In your past."

"Alaston? Would you be the one I saw when I was a child? Why? Why everything?"

"You will be told, human. In due time," a different 'voice' interjected. I turned around toward the direction it came from.

"Algea," the entity introduced herself. I didn't have any reason or any specific knowledge about it but I knew I had to refer to the entity Algea as a "she". It was the thinner and shorter of the entities I had previously noticed. The voices were melodic but they were not truly vocal. I didn't hear them in the physical sense, rather more than in just the physical sense.

"We know of your questions. You, as others are now, will start to be instructed this time, and made aware. So that the same will not happen again."

"Others?"

"Indeed. There are others of your species, as you have discovered. In the course of these events, special others have been selected. As you have been selected."

"Selected? And why do you say you had other names in my past? I never...which past?" I realized suddenly they weren't talking about me and this lifetime.

"The past of your race, as you are guessing correctly. After the First Loss, we decided to take a more proactive role rather than simply limiting ourselves to observation. It seemed to bear fruit. Nevertheless, we could not avoid the Second Loss. It has since been decided not to allow a Third Loss to ever happen."

"I cannot follow you. Which losses? The second one? And what third loss has been avoided?" I turned back to the first entity. "Alaston? I am afraid *I* am at a loss."

"It is time, indeed, for you to start knowing of your past before you understand your present and can walk toward your future." I was in for a cosmic lesson and felt my questions had no more place then. I had to wait.

"Your race is young. And your race is not from the planet you call Earth. Your star system is young, formed not even five billion of your years ago, the way you count them now. There are civilizations in the Universe whose recorded history goes beyond that. In your time, your system is known to be composed of eight major planets and five dwarfs. These small ones were given names in your language: Ceres, Pluto, Haumea, Makemake and Eris. Your star is known to your people as Sun. There is still another undiscovered planet beyond Pluto with a large elliptical orbit which your race has yet to discover. We call it Uribi.

Alaston continued. "In the beginning, your race was prosperous on a planet that is no more but was once home to your race. Its name was Tiamat, the watery planet. Another planet, Eridu—or Earth, in your language—resembled Tiamat as being primarily covered with water. But Tiamat was much larger and richer that Eridu.

"Tiamat is still there in part, occupying its fifth position from your star, between the planets known to you as Mars and Jupiter. 2.8 times the distance between Eridu and the Sun, or some 260 million miles from the Sun if that is more familiar to you. Its ancient position is still vaguely remembered, even after the Second Loss, in some later civilization's numerology where the number five has a central position and a unifying role. It all comes from a once-existing planet, closing the first inner circle of four companions.

"Now it is no longer a planet. What remains of it forms what you call the Great Belt, also known as the Asteroids Belt, occupied by millions of irregularly-shaped bodies. The loss of Tiamat, and the lives which were also lost, constitute what we call the First Loss. This event took place around 65 million years in the past of your time. Your race caused that loss and all subsequent events. Tiamat finally exploded, and the shock disrupted the stability of the solar system. Some from your race left Tiamat in time and survived. Eridu was their destination, a home away from home.

"The mystery of the great rift on Mars comes from the impact of a Tiamat fragment. The moons of Neptune still show evidence of that violent disruption. In the gravity tidal waves that derived, planets were disturbed in their orbits. Mercury, which we call Nebu, played with Venus for a while, traveling with her in a quasi-dual-planet system.

"The gravitational disturbances affected all planetary orbits for millions of years before everything settled and reached the orbits they occupy at this moment. Saturn lost part of its mass in a massive struggle with Jupiter in the modified orbit while gaining its rings in the process. Mars? It once had many more moons. They went lost in the Sun after Tiamat disappeared.

"Pluto and Charon are moons of Neptune that escaped in the aftermath of the cataclysm your race created at the zenith of its evolution. Eridu and the other planets were struck with large fragments from the exploded Tiamat. The planetary system filled with debris, rocks, boulders and icy dust. Many collided with other bodies, others coalesced to become additional moons or displaced existing ones, some got lost in the interstellar space, others became comets, and the rings around Jupiter, Uranus, Saturn, Neptune, Pluto and Rhea started to take shape. For ages, much debris struck with violence when their elliptical orbits crossed, causing massive destruction on larger planets.

"At the time of the Second Loss, your race started to have the suspicion you were not the only civilization in the Universe, even though you occupied only a marginal and peripheral position in the Galaxy. Still, you soon began—again—on a path of self destruction and havoc. This knowledge you have lost because of your pride. Your race believed it was the only one in the Universe; if not, the most advanced one.

"Your pride and rage caused the loss of more than 16 billion lives in Tiamat alone. Your entire civilization almost got wiped out in your self-destructive foolishness. The First Loss, as it is known, had been the largest any civilization in the Galaxy had ever endured and it rapidly plunged its survivors into a struggle to continue surviving on virgin Eridu. Not one race, except yours, has ever destroyed its own planet.

"Eridu has seen the death of many of the largest animals, as well as several families of birds and mammals. Also, marine species have been cut from the evolutionary tree like dead branches. Never to be seen again, never to be remembered, never to evolve. The land got broken and what was left was a cleaved planet.

"Your race waited around Eridu for as long as was possible, then landed on a not yet generous planet for its hospitality. They completed the extinction of the large animals. Your race almost succumbed as it scattered in small and hostile groups, evolving independently because the old rage and hatred had not yet vanished from your minds. You chose the path of isolation, instead of the one of cooperation. Even in your most dire days, even at the cost of your possible extinction.

"Your wisdom, tremendous technology, and scientific achievements were all forgotten. Since then, you walked on Eridu, going backward in knowledge and losing about a million years of evolution. Only very recently has your race begun to find traces of the inexplicable presence of modern artifacts, from times when humans were not supposed to have seen yet the light of day on the planet. And those were only artifacts from the ages after the Second Loss. They might have given rise to questions for your wise ones to answer. It does not matter much now, does it?

"Your race grew again in number, and regained some of its knowledge. You fully populated Eridu and indulged in your old arrogance. Ultimately, your race reached the power from the fission and the fusion of atoms and beyond. Its might rose again for thousands of years. Thousands of years ago. We all watched in amazement at the rebirth of a race and a civilization given up for lost. Your old nemesis though, your pride and rage, again unleashed destructive powers that almost generated another planetarian destruction. Eridu had been shocked with powerful blasts and mighty blows.

"Powerful continents and nations had been annihilated, vaporized, consumed by your folly from enormous nuclear heat and pressure. What remains now on Eridu are large areas of vitrified remnants of cities and their ruins, fused vast green glass slabs where the rocks and the sand melted. Fission and fusion fire, much more powerful than the ones you know, ravaged once flourishing planes and cities in Pierrelatte in Africa; in what you call the Euphrates Valley; and in what then became the Sahara Desert and the Gobi Desert. And the places you know as Iraq, the Mojave Desert, Scotland, the Old and Middle Kingdoms of Egypt, and south-central Turkey and more. What you would today call India, Syria, and Brazil...the entire known world had been vilified by the nuclear fire unleashed again by your race.

"Blackened and shattered stones now cover western Arabia, once a lush and fruitful land. The Sinai Peninsula bears the scars. Some of those memories remain narrated in your most ancient scripts, in a more or less explicit way.

Ancient memories being transcribed when their knowledge was long gone. Events that we refer to as the Second Loss, in a time your race calls pre-historian. Another glimpse of your resurging arrogance.

"We revealed those events to those who had forgotten. Then, the ancient sages lived in a frightened state of mind, and rightly so. Fear justified by the events we revealed, the ones their ancestors witnessed and suffered, or perished from. Eridu was so mistreated that ancient drawings of the celestial bodies could not be made in accord with the current arrangement of the solar system as you know it today. And yet, they were remarkably precise in their times.

"We thought we could help your race avoid reenacting your doom by letting the new civilizations know about ancient facts. Lores of realms from the ancient Sumerian, the people of Babylon, the Indian epic, the glyphs of the Olmec, of the Aztecs and the Mayans are the remaining fruits of those revelations. Those events were unveiled explicitly and still remembered in some of the books you know.

"One, when trying to cover those times, recites: 'Then the Lord rained down fire and tar from heaven upon Sodom and Gomorrah, and utterly destroyed them' was nothing but the old memories of what your race endured once more. Or another, even more explicitly, says: 'Nor is this world inhabited by man the first of things earthly created by God. He made several worlds before ours, but he destroyed them all.'

"Six times, your race was reborn and almost annihilated itself because of cataclysms originated from the First Loss and inflicted onto the entire planetary system. Because of the aftermath from the Second Loss, Eridu remained unstable for a long period. The repercussions from the destruction of

Tiamat persisted for ages before the planets, as they are known to you, settled down. And even after the Second Loss, at about the time Eridu captured its Moon, over six thousand years ago.

"The repercussions from the destruction of the Second Loss persisted in Eridu for thousands of years. Violent earthquakes and unimaginable tidal waves caused repeated vast destruction in Asia Minor, in Persia, Mesopotamia, Egypt, Palestine, in the Caucasus and Cyprus: All destroyed by the most frenzied elements of Eridu and the planetarian system. Several times, during the third and second millennia before the present era, the ancient East was disturbed by stupendous catastrophes.

"The ancient East and West went through massive natural paroxysms. At least five great upheavals put a sudden halt to flourishing new civilizations. At each of these occurrences, life course was disturbed, and the flow of history interrupted, often lost in oblivion. These catastrophes caused the termination of the great periods in your race's recent history. Earthquakes, flooding, and climate change did not spare a single land. These changes moved entire nations to endure large and vast migrations. You were the cause of immense concerns for many of your own.

"Eridu acquired, then lost, a highly inclined ring of meteors and dust about four thousand years ago. Many fell on its surface and over the oceans, causing large tsunamis. The ancients described events that were considered tales and inventions for entertainment of the mighty and powerful of vanished kingdoms, by those who came after them. Tales and inventions which are nonetheless present in all cultures, and in the entire world. When there were no witnesses, we made sure those events were not to be forgotten. To no avail though. The blind did not want to see.

"We helped in avoiding oblivion, so the memory of those events would survive. The same testimony is now present in all quarters of the planet, from all people, in all civilizations. Only those who forget, and do not want to know, dismiss them as myths. As if myths were just the pure invention of poets. Those scars, Dan, are painful even today, for those who do not forget! Those powerful cataclysms are the definite instances of interruption of cultural continuity, which the scholars of your time acknowledged but never explained, while the answer was always in front of their eyes.

"Ahh, those who forget and do not want to know. One of your race, Plato, warned you: '...All this, though told in mythic guise, is true, inasmuch as a deviation of the celestial bodies moving past the earth does, at long intervals, cause destruction of earthly things through burning heat...'

"We walked among men, thousands of years ago, and many of the myths and tales of gods were born in the epics of all men on Eridu. Some of those stories and myths arrived in your times, too; inscriptions, maps, descriptions, carvings of gods' vehicles, and impossible technologies. They could not invent those, unless they had been told or had seen them.

"Your race is dangerous, Dan. Far more dangerous than you might understand now. After the First Loss, you have been under careful watch. What your race caused recurred like a plague brought down upon you a celestial current, each time leaving uncivilized remnants. Wherefore, you had to begin all over again, like children, without knowledge of what has taken place in older times on Eridu.

"For the last thousand years, we and others have been uncertain about your fate, fearing the day when the son of man would reach his might again and emerge corrupted. Your race might have kept an ancestral memory of its old knowledge: a million years have passed since the First Loss, and subsequent devastations on Eridu, before the conditions for the Second Loss were met. Now only a few thousand years have elapsed before your race again became capable of causing events inevitably leading to a Third Loss. This, despite the oblivion of your own primeval history, which only remains in fragments of most ancient scripts from different continents yet all referring to the same events.

"Even more dangerously so, because the power it regained was not balanced by the greatest other achievements that had been reached by previous generations. Painfully unable to stop every and each of past havocs you caused Eridu. What would happen if, one day, your race should break this cycle and impose instead another Loss, not onto itself but onto others? Who would then be blamed the most? Those who have forgotten, or those who still remember and know well?

"For thousands of years, the struggle continued among us, without any party taking the lead, between those who wanted your race to be tested and possibly forgotten in a Final Loss, and those who despised this eventuality and feared a devastation that could have provoked cataclysms similar to the ones following the First Loss. This time, your race would have probably vanished forever, and those who forget would have been forgotten.

"The Cycle of Losses had to be broken, and we had to take action so that those who always forget could never forget again. Your race surprised us most when, in the last few thousand years, you jumped ahead and reacquired old powers. You used those powers immediately as they were discovered and, soon, you were on another uncontrolled path. Eridu is not to be disturbed again. So, we decided to start the Selection."

I was overwhelmed. Alaston did not give me a single moment of pause, where I could have reasoned with him, maybe rejected accusations, spent a word for the beauties the human race had been able to produce. Rationally, I could not believe or accept anything of what Alaston said. It clashed with all I knew and studied. Emotionally, though, I knew it fit, and that he had no reasons to lie or invent things on such a grandiose scale.

Moreover, why lie to me? An infinitesimal grain of dust in the complexity of a Universe his words only alluded to. I was too insignificant in all that I heard to imagine I could be of such an importance for Alaston to need to invent all he'd just recounted. There was only one option: that he had spoken the truth, an unimaginable truth that explained everything. He described horror and anguish, and I knew we were capable of perpetrating all he said. Even in my lifetime, we had been able to accomplish the worst toward each other. Alaston had just given me the Unifying Theory of Human Evolution on Earth.

"Yes, human, there are no reasons for us to invent anything of what your own race has sown and reaped. The things that are happening to you now are the harvest of thoughts and actions sown in the past. Today's thoughts and actions are seeds being sown for a future harvest." I turned toward the new voice.

"Mênis," the entity introduced himself.

"Whoever sows sparingly, will also reap sparingly, and whoever sows bountifully, will also reap bountifully. It is time for your race to sow bountifully. Alas, it proved time

306

and again it cannot do it by itself. The readiness is now here, and it has been deemed acceptable. We want the Selected ones to know, in this one more severe test of affliction." Mênis took a solemn tone.

"They will be given according to their means for the favor of taking part in the relief of their own race, and the breaking of the Cycle of Losses. And they will be given without having to endure the wraths of the past. Those wraths are now repressed and a new civilization has the chance for rebirth unless it will cause another even greater Loss for itself, but we will exert ourselves to avoid that. This too has contributed to the decision to initiate the Selection."

"Mênis. I think I've heard those words before..." I was humbled, uncertain of my role here.

The entity Mênis looked at me intensely and showed an expression of fanatical zeal and determination. Looking deep inside me, he addressed me again.

"Others were told those words before. If they resonate in you now, then the Selection has a chance to bring success. Those same words didn't resonate at all on so many of your race for thousands of years. It is sane and healthy for you to be humble before you'll start the walk toward your future. No sane race could do something as horrible as what yours has perpetrated. Twice!"

That "twice!" slashed like a whip. It felt like a sharp and quick slap on the face to the human race. After all I had heard, an even more hurtful judgment came from the entity I subsequently came to know as Akhos and it caused distress, both in my body and mind.

"Your race scorns everything around it, and its gaze goes beyond in search of that which is inconsistent, with vain hopes. Never have you used your talents to do good, or to benefit others. You enjoyed your arrogance and leveraged your strength for brutal actions and wild deeds. Subduing, mistreating and exterminating those who fell in your hands or crossed your paths.

"For your race, respect, justice, fairness, and magnanimity are virtues only appreciated by those who lack the courage to hurt and are afraid of suffering. Not worthy of those who have the power to impose themselves with such traits.

"Your race learned well that possessions can be stolen, lands and kingdoms can be conquered by destruction. But the life of a sentient being is not found, human, nor can you buy or steal or gain it from the time when it left the cloister of his teeth in a last breath. Always you have been in search of that which is inconsistent and worthless!"

"Akhos, I think the human has been lectured enough. Although our words did not hide anything, it is time to move on with his process. He heard from where the nemesis comes, and why his race had to suffer the inevitable consequences of the original offense it perpetrated. He needs to reach his own aidos, and feel now the reverence and the shame which will restrain men from doing wrong in their future. Only then, can the Cycle of Losses be broken."

Those words came from the last entity, Kratos. He was now holding in his hands a circular disc, in the center of which appeared a four-pointed star turning into an eight-pointed star where wavy lines emanated between the points toward the outer ring. Kratos advanced holding the disc with both hands.

"Dan!" resumed Alaston and he startled me. "Words can only reach you up to a point. What you are receiving now is the Palladium. Our gift to the sons of man. Everywhere on Eridu, the ones who were selected will receive one as they will be ready. It will be a source of protection, and the safeguard we are imposing on your race to ensure the avoidance of a Third Loss. It will change you, as it will change all the others.

"At first you will feel more than hear things. The Palladium will ensure a permanent communication with us and will be your access to the memory, achievements, and knowledge of your race. Memories will not be erased this time. When connected to the Palladium, the Selected ones will be connected to and with each other. You will receive answers, if you learn how to formulate questions.

"The Palladium will give you according to your means— and beyond your means—of your own accord if you can endure it. And it will not be without sufferance. The Palladium will be deaf and silent when you will be deaf and silent within yourself. You will come to know. Expiating a sin does not mean doing something opposite to wallow in guilt, but to use that same guilt to achieve full knowledge of the sin. The fault lies more not in having committed certain acts, rather in having carried them out without reaching their intimate knowledge. And this leads to committing a wrong again and again. When you have intimate knowledge of your acts before you commit them, then you will be able to avoid those wrongs as if they were being done to you. Now, Dan, endure the Palladium."

At this, Kratos raised the disc on top of my head then slowly lowered it. An almost unbearable heat assaulted me as the disc molded around my head, shaping into a sort of a crown. The star shapes and the wavy lines started to pulsate and glued to my skin, while my mind was sucked into the

Palladium, or fusing with it. Or was the Palladium to be sucked into my mind? The burning heat invaded my entire body, flowing down like lava from my head to my torso, to my limbs. I wanted to scream but no sound came out of my wide-open mouth.

I have memory of the pain. I fully remember it as intense, excruciating. Still my brain did not urge me to flee. It wasn't associated with the 'fight or flight' instinct. I believe I was being helped to endure it. Physical pain allows us to survive as we can then avoid the damage it's causing. But I was not being damaged and I did not feel the urge to withdraw from the Palladium, to protect my body from it. My instincts were not triggered.

Algea later told me that they imposed their hands onto me and talked to me while I was going through the Palladium, or the Palladium was going through me. Whatever it was. In any case, the distinction is immaterial. I have no recollection of them around me nor do I have a conscious memory of their words. Then, amid the pain, I started to see and feel.

I felt the disruptions of Tiamat, felt it! I saw a different world, magnificent structures, and I suffered the torment of the lives lost. I saw continents break up, and shores sink, and heard the desperate cries of billions. I felt mountains crumbling down, flattening entire cities with their boulders. I saw oceans boiling, rushing toward a sky which tore like a corrupt canvas. I felt the agony of my ancestors of million years ago. I felt their amazement at seeing those near them vaporized, just a moment before disappearing themselves.

I felt the desperation and the panic, heard the screams of mothers and fathers and children. Of lovers, holding each other until the last deadly moment before being engulfed by fire, by water, by mud, by falling rocks, by roaring blasts, by the air burning their flesh and lungs. I felt all their languages crying "Mom", "Dad", "I love you" the moment death grabbed them with her crooked, fleshless fingers. I heard their last attachment to life spoken in anguish: "Oh God, if only I had one more day, one more hour." or "If only I could hold her, him, them, again."

And I saw this race rise again on Earth, their struggles and forgotten sins repeated. New destructions and new devastations on familiar lands. Flying rods of adverse nations spreading death from above. Depressions on Earth created by immense blasts as if giants were pounding their fists on helpless cities. And the same cries, the same panic and terror...the ancient anguish repeating itself. Again!

I felt all that in waves, crushing over my very essence and purifying it. Voiding me of all strength while removing all remaining debris of consciousness: *How could we have forgotten all that? How could we have the right to another chance? How did we dare? What have we done? Damned, damned, damned!*

What remained in the end was their love, so painfully real. All their last moments of desperate love that gripped the throat and clutched it so tightly that you could hardly breathe anymore. And in doing this, the Palladium had been merciful: I was left with the enduring sensation of a tremendous flood of love, desperate and anguished but nonetheless infinite. An unguent poured over my tormented spirit. The purest love of all for everything that was gone, for everything that could never be, for everyone who'd been lost. And it planted the seeds for the love of everything that will be.

I was exhausted and on my knees. The burning pain had

gone though its memory was vivid. The Palladium had changed me in the process but in ways that I wasn't yet aware of. Kratos moved forward and touched the outer ring of the Palladium. It expanded, the wavy lines detached from my head, and its shape flattened to resume that of a disk with its two pronged stars in their perennial ballet of change. He took it off my head and gravely handed it to me.

"The Palladium is now in you and you are in it. This is happening with all the Selected ones who will share the experience you just had. You will never be the same, human, and the Selected ones will help us in our daunting task."

"I have seen destruction and devastation, and I felt the aches and the afflictions. The madness and the sickness. It is still tormenting and torturing me, it has lacerated me deeply. But there was tremendous love as well, Kratos, at each time…" I stumbled over the words.

The Moîrai all looked at me, and I realized then that I could discern their traits perfectly which I couldn't before the Palladium. They were no longer indistinguishable from each other; I saw that Algea was obviously a beautiful female. Neither was their glow hiding them from sight as before.

"In all these destructions which we have caused, an additional one is missing." The Moîrai were all attentive and listened carefully to my words.

"I saw nothing on the Third Loss!" I could see clearly from their expressions that my remark was not entirely expected. Algea lowered her eyes. Still looking at the ground, she spoke.

"Dan, we have a great burden on our shoulders and an onus, too. We will be judged on how your race will rebirth.

We have not been alone in this decision, but we have the full burden of obligation upon us. The responsibility is ours. If your race had gone through another massive destruction of Eridu, it would not have survived. Leaving you all to your destiny was not an option, and we have been guardians and companions of your race for eons as has happened with other young races. The way you can see us clearly now... It was that way, too, for the son of men in other places, in other times." Algea fully captured my attention. She raised her head and looked straight at me.

"Dîos. During the last few thousand years, that word only meant divine. For your race, it means 'pertaining to the gods'. Before, dîos referred instead to those who were shining, glittering, glowing. Do you understand? When the ancients used dîos to describe someone, the term primarily referred to their glowing, to the emanation of their inner light, the splendor that accompanied them and on which stood their shape. We have been judged to be interfering too much with another race, your race, and thus to have disturbed its evolution.

"Even in light of the First Loss, and of the Second Loss, there were those who pushed for us to step back. Which we did. We were compliant, we stopped walking together with men and retreated. Yet we kept watching and observing your evolution, mostly unseen. As Alaston already told you, your race acts, waiting for the judgments to drastically change." I couldn't help but hold my breath as the enormity of what Algea was revealing went beyond any possible imagination.

"Yes, it was decided then to enforce another Loss. This time controlled, this time without the risk of massive planetarian destruction which your race has demonstrated to be fully capable of. We did so without the tremendous suffering of the past, inflicted on all Eridu life forms, and allowing the remnants of yours to start afresh without enduring millenniums of dark ages. All sentient races have participated in the decision, and the Selection process started thus about fifty of your years ago."

I understood better then the origins of the mythical Golden Age gods, when the people of light, the watu wa mwanga—where did that come from in my mind?—walked with the son of men. My lips were tense when I asked.

"Without suffering, Algea?"

"Without the agony and torments they would have suffered otherwise." Then Algea paused and her tone changed.

"We bent the space and exposed all humans to a sudden vacuum. We tested sudden exposure to extremely low pressure to other life forms and we have been able to be highly selective in the process. The rapid decompression we provoked around those life forms, in the worst cases, produced only the rupture of eardrums and sinuses with bruising and blood seepage into soft tissues. The shock caused an immediate sharp increase in oxygen consumption that subsequently led to hypoxia.

"Any oxygen dissolved in the blood emptied into the lungs trying to equalize the partial pressure gradient. The lungs emptied. Once the deoxygenated blood arrived at the brain, animals lost consciousness within a couple of seconds and died of hypoxia. We created a rapid decompression not taking more than a few tenths of a second, allowing the lungs to decompress rapidly while avoiding the pulmonary barotrauma. It was very natural and clement. The level of pain was minimal and very sudden. Unconsciousness was extremely rapid. So was death."

"You *bent* the space…and killed billions of people?"

Algea's tone changed again. This time, her voice was full of sadness and much compassion. "We gave your race another chance, Dan. The Selected ones will play a crucial role. If you do not see this, and do not see that your race can build a different, better future, then the interruption of the Cycle of Losses will be in vain. You will live the equivalent of many past generations because of the changes you received from the Palladium. Your direct offspring will carry your gene modifications and live long, about two hundred of your years at first, and in good health. Descendants generated via this first generation will live even longer, in the end matching yours and the others, Selected life span."

"You mean Annah, my daughter, and the baby Laura still carries?" But I knew the answer, and a needle of pure pain pierced my throat.

"No, Dan. We mean the ones you will generate from now on, and from other Selected ones and their descendants." Algea lowered her eyes again.

I wasn't surprised Algea knew about my family and I smiled; a sour, bitter smile. I wanted to swallow but couldn't. The enormity of what I had been exposed to was overwhelming. We had been culled, and selected specimens chosen for controlled reproduction. We were going to be bred for a better race; something we humans used to do with animals, selecting specific traits and behavioral characteristics. And in the process, our habitat and environment had been preserved to enhance the chance of success. A surgical process.

"What if I or other Selected ones refuse to cooperate?"

"A percentage probably will, that is why there were so

many chosen. The majority will work with us to generate a better human race. You are already a better human, Dan."

"How many, Algea? How many have been spared?"

The cold explanation from Algea resumed. "Right now, on the planet, there are roughly ten million humans of which two million are the Selected ones. About 10,000 years ago, humans were only about five million. The mortality was very high, and the race which survived the Second Loss was extremely feeble. You were only 300,000,000 about two thousand years ago. Growth will be quite different this time. You will be hundred million on Eridu by 2050 and one billion right after the century.

"It was around year 1800 of your calendar when your race reached the one billion mark. You will be alive when it happens again. Actually, you will still be young. In your long life span, the human race will soon reach numbers close to those at the time we enacted the selection and you will fully populate Eridu. With our help, and your help, it will be a much wiser, much more evolved human race. And, if you allow me…much more humane."

"My race, Algea? It will be your race, the race you will have created. My race will be extinct soon." My mind rushed with agony to Mary, Annah, Laura and our unborn child.

"What is a race, Dan? Just physical bodies, existing at a specific moment in time, or the minds that can inhabit them and are able to evolve over millions of years? The human race will live longer; it will be stronger and better. You and the Selected are already a member of this new race. Don't turn your back on yourself or on your future. Your race can prosper soon and meet the others, too, claiming its rightful place. We are all waiting for this. And it will be a very short wait, rather than a slow, painful progression toward annihilation through a catastrophic, irrecoverable Third Loss."

In their perspective, the selection had been a necessary and right thing to do. Actually, in their words, it had been well-doing in full knowledge while, on the contrary, sparing every human life would have condemned the entire race to oblivion and to a probable Armageddon where we would have killed each other—either slowly or in few nuclear flashes—someday in the future.

I recalled how humans considered gods as distant entities, unreachable to the human mind and difficult to understand when they caused death and destruction. Gods to be revered, and pray to, so that their goodwill would have been the *will of good* we humans could understand and hope for. I realized then that I was missing a crucial piece of information.

"What about the other eight million people, Algea? They too will grow, or will the process entail more exposure to space bending?"

It was an acrid remark, though perfectly legitimate. I suppose they understood my bitterness as Algea had that very human reaction before answering. She lowered her eyes and paused, as if she were searching for the best words. When she spoke, she again sounded emotionless and she did not look directly into my eyes.

"The Selected have a strenuous task, in all their actions, their efforts, and during their life time. Many options have been considered and have been thoroughly evaluated based on everything we know about your race. The Palladium changes the Selected for the better but it cannot fully change their minds, too. Which would have been a great crime.

"You felt love at the end: Your race is capable of doing marvelous things, and terrible ones. It has been deemed worthy of all the efforts required. The wonderful things have been deemed worthy. We could not modify you completely, that would have been equivalent to losing you, only in a different way. You are more inclined now to do marvelous things and fight against repeating the terrible ones. But, basically, you are still the same. The potential is not lost; it has simply been helped toward its fulfillment.

"One of the options was to preserve the Selected, and only them. You would have woken up alone, your wife and daughter unspared. We could have lost you and the others before we could impose the Palladium on all of you. That option was discarded. You needed to go through your own mourning process for the past world and find in yourself the strength to carry on. That strength confirmed you were indeed capable of being part of the Selected: the strength to adapt, to change, and evolve. We could not give or impose too much onto you without losing you." Algea briefly glanced at the others; at Alaston, in particular, who imperceptibly nodded his agreement. Algea resumed.

"The Selected ones are the seeds. Without them, all will be lost. Among the spared ones, the males will not be able to beget. The females can receive the semen of the Selected and generate a new first generation. The women among the Selected will generate descendants that will bear fully all the new traits and genes received with the Palladium. Among the Selected, this is set to happen through the Palladium itself. At first. The descendants of the spared females will be fertile again, and their offspring will carry fully the new traits of the Selected.

"The spared ones are living memories for the Selected. A

motivation not to give up, a reminder of what each Selected has experienced the first time with the Palladium. The respect for the fragility of the spared ones will allow you to grow into a better human; the fragility the rest of the planet has suffered already and that has been abused with terrible intensity by the strongest in your race with disdain and scorn. You will care for the spared ones, too.

"When all the Selected have received the Palladium, the Palladiums themselves will beam upwards. They will signal and announce to everyone about the new start. There is still lots to do, Dan, if you wish and if you can endure it. And there are more things that you will learn and discover. It is a path we will walk together. Every Selected must decide whether to walk in this path, or be lost in the darkness of destructive selfishness. We challenge you to make your life worthy."

The Palladium beamed on its marble pedestal in the center of the square. The beam was visible from miles and miles away and seemed to pierce the sky, uninterrupted. From our hill, two more beams were also visible where other communities prospered and grew as ours did. Mary was pregnant with our second child; my first of the new generation though I will outlive this baby, too. She was as beautiful as ever, even more than ever if possible. Laura gave birth to our lovely baby girl. We called her Hope. She was smart and extremely clever. At one-year-old, she was starting to walk almost without hesitation. I regretted that Hope had been conceived shortly before I received the Palladium but that made her ever more precious to my heart.

Algea was always present and helped us with everything in her power, which was a lot. Alaston made impromptu visits from time to time, always very welcomed. We discussed all possible subjects, present, past, and future. He revealed to me what existed out there; his civilization and others, too. A humbling experience. Every Selected community was followed and helped, instructed closely by its own Moîrai. Little by little, we were just starting to have access to their technology. We were "given according to our means, and beyond our means at times, of our own accord" to rephrase what Mênis once told me. I wondered whether someday he would visit us, too. But I knew every Moîrai was quite busy with their obligations and would be for quite some time.

I still don't know if the Palladium had a role in changing our minds as, bar none, all Selected accepted to work with the Moîrai to rebuild the human race. In one year, over eight-hundred thousand children were born or were due to be and that was just counting the Selected women. No one stepped back from the role that had been planned for us by the Moîrai. The pregnancies were, in themselves, a revelation. Selected women could feel their babies like no woman had ever been able to. They could also feel when the baby, still in the womb, gained self-consciousness. The regrowth numbers that Algea put in front of me only a year before didn't seem unreasonably optimistic anymore.

In the past year—with help from Algea and Alaston— others joined us and the spared ones were making our tasks more bearable. With…grace, should I say? I didn't know many details about the other communities but it seemed everyone got along as nicely as we were.

For example, Jean Claude joined us a month after the Moîrai revealed their plan to me about the Selection process. He was now our Chief Agronomist and had one apprentice: Liliana, a girl from the Italian city of Aosta. Liliana and Jean Claude had a romance going on and, at the moment, they didn't much care that he wasn't going to be able to get her pregnant. They had discussions about Liliana having a baby 'otherwise' but it was entirely their decision. None of the Selected, nor the Moîrai, pushed spared women in that direction. For the moment, Jean Claude and Liliana were happy just getting to know each other.

Federico, too, was from Aosta. Together with Liliana, he was surviving in Aosta when we found them. Luckily for me and Mary, Federico was a truly nice guy. Luckily, because he had eyes for Annah. I wondered whether the spared ones had gone through a sort of selection of their own by the Moîrai. I supposed so. He was our handy man, able to fix and repair practically everything. He said he was our Utility Service Engineer and he knew what to do on every occasion.

At seventeen years old, that was an accomplishment in our new world and he was instructed by both Algea and the Palladium. After all, the spared ones had an important role, too.

I didn't fully understand why everyone had not been allowed to receive the Palladium the way the Selected had. Algea was a bit evasive on the subject and once replied that they, the Moîrai, actually felt they were very lucky to have been able to select so many of us anyway. And I wondered why they didn't select more than just two million? One day, I'll need to be told precisely the reasons.

Nonetheless, the Palladium was able to act as an instructional device for the spared ones, 'according to their means and inclinations' as explained Algea. So Federico, Jean Claude, and Liliana were all extremely knowledgeable thanks to it and knew well what to do to run things smoothly. Two girls from the Haute Savoie joined us when we started our journey from Geneva toward the south, and toward more clement weather conditions, especially during winters. Sarah and Camille were both about nineteen years old, almost twenty now. They took care of our little farm with its few goats, sheep, and poultry and enjoyed their bucolic task a lot.

In the meanwhile, our canine community had also grown and four puppies were happily strolling around following the steps of their parents, Taxi and Tarantula. Tarantula only got pregnant after we settled into our new place. I guess Mother Nature is wiser than any human ever could be.

I was in daily contact with the other Selected, especially the immediate neighbors: Marina, an Italian woman, and Luc, a Swiss guy. From their locations, they could see additional Palladium beams, too. We had come to the conclusion that, on average, we had one Selected and related community about every four thousand square hectares. On average meaning everything and nothing, of course. The beams—and the Moîrai—were making so that all spared ones had joined, or were about to join, a community headed by a Selected. The Palladiums were beacons for all humanity.

Established communities were not evenly distributed throughout all lands or locations. There were higher concentrations in specific, more favorable areas. It was no surprise that the most beautiful places on Eridu had been favored and many communities were growing there. It also favored shared resources and contacts, even among the spared ones. *Location, location, location* still held true in our new world. Communication-wise, distance meant very little. The Palladium was the ultimate channel and a more intimate one, too, as the Selected were able to let others feel and see what they were feeling while in communion with it.

Ironically, after the Palladium experience, I started to call our planet Eridu and the other Selected were doing the same. We used the old term 'Earth' only when talking to the spared ones. We all shared a protective role for them and were animated by a sense of urgency. Their life span was so short compared with ours now and with that of new generations to come...they were weak and vulnerable in comparison. The Palladium must have provoked some subtle changes the Selected were still discovering with its use. For example, I recently started to *know* when some of the others, or one of the Moîrai, wanted to enter in communion with me. I simply knew that. The same happened to the others.

We Selected were organizing ourselves, pointing out to each other where and how other communities could help growth and prosperity. Many had relatives who had been spared, the way Mary and Annah had been from the very beginning or at the very end of it all. It enhanced our collective sense of duty toward all spared ones and I believe it reinforced the protective feeling we Selected shared when talking about them. When all the spared ones were gone and only new generations remained alive, we would enter a new age for those who would carry on and evolve. Their short lifespan represented for everyone a sort of transitional period, where we would have lots to learn and discover about ourselves, and the others.

We established our group on a hilltop in Lazio, a central region on the Italian peninsula located about 90 miles north of Rome. The borough we chose to be our home during the transition was founded by the Etruscans over 2500 years ago. The little town was situated atop a plateau overlooking the Tiber River valley. Our community could grow easily and comfortably there before any need arose to occupy other areas.

The burg had a peculiar and unique history, having been practically deserted to become a sort of ghost town at the end of the 90s. Since then, it had enjoyed renewed interest as a haven of peace and an oasis of detachment, almost secluded from modern life. Most of its centuries-old houses had gone through intense renovation by wealthy people years before and the town was now a little jewel unto itself.

Mary had read about it and became fascinated. She always wanted to visit and spend a holiday away from everything. She influenced me into choosing this location for us. It was our home now, a sort of an island in the surrounding countryside. I consulted with other Selected and we would not be far away from other communities either.

We had the impression that—through the stone portal gate—we were being admitted into a supernatural world, surviving in another dimension. It was not far away from the truth. The name itself, Civita, had prophetic significance to me as it meant a body of citizens who constituted a social entity. Very much like a city-state, with shared responsibility and a common purpose. The town itself contributed to our growing sense of community.

With help from the Moîrai, the town church—named after an Italian saint, Donato—had been transformed into our agronomy lab and produce farm. It was the realm of Jean Claude and Liliana and it provided all we needed for our diet, in addition to what we had from our small animal farm, thanks to Sarah and Camille. Algea had also been instrumental in equipping us with multi-junction solar cells that rendered us completely autonomous as they directly converted light into energy, able to capture the whole solar spectrum with high efficiency. From that point of view, the entire town did not need any other traditional supply. The Moîrai reassured us all, the Selected, that we would not need to rely on our old sources of energy in the future.

Jean Claude was at work with expanding the variety of sprouts and plants. Especially the enhanced ones provided by Algea. By themselves, they were reducing the need for us to get animal proteins.

"How is the crop production, JC? And the hydroponic farm?"

"Amazing, Dan, simply amazing. Look, aren't they just perfect?" he said while showing me the lettuce, onions and radishes which were almost ready for our consumption. Indeed, they were astonishingly healthy and lush. "And the new aeroponic installations...they are already showing progress over the hydroponics system. Meaning, we need much less water."

Rows and rows of plants were suspended in a semi-closed environment. The plants' dangling roots and lower stems were constantly sprayed with a nutrient-rich water solution by a high pressure diaphragm pump that kept plants germ-free at the same time. I had to admit to Jean Claude that I had never before seen plants so beautiful and strong-looking as those we had in our agronomy lab. We could not have achieved so much in so little time if it had not been for Algea's support, and the Palladium itself.

"I think we are going to receive more people next week. I am discussing this with Marina and she is not against moving here, to Civita, with us. It will be more pleasant and both communities would profit from each other. We might even put the ancient olive press to work again."

"That would be nice. The town is large enough to welcome many more people."

"Yes, I thought that, too. It could happen next month if we decide on it."

"Is there any reason not to?"

"Not really. It is just a matter of organizing their move here. By the way, have you seen Federico?"

Overhearing our conversation, Liliana raised her eyes from the spinach and carrot plants she was taking care of. With the air of revealing a secret plot, she told me that Federico had finished checking the additional solar cell installation for the morning, and then had rushed to meet someone at Saint Mary's Gate. He was going there with a bunch of flowers in his hands.

"He asked me what flowers a girl would like." Liliana smiled and winked at me. I knew what she meant and I smiled back.

"How is Snowball?" I nodded toward the puppy crouched at her feet.

"Oh, Snowy? I love her. We are really good friends. Isn't she adorable? By the way, Annah was with Tarantula." Couldn't hide anything from Liliana, apparently, and I mentally thanked her for the information. I exchanged a glance with JC who rolled his eyes and gestured as if saying "and you haven't seen anything yet, my friend."

Really, there was nothing to worry about but knowing Tarantula was with Annah comforted me just the same. I would have given Annah a bit of privacy before going to look for her because her world had changed, too. And she was growing up fast.

"Ah...almost forgot, JC. I brought you the manuscript with our story. Everything that has happened since February; the first days, how we met Laura, how we discovered the Moîrai were among us and behind all the events, and why."

"Excellent. Thanks, Dan. Your memories cannot be lost. Will you share them with all the others?"

"Certainly. The Selected are starting to discover we are growing shared memories. Individual souls part of a universal intellect like cobwebs enveloping us without our noticing as we walk on a country path. I have yet to get used to it. For all others...yes, it will be important. It is the best of my recollection."

JC took the manuscript from my hands as if it were the most precious object on Eridu.

"I will make copies but first I want to read it myself. Ah, you even gave it a title. 'Daimones'...very appropriate."

I smiled and nodded.

"Watu wa wmanga" voices from a radio broadcast burst into my mind and soon faded like sparks from a damaged wire. I remembered things and tears watered my eyes. JC noticed my expression changed, as if a shadow had passed and obscured my face.

"What?"

"Nothing. It's what they are." I left without further explanation.

Everyone but the Selected had lost everything; we had been spared the pain of losing everyone we loved. I reasoned that, even with the best intentions, cruelty was always around the corner.

— o —

Saint Mary's Gate was the only access to Civita. Via a mostly-pedestrian and long structure that bridged a deep chasm, it was the only connecting route to our town. As the day was sunny and warm, I decided to take a walk there. In the square, Mary and Laura enjoyed the sunlit balm while watching Hope who was playing at their feet and climbing on top of Taxi who patiently endured having his ears pulled by a laughing little girl.

It was going to be an excellent idea to have Marina and her people joining us. We all would profit from being a larger community. Although small, Civita was still way too large for us. Together, it would be easier...for many reasons. Sharing the transitional period with another Selected by my side was going to be good.

I stopped and enjoyed the scene for a moment when Annah and Federico showed up, Tarantula trotting gently beside them. Annah held a beautiful bouquet of flowers and she was radiant. Oh, my little lovely girl. Her eyes met mine and she smiled happily. Federico was a bit shy and, when he saw me in the square, he blushed lightly. Those signs were unmistakable. *Some things will never change...* but I could not finish the thought. Taking a glance at Mary revealed she understood as well. Looking at both youngsters lightly touching their hands in secret while walking up toward the square, she was smiling too. Laura stood up and brought Hope with her as she approached me.

"Here, she has been missing her Dad all day, you know."

Beautiful Laura, beautiful Hope. I was a lucky man. Extremely lucky. In due time, my descendants will probably join a community of sentient beings I could only try to imagine now, carrying my genes to all corners of the galaxy. Algea says I will witness things my mind cannot grasp at this time and I believe her. These few years of learning, the duration of the life time of the spared ones, would reveal much of what is expected of us, as a race, in the future.

I stared at the Palladium. A long path was laid in front of us all. I took a last intense look at my family, one after the other: Mary, Laura, Annah, Hope. And I thought of the new baby, too. Will it be a boy this time? I couldn't wait for when the baby started to think for the first time in Mary's womb...I couldn't wait to welcome this new life. Yes, I surely was a lucky man.

They saw me smiling, and they smiled back. It is a moment I will never forget, carved in my mind and in my heart. Their lives, and that of Mary's new child, will pass in front of my eyes like a breeze at the end of a warm day. It will stop blowing rapidly...and too painfully. I and others have a huge price to pay just for having been selected. I hope the Palladium will change *me* to be strong enough for when I will lose the ones I cherished the most in this life...

I loved them from the moment they entered my life, and I will love them dearly until the moment they leave theirs.

- The Beginning... -